The Admira
trap" was s
Operations,

The one man who might have saved the day—the best intelligence officer in the Navy, who spoke the most fluent Japanese and best understood Japan—was Capt. Ellis M. Zacharias, exiled to sea duty by the ranking admirals' "club," whose motto was "Keep Zach Out."

For some inexplicable reason, the Navy brass were convinced that Navy intelligence in Hawaii had a "purple magic" machine—essential for decoding Japanese messages. Meanwhile, in Honolulu, Adm. Kimmel asked his intelligence chief, *"What* is a purple machine?" The chief had no idea.

In Honolulu, at 1742 Nuuanu Avenue, at the Japanese consulate, Consul General Nagao Kita directed a cadre of 217 assistant consuls fanned out all over the islands—where twelve would have sufficed for normal consular business.

Shortly before the Pearl Harbor attack, this message was sent from Tokyo to Consul General Kita: *With regards to warships and aircraft carriers, we would like to have you report on those at anchor... tied up at wharves, buoys, and in docks.* This message, intercepted, sat in its "Top Secret" pigeonhole for two weeks before it was deciphered, and was never passed on to Adm. Kimmel.

> These, and other, reasons, are why the critics have called A. A. Hoehling's *December 7, 1941:* THE DAY THE ADMIRALS SLEPT LATE "Enthralling..."—*America*
> and
> "The best picture yet..." Walter Lord, author of THE DAY OF INFAMY, in *The New York Times Book Review*

BY THE SAME AUTHOR

Last Train from Atlanta
A Whisper of Eternity
Lonely Command
The Fierce Lambs
The Great Epidemic
Home Front USA
Who Destroyed the *Hindenburg?*
The Great War at Sea
They Sailed into Oblivion
America's Road to War, 1939-1941
Thunder at Hampton Roads
Vicksburg, 47 Days of Siege
The *Franklin* Comes Home
The *Lexington* Goes Down
The *Jeannette* Expedition
Epics of the Sea
Great Ship Disasters
Disaster: Major American Catastrophes
Women Who Spied
Lost at Sea
Damn the Torpedoes: Naval Incidents of the Civil War
After the Guns Fell Silent, a post-Appomattox Narrative
The Fighting Liberty Ships: a Memoir

WITH MARY HOEHLING

The Last Voyage of the *Lusitania*
The Day Richmond Died

DECEMBER 7, 1941: THE DAY THE ADMIRALS SLEPT LATE

BY A. A. HOEHLING

(Previously published as THE WEEK BEFORE PEARL HARBOR)

ZEBRA BOOKS
KENSINGTON PUBLISHING CORP.

ZEBRA BOOKS

are published by

Kensington Publishing Corp.
475 Park Avenue South
New York, NY 10016

Copyright © 1963 by A.A. Hoehling

All rights reserved. No part of this book may be reproduced in any form or by any means without the prior written consent of the Publisher, excepting brief quotes used in reviews.

If you purchased this book without a cover you should be aware that this book is stolen property. It was reported as "unsold and destroyed" to the Publisher and neither the Author nor the Publisher has received any payment for this "stripped book."

Third printing: November, 1991

Printed in the United States of America

This book is dedicated to the dead
of Pearl Harbour who paid
the full price of Washington's apathy.

*In a sense the Pearl Harbour tragedy
was a Waterloo of American evaluation,
estimating and planning.
And that should now in retrospect
be our greatest warning.*

Rear-Admiral Ellis M. Zacharias

CONTENTS

Foreword	9
Dramatis Personae	11
1 The President comes home	15
2 The Commander-in-Chief and his lieutenants	18
3 The lieutenants' lieutenants	39
4 Trouble on the second deck	57
5 "Magic"	80
6 Honolulu	93
7 "A bare chance of peace..."	115
8 The Fourteen-Part Message	127
9 The Mori message	137
10 Properly alerted	148
11 Saturday night in the Pacific	170
12 "This means war"	179
13 For delivery at one o'clock	195
14 A "last effort for peace"	205
15 Sunrise at Pearl Harbour	221
16 "... that was an excitement, indeed"	227
Epilogue	239
Appendix	262
Acknowledgements	272
Bibliography	274
Index	277

FOREWORD

On Sunday, December 7, 1941, I was an Ensign on duty in the public information section of the Navy Department. That morning war came with shocking suddenness. When I reported to the old building on Constitution Avenue for the afternoon watch, the yellowing halls were vacant; the office warrens were dark—silent. Almost no one was there.

I wondered then—and I still wonder—how could this be? Had no one expected the raid on Pearl Harbour?

Since that time I have talked or corresponded at length with all possible principals in what might be termed "the Pearl Harbour case." They range the entire military scale from Admiral Stark, the senior member of this fast dwindling band, to General Marshall's orderly. With two or three noteworthy exceptions, most of them live in retirement in scattered havens of the world from Florida to Tokyo.

Only a few have chosen to remain in the areas associated with the Pearl Harbour tragedy: Washington and Hawaii. Nearly all of those in positions of responsibility in Washington, Pearl Harbour and Manila on that fateful day have searched their memories to contribute fragments to the vast and generally vexatious mosaic. This book, employing earlier material such as the official inquiries only as a backstop, is based directly on their words and letters to me.

I have tried to pursue the Pearl Harbour case without bias or preconceptions. But, in reflecting upon the staggering complexity of the incident, I am convinced that there persists today a tendency by historians to oversimplify the chain of events and circumstances which led up to that Sunday morning in December. This is curious, indeed, considering not only the conflicting international desires in 1941 but also the especially snarled web of executive prerogative in virtually every capital of the world.

Villains there were in Berlin and Tokyo in 1941, and knaves in Rome. When the focus is on Washington, the distinction between heroism and villainy begins to blur, and it is not easy to distinguish between errors of omission or of commission. This study is aimed at probing for the highlights, no matter how shadowy, in the befogged canvas of the Pearl Harbour case, a canvas that from a distance seems to be an all-pervading grey.

DRAMATIS PERSONAE

WASHINGTON

Franklin D. Roosevelt, *President of the United States*
Cordell Hull, *Secretary of State*
Sumner Welles, *Under Secretary of State*
Henry L. Stimson, *Secretary of War*
Frank Knox, *Secretary of the Navy*
Harry Hopkins, *Roosevelt's "man Friday"*

NAVY DEPARTMENT

Admiral Harold R. Stark, *Chief of Naval Operations*
Rear-Admiral Royal E. Ingersoll, *Assistant Chief, Naval Operations*
Rear-Admiral Richmond Kelly Turner, *Chief,
War Plans Division Naval Operations*
Rear-Admiral Theodore Stark Wilkinson, *Chief,
Intelligence Division Naval Operations*
Rear Admiral Leigh Noyes, *Chief,
Communications Division Naval Operations*
Commander Laurence E. Safford, *Chief,
Security Intelligence Communications*
Captain Roscoe E. Schuirmann,
Central Division (liaison with State Department)
Commander Arthur H. McCollum, *Chief,
Far Eastern Section Intelligence*
Lieutenant-Commander Alwin D. Kramer,
Translation Section Communications
Lieutenant Lester R. Schulz,
White House communications duty officer

Rear-Admiral Ross T. McIntire, *White House physician*
Captain John R. Beardall, *White House Naval Aide*

WAR DEPARTMENT

General George Catlett Marshall, *Chief of Staff*
Major-General Henry H. Arnold, *Deputy Chief of Staff for Air*
Brigadier-General Sherman Miles, *Chief of Intelligence (G2)*
Brigadier-General Leonard T. Gerow, *Chief, War Plans Division*
Colonel Walter Bedell Smith, *Secretary, General Staff*
Colonel Hayes A. Kroner, *Head, Intelligence Branch, G2*
Colonel Rufus S. Bratton, *Head, Far Eastern Section, G2*
Lieutenant-Colonel Carlisle C. Dusenbury, *Assistant to Bratton*
Lieutenant-Colonel Thomas J. Betts, *Head,*
Situations Section (China desk) G2
Colonel Otis K. Sadtler, *Signal Corps, operations officer*

HONOLULU

HAWAIIAN DEPARTMENT

Lieutenant-General Walter C. Short, *Commanding General*
Colonel Walter C. Phillips, *Chief of Staff*
Lieutenant-Colonel Kendall J. Fielder, *Chief, G2*
Lieutenant-Colonel George W. Bicknell, *Assistant to Fielder*
Major-General Frederick L. Martin, *Commanding,*
Hawaiian Air Force (under Short)

UNITED STATES PACIFIC FLEET

Admiral Husband E. Kimmel, *Commander-in-Chief*
Lieutenant-Commander Edwin T. Layton, *Fleet Intelligence Officer*
Captain Ellis M. Zacharias,
Commanding cruiser U.S.S. Salt Lake City

FOURTEENTH NAVAL DISTRICT
(Pearl Harbour, headquartered)

Rear-Admiral Claude C. Bloch, *Commandant*
Rear-Admiral P. N. L. Bellinger, Jr.,
Hawaiian and Pacific Fleet Air Commander
Captain Irving H. Mayfield, *Intelligence Officer*
Commander Joseph J. Rochefort, *Communications Security Unit*
Robert L. Shivers, *Agent, Federal Bureau of Investigation*

MANILA

General Douglas MacArthur, *Commanding General,
United States Army Forces in the Far East*
Admiral Thomas C. Hart, *Commander-in-Chief, Asiatic Fleet*
Major-General Lewis H. Brereton, *Commanding, Far East Air Force*

1
THE PRESIDENT COMES HOME

A few minutes before noon on Monday, December 1, 1941, the President of the United States was assisted from his armoured, bullet-proof Pullman car at Washington's Union Station. Franklin D. Roosevelt's Thanksgiving vacation in Warm Springs, Georgia, previously postponed, had been interrupted late Saturday by a telephone call from an ill and worried Secretary of State. Come home, the white-haired Cordell Hull requested.

The lean, distinguished seventy-year-old Tennessean warned Roosevelt of "the imminent danger of a Japanese attack." During the past few days the Secretary had made no secret of his belief that "the situation diplomatically" was "hopeless." He had said so to a regular caller at the Department of State, Lord Halifax, the British Ambassador. To his colleagues in the Cabinet, Secretary of War Henry

L. Stimson and Secretary of the Navy Frank Knox, he had voiced the warning that "Japan might move suddenly, with every possible element of surprise."

Roosevelt himself shared Hull's concern. Addressing a dinner attended by his Warm Springs neighbours and fellow infantile paralysis sufferers, he had noted:

"In days like these our Thanksgiving next year may remind us of a peaceful past. It is possible that our boys in the military and naval academies may next year be fighting for the defence of these American institutions of ours."

Roosevelt's face was lined this Monday morning, mirroring his concern over the times as well as a recurrence of the pain caused by his chronic sinus infection. His familiar smile was singularly absent. The cigarette smouldered from its holder, as always, but the customary jaunty angle had become more of a droop.

The President, now fifty-nine, was tense, preoccupied, possibly less self-confident than he had been a few months previously when he returned from the Atlantic Charter conference with Prime Minister Winston Churchill. There was, as a matter of fact, ample cause for preoccupation. In Europe, Hitler remained master. France, Belgium, Holland, Norway, Denmark, Poland, Austria, Greece and most of the Balkans had been crushed by the German war machine. England, shaken and reeling, held, but at an incalculable price. Stalled by winter, the Nazis were experiencing in Russia their most dramatic reverses.

Japan, though some of her armies might have been as absorbed by the wastes of China as Germany's by those of the Soviet Union, had planted the Rising Sun from Manchuria to Indo-China. The same flag flew from scores of Pacific islands, many of them under mandate from the League of Nations, and it was increasingly clear that Japan contemplated some new move in that vast ocean.

This was the darkening international complex that brought Roosevelt home as fast as the Southern Railroad locomotive could haul his special train over the often mountainous route from western Georgia. Indeed, there appeared not a minute to lose—waiting at the White House to confer with him, even as the President was being driven from the station, were Hull, Admiral Harold R. Stark, Chief of Naval Operations, and Harry Hopkins.

What would lie ahead for these men? What were the many forces which brought them together in a common bond of concern? Certainly, Roosevelt seemed to sense the imminence of the "rendezvous with destiny" he had in the past so dramatically forecast. Hull was alarmed, and possibly others as well.

And yet, this week, which started out on such a vibrant note of alarm and with such apparent speed, would end in what amounted to a doze. The date with destiny was kept, but no one in Washington would find any glory in it.

2
THE COMMANDER-IN-CHIEF
AND HIS LIEUTENANTS

There had never dwelt in the White House a President whose health was so imperfect and yet who managed to drive himself—and his lieutenants—so unremittingly. While every President except Grover Cleveland between the Lincoln and Theodore Roosevelt administrations had, in combat, survived the perils of the Civil War, none had overcome so shattering a personal experience as poliomyelitis to rise to the nation's highest office.

Nor had there ever been a Chief Executive, with the conceivable exceptions of Wilson and Harding, whose health was the object of so much secrecy, if not actual deception. The President, who had a tendency to high blood pressure and overweight, was bedevilled by headaches. Whether Roosevelt's sinus condition, his high blood pressure or something else entirely caused these headaches, Dr. Ross T. McIntire, the White House physician, never adequately explained.

Rather regularly, Dr. McIntire drained the President's sinus cavities. This semisurgical process brought momentary relief from pressure and congestion, but it also had an irritating effect which caused the next seizure to be more distressing and possibly even momentarily incapacitating. Eleanor Roosevelt herself thought her husband was submitting far too frequently to the ordeal. However, Dr. McIntire was an ear, nose and throat specialist. Who would question his treatment?

There was no doubt that Roosevelt's dedication to his job had told on him after nearly nine years. His hair was grey and thin, his face heavier and more deeply lined than it had been even a year or two before. He had acquired the habit of throwing back his head before answering a question. With constrained nervousness he fitted one cigarette after another into its holder. While his verbal riposte was as agile as ever, he appeared cross at his Press conferences this first week in December, as close to bad temper as the correspondents had ever noticed in this man who had a reputation for equilibrium. There was no doubt he was overworked and "overworried."

Roosevelt probably spent more time on the job than had any President before him. His was a restless, peripatetic vigour. He retired well past midnight after reading in bed for an hour or two, but slept until nine. He enjoyed, still abed, an ample breakfast of scrambled eggs, kippers, toast and coffee. The herring, a special favourite, was a taste Roosevelt shared with Churchill.

During this early meal, however, he would scan the first of six newspapers, the confidential mail and the day's visiting list. From slightly after 10 a.m. until 1 p.m. he kept general appointments and continued his engagements after lunch until at least five o'clock, an intensive schedule to which few executives, irrespective of their business or profession, could so continuously adhere. He had a habit of saving the afternoon's final two hours for private conversations—with close advisers such as Judge Samuel Rosenman, Admiral Stark, and General Marshall. Harry Hopkins, since he lived in the White House, was generally an evening caller.

Roosevelt did not keep a personal diary. What transpired during these tête-à-têtes filtered out later in abbreviated snatches from those who visited with him, if, indeed, it ever did at all. However, what dominated the President's mind in 1941 was not a secret. This he clearly expressed in his "fireside chat" of March 15, when he discussed his Lease-Lend measure (as he referred to it) and the $7 billion primer charge. In promising "total effort" on the part of the United States towards helping Great Britain, China and Greece, Roosevelt declared:

"Our country is going to be what our people have proclaimed it must be: the arsenal of democracy!"

Not everyone shared his thoughts and approved of his pronouncements on this matter. In fact, it sometimes seemed that Roosevelt was jousting with fate quite alone. But perhaps the most adamant "one-man" President since Lincoln, he was accustomed to making his own decisions, big and small.

As a result, his trusted aides-de-camp this winter, early in his third term, were few in number, instruments for obeying "the chief's" orders.

His Cabinet, according to Attorney-General Francis Biddle, one of its number, "was not a group of outstanding men." Another was Cordell Hull, from Pickett County, Tennessee, weary from sparring with the Japanese. His problems with them began in 1933 when he first became Secretary of State.

As a Spanish-American War Campaigner with the 4th Regiment, Tennessee Volunteers, and later as a United States congressman, Hull had proved his scrappy, stubborn qualities. When he swore—as he often did—the oaths shocked listeners, for the language somehow did not mesh with the silver hair, soft features and mild manners that gave him a benevolent and detached air.

Not a student nor even a man of unusual intellect, Hull was nevertheless aware that Japan had been a troublesome prodder of the Western world ever since 1853 when Commodore Matthew Perry paid his visit to the Mikado. In 1895 Japan attacked China without warning, and a decade later attacked Russia. The land of the Rising Sun played opportunist on the side of the Allies in World War I in order to secure Germany's Asiatic and Pacific possessions. She invaded Manchuria in 1931, and then paused only long enough to avow "We want no more territory" before launching wholesale aggression in China in 1937.

Hull had every reason to believe that Japan's duplicity could find an equal only with Germany's and that her thirst for conquest was insatiable. He had piloted the nation's foreign affairs through an exceptionally rocky channel after Japanese aircraft bombed and sank the U.S.S. *Panay* in the Yangtze River. Apologies as well as indemnities were forthcoming from Tokyo, but there was little doubt that Japan was committed to a course from which there could be no turning back.

This was illustrated again in September, 1940, when Japan entered into the Tri-Partite Pact with Germany and Italy. "If the United States," warned Premier Prince Fumimaro Konoye, who was considered a moderate, "refuses to understand the real intentions of Japan, Germany and Italy and continues persistently its challenging attitude and acts ... those powers will be forced to go to war."

As the new year commenced, Joseph Grew, Ambassador to Japan, wrote in his diary, "there is a lot of talk around town ... that the Japanese, in case of a break with the United States, are planning to go all-out in a surprise mass attack on Pearl Harbour."

Roosevelt, on January 6, 1941, went before Congress and issued a grave warning: "The future of all American republics is today in serious danger." Among other rearming necessities, he asked for a $½ billion "two-ocean fleet" expansion, and a 20 per cent increase in the Navy's enlisted strength.

In February, however, better relations with Japan appeared in prospect with the appointment of tall, pumpkin-faced Kichisaburo Nomura as ambassador to Washington. Naval attaché to the same capital during World War I, the suave, poker-playing, whisky-drinking Nomura had acquired "the Western outlook." Although he assumed his task loyally and with apparent enthusiasm, Nomura at sixty-three had reason to regret his appointment; he had been plucked out of a snug retirement as head of Japan's "Peers" school, an institution without parallel in other nations. Its aim was to instill tradition, etiquette and "culture" in scions of the nobility. Personable and reassuring, Nomura, while chain-smoking, echoed placating words from Tokyo: the two governments would work together to avert war. There were no issues, he emphasized, which could not be settled by mediation.

Nomura's air of sincerity evoked Hull's commendation, voiced privately, "This is a Japanese I think we can trust." But, more than anything else, Hull wanted peace and an end to conflict. He was physically tired, and tired, as well, of being circumvented by the man in the resplendent white mansion across the street from his own weathered, grey, Victorian State Department.

The President listened to Nomura's avowals of friendship, and then asked Congress for additional funds to fortify Pacific bases such as Guam, Samoa and Hawaii. Great Britain, herself uneasy, flew soldiers and equipment to bolster her northern Malaya outposts and sowed a minefield at the approaches to Singapore.

In May, two months after Roosevelt had signed into law his Lease-Lend bill (known later as "lend-lease") designed primarily to aid England in her battle against Nazi Germany, Tokyo presented a "peace proposal." The United States, the terms suggested, should demand that Chiang Kai-shek negotiate with Japan and that the two powers, America and Japan, work together for the admitted purpose of exploiting in the South-west Pacific such natural resources as rubber, oil, tin and nickel. Premier Konoye, a pawn of the militarists and lately in poor health, assured Ambassador Grew that his country's southward expansion would be carried out only by peaceful means, "unless circumstances render this impossible."

Cordell Hull patiently listened to everything the Japanese suggested, no matter how implausible or impossible. Not only was the Secretary of State aware that our Army and Navy could not back up a "tough" policy in the Pacific, but he was also in the vortex of a national indecision. One day he might be called a warmonger if the administration suggested increased military strength; the next day, a pacifist if another segment of the population demanded embargoes and other constraining or menacing measures against Japan.

The events of the summer seemed to move too fast for the old, sick Hull. On June 22, Hitler attacked the Soviet Union. Ambassador Grew, realizing immediately what this development meant in Asia, advised the Secretary of State:

"The army and other elements in the country see in the present world situation a golden opportunity to carry into effect their dreams of expansion. . . . She has submerged all moral and ethical sense and has become frankly and unashamedly opportunist, seeking at every turn a profit by the weakness of others."

On July 2 Japan showed she was preparing for something major. Nearly two million reservists and conscripts were ordered to the colours. Merchant vessels operating in the Atlantic were recalled, while restrictions were imposed upon travel in the home islands. Censorship of mail and other communications was imposed, hinting at coming military operations. Tokyo news agencies, charging that the Philippines were being used as a "pistol aimed at Japan's heart," thumped that the United States was plotting "encirclement."

Brooding over this allegation, Hull called a Press conference. He accused Nomura's government of "trumping up" charges, then added, in effect, that Japan must really be encircling herself.

On July 21 Japan's new Foreign Minister, Admiral Teijiro Toyoda, billed as a "moderate," declared, "Our foreign policy is centered on the Axis and is flanked by the neutrality treaty with the Soviet Union." That was all Hull needed to hear. Within the week the United States in concert with England "froze" Japanese assets in their respective countries; imports and exports, all financial transactions were subject to government licencing. Japan was hurt in the areas for which the blow was intended: her critical dependence on oil, iron and iron ore, aluminium, manganese, scrap metal, coal, wool, virtually all raw materials. American and British economists agreed that Japan would be bankrupt within six months.

Roosevelt, as he said meaningfully to his Secretary of State, was through with "babying along" the Japanese . . . the Japanese whom he had once branded "Prussians of the East."

In retaliation, Tokyo froze American and British assets, though it was an empty enough gesture. As July ended, the Navy gunboat *Tutuila*, attached to the Yangtze patrol, was hit during an air raid on Chungking. No lives were lost. An apology sped from Tokyo.

On August 17, upon his return from his meeting with Churchill at Placentia Bay, off the Newfoundland coast, Roosevelt advised Japan that Great Britain and the United States had "solemnly agreed" to resist the desires of other nations for expansion through force.

Tokyo replied with a suggestion that the Premier and the President meet. The State Department countered, in a more placating tone, that any such talks must be predicated upon Japan's conceding the basic principles of territorial integrity, the sovereignty of nations, "non-interference" in others' internal affairs and maintenance of the *"status quo"* in the Pacific. These *"sine qua nons"* had been reiterated many times by the United States.

And so the clouds over the Pacific grew darker.

Premier Konoye wrote in his diary after an Imperial Conference on September 6:

"In view of the present pressing situation, the offensives of the United States, Britain, the Netherlands, etc., towards Japan and the flexibility of the national power of the Empire, the enforcement of measures regarding the southern regions shall be made as follows:

"1. The Empire shall complete war preparations with the last decade of October as the aim under the determination not to mind war with the United States (Britain and the Netherlands) for the purpose of guaranteeing its self-existence and self-defence.

"2. In parallel to it, the Empire shall have recourse

to diplomatic means in dealing with the United States and Britain and endeavour to have its demands attained.

"3. In case there is found no way still for attainment of our demands even in the first decade of October, the Empire shall at once determine upon war with the United States (Britain and the Netherlands)...."

Early in September, with Germany still rampaging in Russia and her U-boats marauding the Atlantic, Roosevelt delivered a blistering attack on the Axis powers. He ordered the Navy to shoot the warcraft of these nations on sight "like rattlesnakes." And in Japan, the following month the Konoye régime fell. Its obituary, published October 17, explained blandly: "The Cabinet found it difficult to reach an agreement of views concerning the manner of executing national policy."

The new Premier was Lieutenant-General Hideki Tojo, most recently War Minister and before that the supreme commander of one of Japan's armies—the Kwantung—in China and Manchuria. A hard, humourless man, he had once been chief of the Gestapo-like Japanese gendarmerie. Called *"kamisori,"* or "razor blade," Tojo, descendent of two generations of samurai warriors, did not disguise his martial intent. "Japan," he asserted, "must be able to fight China and Russia at the same time ... the nation should move as one cannon ball of fiery resolution."

In mid-November Hull was confronted by a second Japanese envoy, Saburo Kurusu, tough, devious, signer of the Tri-Partite Pact as ambassador to Berlin.

As short as Nomura was tall, Kurusu had once been consul in Chicago, had married an American woman and was considered to possess "American understanding."

Now, if ever, it seemed to Hull, was the time to call a truce. Though he remained convinced that "these fellows mean to fight," he sought at least a reprieve in a "cooling off" period. But a Japanese note to the United States, on November 20, was not the answer; on the contrary, it was "an ultimatum." As Hull interpreted it, "the plan thus offered called for the supplying by the United States to Japan of as much oil as Japan might require, for suspension of freezing measures, for discontinuance by the United States of aid to China, and for withdrawal of moral and material support from the recognized Chinese Government . . . the proposal contained no provision pledging Japan to abandon aggression and to revert to peaceful courses."

At the same time the State Department was working on a *modus vivendi* of its own, aimed at the withdrawal of Japanese forces from China and also from French Indo-China where they had been, by agreement with the Vichy Government, since the fall of France. In return, the United States would relax its freezing order and allow export again, in reduced quantities, of such commodities as petroleum.

The *modus vivendi*, as might have been expected, never reached the Japanese. It was vetoed in advance by Great Britain, Australia, the Netherlands and, most vehemently, by China. Secretary of War Stimson himself wrote of it in his diary:

"It adequately safeguarded all our interests, I

thought as I read it, but I did not think there was any chance of the Japanese accepting it, because it was so drastic. In return for the propositions which they were to do: namely, to at once evacuate and at once to stop all preparations or threats of action, and to take no aggressive action against any of her neighbours, etc., we were to give them open trade in sufficient quantities only for their civilian population."

On November 26 a Ten-Point Note, attempting in somewhat different language and overtones to "adjust the whole situation in the Far East," was sent from the State Department to Tokyo.* To Hull, who was by his own evaluation "hopelessly overworked," it seemed all that he could do. "I have washed my hands of it," he told Stimson. "It is now in the hands of you and Knox—the Army and the Navy." Haunted by the spectre of failure, humiliated by the realization that his Commander-in-Chief could and often did by-pass him, Hull as one associate described it, was hurt "deep inside."

But he could neither rest nor wash his hands of his almost overwhelming burdens as Secretary of State. And he certainly could not shift his personal responsibilities to the Under Secretary, the tall, aloof and extremely strange Sumner Welles. Hull disliked and distrusted him. He was, in fact, fearful of ever turning his back on his assistant, an unfortunate state of affairs in these, the final, critical weeks of 1941.

Not only were Nomura and Kurusu regularly importuning Hull, but the concerns of his own far-flung posts and out-posts were pressing and constant. As

* See Appendix for complete text of the Ten-Point Note.

November turned into December, for example, he forwarded instructions to Far Eastern consular staffs for dealing with "any sudden emergencies." These included the burning of confidential files, seals, codes, ciphers, extra passports, and also the termination agreements for alien employees.

Worry over the Japanese possessed and dominated the old fighter of the 4th Tennessee Volunteers. He could not seem to rid himself of terrible presentiments. Early in the first week of December, with exceptional bluntness he told Captain Roscoe E. Schuirmann, his naval liaison: "I know you Navy fellows are always ahead of me, but I want you to know that I don't seem to be able to do anything more with these Japanese and they are liable to run loose like a mad dog and bite anyone."

Before the Press, Hull, pale with emotion, accused the Japanese government of pursuing a policy "of conquest and military despotism," while noting that seven months of negotiation had done "nothing to bridge the broad gap between the Japanese position and that of the United States."

Henry L. Stimson shared Hull's forebodings for the future. In failing health, and at 74 the oldest member of the Cabinet, the Secretary of War managed to keep going through prolonged hours of rest at his estate, "Woodley," in the Cleveland Park section of Washington. Something of a fixture in American cabinets, the wealthy New York attorney had served as Secretary of War under Taft and as Secretary of State under Hoover. In World War I he had received a colonel's commission to go overseas with the American Expeditionary Force. But in spite of his long experience,

Stimson was a newcomer to this administration. He was Roosevelt's third Secretary of War, having been appointed only in 1940.

With thin, greying bangs of hair over his forehead, Stimson looked like a schoolboy who somehow had grown old without ever graduating. His manner at a Press conference was halting, uncertain, like that same superannuated schoolboy. His poor presence in front of groups was unfortunate, for it in no way bespoke the keen mind within the unprepossessing frame. Perhaps for this simple reason, Roosevelt did not often avail himself of his Secretary's accumulated store of wisdom, preferring bolder counsel.

Thus, Stimson was not a frequent visitor at the White House, nor was his presence much more strongly felt in the War Department, where he left military decisions to Chief of Staff George C. Marshall. His influence, nonetheless, and his innate wisdom made surreptitious impact. He could filter suggestions upward through many channels, and he was often the one to ask the kind of questions which caused his listeners to think and then, possibly, to act.

As a faithful diarist, Stimson also was to make an inestimable contribution to history, especially his seemingly dispassionate recordings of the informal "war council" meetings called at irregular times at the White House. Present were the Secretaries of State, War and Navy and, usually, the Chief of Staff and the Chief of Naval Operations.

On November 26, the day the Ten-Point Note went off to Tokyo, Stimson wrote a provocative paragraph:

"(The President) brought up the event that we

were likely to be attacked (perhaps as soon as next Monday) for the Japanese are notorious for making an attack without warning, and the question was what we should do. The question was how we should manoeuvre them into the position of firing the first shot without allowing too much danger to ourselves. It was a difficult proposition."

In a telephone conversation with Stimson the following day, Roosevelt confirmed that talks between the Japanese envoys and the State Department were at least temporarily called off "but that they had ended up with a magnificent statement prepared by Hull. I found out afterwards that this was the fact and that the statement contained a reaffirmation of our constant and regular position without the suggestion of a threat of any kind."

On November 28, the day the President was to leave for Warm Springs, Stimson called upon Roosevelt in his bedroom and found him eating breakfast from a tray. The Secretary of War wanted to discuss the Japanese convoys reported to be moving towards Indo-China.

"He," Stimson reported, "branched into an analysis of the situation himself as he sat there on his bed, saying there were three alternatives and only three that he could see before us. I told him I could see two. His alternatives were—first, to do nothing; second, to make something in the nature of an ultimatum again, stating a point beyond which we would fight; third, to fight at once. I told him my only two were the last two, because I did not think anyone would do nothing in this situation, and he agreed with me."

Of a war council meeting later the same morning, Stimson noted:

"It was the consensus that the present move (by the Japanese)—that there was an Expeditionary Force on the sea of about 25,000 Japanese troops aimed for a landing somewhere—completely changed the situation.... It was now the opinion of everyone that if this expedition was allowed to get around the southern point of Indo-China and to go off and land in the Gulf of Siam, either at Bangkok or further west, it would be a terrible blow at all of the three powers, Britain at Singapore, the Netherlands and ourselves in the Philippines. It was the consensus of everybody that this must not be allowed.... It was also agreed that if the British fought, we would have to fight....

"I said there ought to be a message by the President to the people of the United States and I thought that the best form of a message would be an address to Congress reporting the danger."

The day after the President's sudden return from Warm Springs, it was still possible that he would address Congress, according to Stimson. He wrote on December 2 that Roosevelt "is quite settled, I think, that he will make a message to the Congress and will, perhaps back that up with a speech to the country."

Stimson's opposite in the Navy Department, Frank Knox, had neither the perspicacity, vision nor reportorial ability that distinguished the Secretary of War. The publisher of the Chicago *Daily News*, now 67, had been recruited from Republican ranks, about all that the jovial, outgoing Knox had in common with Stimson. He had been a Rough Rider at Colonel "Teddy" Roosevelt's side in the Spanish-American

War, and in 1936 he was Alfred M. Landon's teammate in the disastrous 1936 presidential election.

A heavy-set man of rather square build, Knox wore Wilsonian pince-nez glasses. Otherwise, he bore little resemblance to the President from Princeton, or to any other high-placed statesman. Honest in his ethical code and unassuming of nature, he had admitted he knew nothing about the Navy. He was also unhesitant about confessing his fun at "playing sailor."

Quite possibly a better administrator than the lawyer Stimson, Knox had brought in a number of able civilian aides to help him re-organize the Navy Department. His critics who were also his friends subsequently were to say that he had not gone far enough in allowing the Annapolis "club" to prevail whenever there was a showdown. However, Knox knew that his job was a sort of consolation prize, and considered Roosevelt as the real head of the Navy—a man who had dearly loved the sea service even before he was Assistant Secretary of the Navy during the First World War.

"I believe I understand the Navy," Roosevelt had once confided to Admiral Stark. "I have to take *their* [the Army's] word for what they say."

If Knox was not shepherded into the full confidence of the White House, neither was he a well of information about his own department, even though he was Secretary of the Navy. In fact, Knox was not taken too seriously by the admirals, or even the captains. His newspaperman's instinct to print or at least to tell a story was in marked variance with the inclinations of men who had been trained to "keep quiet—don't talk." There was some truth to the abiding concern that Knox would rush into Press release intriguing bits of intelligence. His naval aides could well draw in a breath whenever they saw Knox's rotund face light up as he reached for his telephone.

He liked to talk. As an example, on the evening of December 4, he and Mrs. Knox were entertaining Donald Nelson, of the Office of Production Management, in their apartment at the Wardman Park Hotel.

"Don," Knox volunteered during dinner, "we may be at war with the Japs before the month is over."

"Is it that bad?" Nelson asked.

"You bet your life it's that bad," Knox rejoined.

Knox, of course, knew that the international situation was going from bad to worse. In fact, he had written to the Secretary of War:

"The security of the U.S. Pacific Fleet while in Pearl Harbour and of the Pearl Harbour Naval Base itself has been under renewed study by the Navy Department and forces afloat for the past several weeks. This re-examination has been, in part, prompted by the increased gravity of the situation with respect to Japan and by reports from abroad of successful bombing and torpedo-plane attacks on ships while in bases. If war eventuates with Japan, it is believed easily possible that hostilities would be initiated by a surprise attack on the fleet or the naval base at Pearl Harbour.

"In my opinion, the inherent possibility of a major disaster to the fleet or naval base warrants taking every step as rapidly as can be done, that will increase the joint readiness of the Army and Navy to withstand a raid of the character mentioned above."

Knox, though overweight, appeared otherwise robust despite the burden of his advancing years. If his fellow Cabinet members Stimson and Hull were in failing health, that of a fourth and especially close adviser to the President had long since failed. Harry Hopkins, from Grinnell, Iowa, former Secretary of Commerce and WPA administrator, was principally concerned with the Lease-Lend programme. And a visit to Russia in the summer of 1941 had done nothing to improve his gaunt, cadaverous aspect. A widower, he had moved into the White House with his nine-year-old daughter Diana as a semi-permanent resident. But for the entire month of November he had been at the old Naval Hospital, near the Potomac River, under treatment for chronic internal disorders.

Hopkins, whose instincts were those of a social worker, was outspoken, a chancy politician. The sight of him could and did elevate the blood pressure of the irascible Harold Ickes, Secretary of the Interior. His position in the Executive Department, in spite of prevalent Republican opinion, was in no way analogous to that of Colonel Edward M. House in the Wilson administration. House, a sombre, inscrutable Texan, sought passionately to influence the President's decisions, to urge him, as a prime example, to bring the nation to Britain's side in the war against the Kaiser. Harry Hopkins was a sounding board, a valuable companion and a patient listener to Roosevelt's ideas who, if he guided the President, did so most indirectly. He was perhaps more comparable to Mark Sullivan the newspaperman, a favourite of Herbert Hoover's at breakfast and on the handball court.

"He knows instinctively," observed the columnist Raymond Clapper, "when to ask, when to keep still, when to press, when to hold back; when to approach Roosevelt direct, when to go at him roundabout... quick, alert, shrewd, bold, and carrying it off with a bright Hell's bells air, Hopkins is in all respects the inevitable Roosevelt favourite."

As, in some respects, Roosevelt's *alter ego* in 1941, Hopkins found it prudent to be a figure in the shadows, and providentially a step or two away from the turbulence which attended public office at the Cabinet or administrative level. He would never utter in public the sort of frank comment that often found its way into his personal memos to Roosevelt. For example, he commented in such a note in October:

"It seems to me that if our naval officers would spend more time getting our own Navy ready to do its job and less on criticizing the British we would be better off."

In the past year Harry Hopkins, in spite of sojourns at the Naval Hospital, had been at Roosevelt's side more than any other official of the administration. He was, however, a security risk of a sort, apparently preoccupied most of the time and consummately careless about secret papers. Once a Navy intelligence officer had to dash to a dry cleaning establishment on the fringes of Washington to retrieve a particularly confidential dispatch from the trousers pocket of one of Hopkins' suits. As a matter of fact, Harry Hopkins did not own many clothes; those he wore invariably looked as if they had been slept in.

Once a socially enthusiastic drinker, Hopkins demonstrated his strong will by obeying his doctors scrupulously when he was ordered never to touch alcohol again. Even with abstinence and the dedicated efforts of the best specialists to keep the waning spark alight in his emaciated body, Hopkins was daily amazed that he continued to live at all.

Hopkins, Hull, Stimson, the President himself—never had leadership of a nation been so dominated by illness and failing health. Knox, slowed down by corpulence and advancing years, would not live even to see the Normandy invasion. The coincidence of so much age and illness in the top posts of an administration was more tragic than curious in this period of American history.

3
THE LIEUTENANTS' LIEUTENANTS

Admiral Harold R. Stark, the luxuriantly white-haired and buoyantly healthy Chief of Naval Operations, was Roosevelt's most personal link with the nation's military. He called the high naval officer "Betty," an old Annapolis nickname, and had done so since 1914 when he first met Stark. At that time Stark, commanding the destroyer *Patterson*, was taking the Assistant Secretary of the Navy across Passamaquoddy Bay to his home on Campobello Island, a short journey punctuated by some of the rockiest channels along the New England coast.

By Stark's side on the bridge, Roosevelt, the enthusiastic yachtsman, finally asked:

"May I relieve you for a while? I am an experienced navigator and I know the coast."

Firmly but politely, the 34-year-old lieutenant replied: "I am in command here and responsible for the ship. I doubt your authority to supersede me. If you can offer any helpful suggestions I shall be glad to hear them."

Apparently, plain talk impressed Roosevelt. The two men remained firm friends, with a respect for each other's abilities.

Harold Stark came from a wealthy family in Wilkes-Barre, Pennsylvania, and distinguished himself as a member of Annapolis' Class of '03 for his athletic ability and as the leader of the Academy choir. All his life he was a practising advocate of physical fitness. He frequently strode out of the old red-brick building at the Naval Observatory, known as Quarters "A," reserved for the Chief of Naval Operations, down the Massachusetts Avenue hill and ultimately to the long, weathered stucco structure on Constitution Avenue which had been the Navy Department since World War I. It was at least half an hour's walk.

Unlike a number of his contemporaries—including Chester W. Nimitz and Ernest J. King—Stark was not attracted to the infant submarine and aviation branches of the Navy. He was devoted to ships and to cannon, and he quickly became a "big gun expert." During World War I he won the Distinguished Service Medal for leading a flotilla of broken-down, but partially reconditioned destroyers from the Philippines to the Mediterranean to harry German and Austrian submarines. He also served on the staff of the outspoken Admiral William H. Sims until 1919. He was commanding the cruiser division of the United States Battle Force in 1939 when Roosevelt decided to jump his firm-minded, soft-spoken friend over ten other admirals to become Chief of Naval

Operations. His predecessor, Admiral William D. Leahy, was retiring and also readying himself to become ambassador to France.

Humiliated that the United States Navy was in third place among the world's fleets—Britain led and Japan ranked second—Stark dedicated his efforts to "building a Navy second to none." It would be a hard fight with an economy-minded Congress, but Stark knew the "Boss" was behind him.

A year after Stark became CNO, Roosevelt inspired a radical shift in naval positioning. In May, 1940, he ordered the Pacific Fleet to be moved from California to Pearl Harbour, 2,000 nautical miles west of San Francisco, 3,430 miles south-east of Tokyo, an immensely strategic position astride the Pacific sealanes. The President not only envisioned Pearl as an excellent lair for operations in all directions but thought the mere presence of the battleships in the Pacific would serve as a deterrent to Japan.

Admiral James O. Richardson, Pacific Fleet commander, however, could see only the former installations at San Pedro, San Diego, Mare Island and Bremerton on Puget Sound as the proper base complex for "the heavies." He denounced Pearl Harbour as a "God-damn mousetrap." Since he did not take to individuals who so openly criticized him, Roosevelt asked Stark to pick a successor for Richardson. He did so in the person of Admiral Husband E. Kimmel, 59, a tall, blond Kentuckian, as "tough" as Richardson but far more diplomatic. Kimmel, promoted over several officers with more seniority, possessed an excellent record as a commander and administrator, was liked by his associates and had been a long-standing friend of Stark's.

If Kimmel went to Hawaii with misgivings, he at least had every reason to assume that the Chief of Naval Operations would keep him advised of the changing international atmosphere and—surely—support him if the going became turbulent. He formally assumed command on February 1, 1941, and a few weeks later decided to put in writing his desires to be "rung in." He wrote to Admiral Stark:

> I have recently been told by an officer fresh from Washington that ONI [Office of Naval Intelligence] considers it the function of Operations to furnish the Commander-in-Chief with information of a secret nature. I have heard also that Operations considers the responsibility for furnishing the same type of information to be that of ONI. I do not know that we have missed anything, but if there is any doubt as to whose responsibility it is to keep the Commander-in-Chief [of the Pacific Fleet] fully informed with pertinent reports on subjects that should be of interest to the Fleet, will you kindly fix that responsibility so that there will be no misunderstanding?

Kimmel's position in this "mousetrap" was not favourable. The Japanese out-numbered by almost two to one United States naval strength in the Pacific, which consisted of 102 effective vessels, including the Asiatic Fleet, under command of Admiral Thomas C. Hart, subordinate to Kimmel. At 64 the peppery, able Hart from Connecticut, had been kept on active duty past retirement age. Air patrol out of Hawaii was inadequate, with only fifty-seven lumbering, superannuated twin-engined flying boats available for reconnaissance. Eight other PBYs were out of commission, awaiting repairs, which perhaps would never be made considering what Kimmel characterized as "the almost total lack of spare parts."

The Pacific Fleet commander was compelled to refuse the repeated requests of Rear-Admiral Claude C. Bloch, Commandant of the Fourteenth Naval District, centred at Honolulu, for effective offshore patrol. "We'd have so many under maintenance," he informed the tall, lean Bloch, who had, like Hart, passed retirement age, "if we frittered them away in distance reconnaissance that we'd have none ready for a real attack." He mentioned, besides, the need to "maintain our training status." He considered Hawaii in part a training station.

As Kimmel grew familiar with his new command, Stark gave his Pacific Fleet chief every reason to trust the Navy Department. On April 1 he advised Kimmel and naval district heads:

> Personnel of your naval intelligence service should be advised that because of the fact that from past experience shows the Axis powers often begin activities in a particular field on Saturdays and Sundays or on national holidays of the country concerned, they should take steps on such days to see that proper watches and precautions are in effect.

On May 27 Roosevelt proclaimed an "unlimited national emergency," which placed a particular strain upon the Navy. Stark knew only too well that the President's assertion, "We do not accept and will not permit this Nazi 'shape of things to come' " meant an immediate broadening of the Navy's operations in the

Atlantic. There, officers already were quipping cynically that they were "waging neutrality." The legalistic ramifications of a neutral power convoying the merchant ships of a belligerent were themselves many and complex, to say nothing of the neutral actually attacking another nation's submarines.

Hitler's invasion of Russia still had not involved the United States in the "shooting war" as the summer wore on. However, on July 7, Stark felt it wise to advise Kimmel:

> Japan is preparing for all possible eventualities regarding Soviet in order join forces with Germany in actively combating communists and destroying communist system in Eastern Siberia. At same time Japan cannot and will not relax efforts in the south to restrain Britain and the United States. New Indo-China bases will intensify restraint and be vital contribution to Axis victory.

The Chief of Naval Operations ordered the approaches to Manila mined, and he continued to wrestle with the vexatious problem of how to defend the immensity of the Pacific while fighting in the relatively limited Atlantic. In August, Stark dispatched an unusual order to the Commander-in-Chief of the Pacific Fleet.

> ... destroy surface raiders which attack or threaten United States flag shipping. Interpret an approach of surface raiders within the Pacific sector of the Panama Naval coastal frontier or the Pacific south-east sub area as a threat to United States flag shipping.

In September, however, when a puzzled Kimmel

asked about bombing submarine contacts "without waiting to be attacked," the Chief of Naval Operations cautioned restraint, urging that the longer the *status quo* could be maintained in the Pacific the better. A "strong warning and a threat of hostile action" by United States naval ships was recommended by Stark as the safer course of action.

When Tojo bullied his way into the premiership in October, Stark, much more concerned than he was after the Nazis had mocked their "friendship" treaty with the U.S.S.R., cabled Admiral Kimmel:

> The resignation of the Japanese cabinet has created a grave situation. If a new cabinet is formed it will probably be strongly nationalistic and anti-American. If the Konoye cabinet remains, the effect will be that it will operate under a new mandate which will not include *rapprochement* with the U.S. . . .

Stark went on to mention the possibilities that Japan might attack Russia, or even Great Britain and the United States, and then warned that Kimmel should "take due precautions including such preparatory deployments as will not disclose strategic intention nor constitute provocative actions against Japan."

As was his habit, Stark followed up this formal communication with a note to his Pacific Fleet commander: "Personally I do not believe the Japs are going to sail into us and the message I sent you merely stated the 'possibility' . . . in any case after long pow-wows in the White House it was felt we should be on guard, at least until something indicates the trend."

Then, before sealing the letter, he postscripted: "Marshall just called up and was anxious that we make some sort of a reconnaissance so that he could feel assured that on arrival at Wake, a Japanese raider attack may not be in order on his bombers. I told him that we could not assure against any such contingency, but that I felt it extremely improbable and that, while we keep track of Japanese ships so far as we can, a carefully planned raid on any of these island carriers in the Pacific might be difficult to detect. However, we are on guard to the best of our ability and my advice to him was not to worry."

In response, Kimmel stationed submarines off Wake and Midway islands, reinforced Wake and Johnston with additional Marines, ammunition and stores, and shipped more Marines to Palmyra Island. He directed an alert status in the outlying islands, placed on twelve-hour notice certain vessels of the fleet which were in West Coast ports, held six submarines in readiness to depart from Japan, and delayed the sailing of one battleship from the Mare Island Navy Yard in San Francisco. He could not, however, improve upon one imponderable: fuel for his fleet. He still had only four sea-refuelling tankers. Others had been snatched away to satisfy the appetite of the Atlantic Fleet in the undeclared war against Hitler's Kriegsmarine.

At Fourteenth Naval District headquarters, Admiral Bloch complained that the U.S.S. *Sacramento*, an old gun-boat "of negligible gun power" had been the only new vessel added to his local defence forces in the past year. He desperately desired fast, small craft and single-engined VSO patrol planes to snoop out the enemy submarines which he was certain lurked over western horizons. Kimmel endorsed his fellow admiral's appeal, while speeding it on to Washington:

"There is a possibility that the reluctance or inability of the Department to furnish the Commandant, Fourteenth Naval District, with forces adequate to his needs may be predicated upon a conception that, in an emergency, vessels of the U.S. Pacific Fleet may always be diverted for these purposes. If such be the case, the premise is so false as to hardly warrant refutation."

Admiral Stark replied that nothing additional could be supplied except a few sub-catchers, and maybe some "privately owned" ships as auxiliaries, but *no* planes were available.

In Washington, as another winter approached, no results whatever accrued from Nomura's talks which had commenced the previous February. Nonetheless, Stark counselled caution. In a long appraisal of the situation to Roosevelt, he emphasized these conclusions, to which General Marshall also subscribed:

"That the dispatch of United States armed forces for intervention against Japan in China be disapproved. . . .

"No ultimatum be delivered to Japan. . . .

"War between the United States and Japan should be avoided."

But in the sanctuary of his own level-headedness, Stark had made up his mind that war *was* coming.

Meanwhile, in spite of the manifestly careful attitude of the United States, Japan's intentions grew daily more ominous. These included a continuing movement of her military and naval forces in the East and withdrawal of her flag and merchant vessels from western hemispheric waters.

"Things seem to be moving steadily towards a crisis in the Pacific," Stark wrote Kimmel on November 7. "Just when it will break, no one can tell. The principal reaction I have to it all is what I have written you before; it continually gets 'worser and worser!' ... two irreconcilable policies cannot go on for ever ... it doesn't look good."

On November 24 Stark became sufficiently concerned to cable Kimmel:

> Chances of favourable outcome of negotiations with Japan very doubtful. This situation coupled with statements of Japanese government and movements their naval and military forces indicates in our opinion that a surprise aggressive movement in any direction including attack on Philippines or Guam is a possibility. Chief of Staff has seen this dispatch concurs and requests action. Addressees to inform senior Army officers their areas. Utmost secrecy necessary in order not to complicate an already tense situation or precipitate Japanese action. Guam will be informed separately.

The next day Stark mailed a personal letter to Kimmel:

"... neither [Roosevelt nor Hull] would be surprised over a Japanese surprise attack. From many angles an attack on the Philippines would be the most embarassing thing that could happen to us. ... I do not give it the weight others do. ... I have generally held that it was not time for the Japanese to proceed against Russia. I still do. Also I still rather look for an advance into Thailand, Indo-China, Burma Road areas as the most likely.

"I won't go into the pros and cons of what the United States may do. I will be damned if I know. I wish I did. The only thing I do know is that we may do most anything and that's the only thing I know to be prepared for; or we may do nothing—I think it is more likely to be 'anything.'"

Two days later, November 17, Stark sent a strong message to Kimmel:

> This dispatch is to be considered a war warning. Negotiations with Japan looking towards stabilization of conditions in the Pacific have ceased and an aggressive move by Japan is expected within the next few days. The number and equipment of Japanese troops and the organization of naval task forces indicate an amphibious expedition against either the Philippines, Thai or Kra Peninsula or possibly Borneo. Execute an appropriate defensive deployment preparatory to carrying out the tasks assigned in WPL46. Inform district and Army authorities. A similar warning is being sent by War Department....

Stark, as was his custom, telephoned Roosevelt about his "war warning." In this case, the Chief of Naval Operations was so sure of himself that he had not consulted the President prior to its transmission. "That's all right, Betty," approved Roosevelt, who addressed almost everyone, including "Winnie" Churchill, by his or her first name.

Thus Stark had increasing reason to feel that he was both carrying out the Commander-in-Chief's desires and that he *understood* him, regardless of whether this understanding was obtained through formal conversation, by communication, or by innuendo: the inflection of Roosevelt's voice, even a nod or an expression or the especially vital eyes which could convey so much.

As Stark has recalled with nostalgia to this writer, few nights went by without his either receiving a call at Quarters "A," Observatory Circle, on the private line from the White House or his telephoning Roosevelt just to chat about the day's developments. A midnight conversation was not at all unusual, since Roosevelt was in the habit of reading mysteries in bed until long after that hour, when, in fact, the city beyond his windows had grown very quiet.

On the daily list of White House callers, Stark's name appeared with significant frequency. He arrived at the back door of the Executive Mansion, often without an appointment, sometimes without a prior telephone call. His comings and goings were as easy and natural as though he were a member of the family.

Quite the opposite was the Chief of Staff's relationship with the President of the United States. General Marshall, 61, the same age as Stark, moved and thought slowly. He was a stickler for tradition and protocol. He rarely called at the White House in 1941 or telephoned Roosevelt on his own direct wire from "House No. 1," reserved for the Chief of Staff at Fort Myer, Virginia, adjoining Arlington National Cemetery, across the Potomac River. A sombre, perhaps shy man, Marshall, since becoming Chief of Staff in 1939, had chosen Harry Hopkins as his pipeline to the President. This meant, naturally, that the Army's story—and the Army's needs—were invariably heard secondhand at the White House.

While his relationship with Stark was somewhat less stiff and his communication somewhat more direct, Marshall nonetheless tended to bury himself in his ample office on the second floor of the Munitions Building. The weathered structure was connected by ramps to its twin, the Navy Department, but between the Chief of Staff's office and the Chief of Naval Operations' own blue-green "cabin," in identical centre locations in their respective buildings, there was a distance equivalent to four city blocks. It was far easier to use the intercom than to visit in person.

Graduate of the Virginia Military Institute, Class of '01, Marshall, a native of Pennsylvania, could reflect on an Army career that was not entirely satisfactory. He had long been in the unusual but unenviable position of protégé of one military great—General John J. Pershing—but something else again to another, General Douglas MacArthur. Marshall, who had never held a field command, had served in the planning and operations section of the AEF headquarters, Chaumont, in 1918. When MacArthur, a hell-for-leather brigadier-general with the Rainbow Division, had been accidentally captured by his own men during the confusion of the Meuse-Argonne campaign, there arose the possibility that MacArthur blamed Marshall for the mix-up in planning that had caused such an indignity.

In any event, Marshall's career waned after Pershing retired and MacArthur's star was on the ascendancy. The inherently reserved V.M.I. alumnus was awarded the most minor of Army duties during the period when MacArthur was Chief of Staff. At 56 he was one of the oldest colonels in the service when another Chief of Staff, Malin Craig, approved Marshall's promotion, at long last, to brigadier-general. In 1939 it was probably the combination of Craig and Pershing, who was in retirement but was the active chairman of the American Battle Monuments Commission, that persuaded Roosevelt to approve Marshall for the top Army command. Even so, the reticent general did not at that time develop an easy acquaintanceship with the President. He was not, as Stark, a frequent "back door" visitor.

As Stark was occupied with fashioning a Navy that would no longer take second place to Japan's, Marshall was charged with moulding an Army that would not look—or operate—like a relic from the post-Armistice occupation in Germany. He was especially concerned about the extension of the Selective Service Act.

At approximately the same time that Kimmel went to Pearl Harbour the Army's Hawaiian Department received a new commanding general: Walter Campbell Short, 61 years old, blond, smooth-faced Midwesterner, a meticulous "spit-and-polish" officer. He was commissioned in the regular Army shortly after taking his B.A. from the University of Illinois the same year that Marshall completed his training at V.M.I. Although rather cold of manner, he was known as fair in his dealings with subordinates, one who never spoke unkindly of others. "Superconscientious," he possessed an aptitude for teaching that won him a Distinguished Service Medal for his action in the Saint-Mihiel and Meuse-Argonne campaigns during World War I. The citation noted that "he efficiently directed the instruction and training of machine-gun outfits at every available opportunity during rest periods."

After the war, Major Short served in Washington for three years with the Far Eastern Section of the Military Intelligence Division, although his only experience in the East had been a four-month tour of duty at Malabang, the Philippines, in 1907. He went back to teaching at the Command and Staff School, Fort Leavenworth, where he had previously served as an instructor, but left again for Washington in 1930. As a brigadier-general, Short was commanding officer of the First Army Corps, headquartered in Columbia, South Carolina, before he was promoted to lieutenant-general and hand-picked by Marshall for the Hawaiian command: a kind of holding force, comprising two infantry divisions, supporting ground troops, coast artillery and air units. The 43,000 troops which this "department" represented, while obviously inadequate to repel a determined invasion, were intended to protect the fleet and naval installations.

Short realized that he was assuming a command inadequately prepared to defend itself. Soon after reaching Hawaii, he asked of his Chief of Staff:

"I would appreciate your early review of the situation in the Hawaiian Department with regard to defence from air attack. The establishment of a satisfactory system of co-ordinating all means available to this end is a matter of first priority."

On March 6 he advised General Marshall:

"One of the first projects which I investigated in this department was the Aircraft Warning Service which I believe is vital to the defence of these islands.

At the present time the maximum distance an approaching aeroplane can be detected is about five miles... The Navy is vitally interested in this project. At present with the fleet in Hawaiian waters, there is no adequate warning service.... I believe that this matter is sufficiently important to be brought to the attention of the Secretary of War."

But in reply Marshall told his new Hawaiian lieutenant that he could not help the "deficiencies" of the Army about which Short had complained, including the lack of planes and anti-aircraft guns.

"My impression of the Hawaiian problem," added Marshall, "has been that if no serious harm is done us during the first six hours of known hostilities, thereafter the existing defence will discourage any enemy against the hazard of an attack. The risk of sabotage and the risk involved in a surprise raid by air and by submarine constitute the real perils of the situation."

Short went to work with energy and enthusiasm. Every beach where a landing was possible was studied and emplacements, dug-outs, obstacles and other works positioned. Since funds were low, much of the material for breastworks was "scrounged" from salvage, even as the Union soldiers had to make-do at Bull Run.

"We did a most thorough job," Short himself was to report. "We made a very decided overhaul, and put on a great many additional sentinels, particularly around the waterfront where there was danger of fire from petrol, and so forth.... Our problem was to meet internal disorders."

Walter Short had been decorated for proving he could instruct men in 1918 even during the fury of battle. Now he could train them in Hawaii, undistracted by combat. He continued to prove himself "relentless in his demand for superb physical fitness and thorough knowledge of weapons and their use." But out in the scenic expanses of Schofield Barracks, sixteen miles north-west of Honolulu, where Major General Maxwell Murray was in command of the 25th Division, the soldiers drilled under a drenching sun in uniforms almost identical to the ones their fathers wore when they went "over there," and carried the same Enfield and Springfield rifles, and shouted their "hup-two-three!"—preparing for the same kind of war that General Pershing had fought long ago.

Marshall, who also had to make-do with what tools were available while shopping around for such new ones as Congress would permit him, apparently was satisfied with Walter Short's approach to his area's problems. On July 7 he sent a message similar to the one Stark had transmitted to Kimmel:

> For your information stop Deduction from information from numerous sources is that the Japanese government has determined upon its future policy which is supported by all principal Japanese political and military groups stop This policy is present one of watchful waiting involving probably aggressive action against the maritime provinces of Russia if and when the Siberian garrison has been materially reduced in strength and it becomes evident that Germany will win a decisive victory in European Russia stop Opinion is that Jap activity in the south will be for the present confined to seizure and development of naval comma army and air bases in Indo-China although an advance against the British and Dutch cannot be entirely ruled out stop The neutrality pact with Russia may be abrogated stop They

have ordered all Jap vessels in U.S. Atlantic ports to be west of Panama Canal by first of August stop Movement of Jap shipping from Japan has been suspended and additional merchant vessels are being requisitioned.

In late November Marshall co-ordinated a "war warning" message with that sent by the Chief of Naval Operations, advising Short:

> Negotiations with Japan appear to be terminated to all practical purposes with only the barest possibilities that the Japanese government might come back and offer to continue. Japanese future action unpredictable but hostile action possible at any moment. If hostilities cannot repeat not be avoided the United States desires that Japan commit the first overt act. This policy should not repeat not be construed as restricting you to a course of action that might jeopardize your defence. Prior to hostile Japanese action you are directed to undertake such reconnaissance and other measures as you deem necessary but these measures should be carried out so as not to repeat not to alarm civil population or disclose intent ... undertake no offensive action until Japan has committed an overt act.

The commanding general in Hawaii immediately responded: "Department alerted to prevent sabotage. Liaison with Navy." This "No. One" was the lowest state of alert, and its declaration was scarcely noticeable by Hawaiians in movements of either soldiers or guns. Alerts "Two" and "Three" specified danger of enemy attack.

Since Marshall did not comment on Short's acknowledgement, the assumption had to be that the Chief of Staff agreed the Hawaiian Department's anti-sabotage alert was sufficient.

4
TROUBLE ON THE SECOND DECK

Even though they adjoined, the two elongated buildings along Constitution Avenue which the Army and the Navy called home were worlds apart in direct communication or even in basic human understanding. Covered ramps connected the three levels of both buildings, there was a spiderweb complex of interlinking telephone circuits, and messengers, individually certified in an ascending scale of security, constantly scurried between the Navy Department and the Munitions Buildling but nothing could chip at the "inter-service rivalry" that separated the two, a kind of impregnable monolith which defied both time and reason.

Navy personnel considered they were crossing into "foreign," or at best unfriendly, territory when they tramped over the creaking causeway into the Munitions Building. Army men reflected the same provincial attitude, so definite that a man in Army uniform felt conspicuous and most uncomfortable when he paused for a soft drink at one of the Navy Building's several refreshment stands. While Admiral Stark praised the co-operation he received from his opposite, General Marshall, and there was an intercom on the desk of each of the two top-ranking officers, aides recalled very little, if any, reciprocal visiting down the long, barrack-like corridors.

Moreover, rivalry existed not only *between* the services. It extended to an even more pernicious intraservice rivalry, attaining an unenviable peak of absurdity within the office of Naval Operations itself. Actually, this rivalry involved just three admirals, but three whose duties were of incalculable importance to the efficient functioning of both Atlantic and Pacific Fleets. They were the Chief of War Plans (OP 12), Rear-Admiral Richmond Kelly Turner; Chief of Naval Intelligence, Rear-Admiral Theodore Stark Wilkinson; and Chief of Communications, Rear-Admiral Leigh Noyes.

The most aggressive and powerful of the group was 56-year-old, greying, hard-boiled Admiral Turner. Fifth in the Naval Academy's Class of '08, but always bitter that he never made first place, the slender, sharp-featured Kelly Turner represented a curious complex of human ingredients which included brilliance in certain areas of skills and judgement but stopped short of greatness. His own nemesis was his domineering intolerance of divergent opinion, his impatience, and his hot temper. It was scarcely surprising that the Admiral was referred to interchangeably as "Terrible Turner" and "Turn-to-

Turner." "They should have known better!" was his familiar "amen" after excoriating staffers for what he adjudged failure in performance. On the other hand, he gave his critics something to ponder in his softer approach towards very junior officers and enlisted men.

Turner was born in Oregon but grew up in Stockton, California. Possessed with a near mania to be a military man, he played with tin soldiers, built ship models, and spent an inordinate amount of time out of doors, shooting sparrows, hawks, coyotes, foxes, skunks—often, it seemed to his uneasy mother, anything that moved across the valley scrub. Nonetheless, young Turner was a good student; when he was in ninth grade he won a national history contest, the prize for which was a trip to Philadelphia and the Republican Convention which renominated William McKinley for President.

Turner was a striking figure and a sulphuric personality from his undergraduate days on into his naval career. "Abrasive as a file," he was distinguished by a lantern jaw and heavy, black Mephistophelian eyebrows which, as he grew older, augmented his menacing aspect. He served on battleships during World War I, later won his wings as a naval aviator, but had no duty of note until 1927 when he attended the Geneva Disarmament Conference. After that however, he was once more immersed in a slough of service obscurity, punctuated by such special assignments as the Naval War College, in Newport. This postgraduate course was looked upon by officers not "tapped" for it as a fashionable, extravagant finishing school—"that God-damn war college farm."

Kelly Turner, off duty, was a devoted husband. He and his wife, Harriet, childless, enjoyed a hobby of raising Lhasa terriers and prize roses. He also golfed and fished. His name did not appear noticeably in the papers until 1939 when, as captain of the cruiser *Astoria* he bore home the ashes of Hirosi Saito, who died while Japanese Ambassador to the United States. Those who had felt Turner's sting observed that this funeral voyage gave the sharp-tempered, opinionated officer the notion that he was an authority on the Orient. They quipped that this was his only basis for familiarity with Japan.

Whether or not there was substance to this dig, Turner became the War Plans director late in 1940, at a time when the Pacific was increasingly charged with peril. At once he decided that Japan was going to attack Russia, an encore to its sneak attack on Port Arthur in 1904. In testament to this conviction, he commenced a succession of often Delphic dispatches to the fleet and naval outposts. His warnings, meant only to be helpful, culminated in a preposterous example of confusion in February, 1941. On the day Turner sent a general dispatch that Japan might move northward against Russia, Naval Intelligence was alerting the same recipients to expect Tokyo's force to drive southward.

That Turner was perhaps an heir apparent in the Navy hierarchy had become a supposition in the Japanese Embassy. Nomura and one or two other emissaries of standing visited with the War Plans Admiral, entertained him and sought on several occasions to elicit his opinions. He talked freely: Tokyo, he asserted, must withdraw her troops from China;

the United States wanted "not just a pretence but a definite promise"; if the Japanese should advance into Siberia, the President would be placed "in a terrible predicament"; Japan should set aside her "obligations" toward the Tri-Partite Alliance. Turner said nothing that Hull had not already voiced or that any American might not desire, and Nomura gained little from his careful cultivation of this naval officer.

Turner slowly became convinced in his own mind, however, that aggression in the East, including "striking us in the Philippines," would be accompanied by some sort of "amphibious operations against Hawaii simultaneously." He thought, in fact, that an "attack on Hawaii" was "inherent in war with Japan." He attempted to ring the islands with radar picket boats, although his desires were frustrated from the start because of the mesozoic state of radar evolution and meagre production of the precious equipment. The number of fleet ships so equipped was inconsequential. (The Army itself, by Thanksgiving time, had succeeded in operating only six radar outposts on Oahu's headlands, and these between 4 and 7 a.m. "the most dangerous hours of the day for an air attack," in General Short's estimation.) Turner rated Japanese naval potential not very highly compared to the United States fleet. Even so, his concern for Hawaii grew. An aide recalled (to this author) that Turner had endeavoured, unsuccessfully, to specify in the recent "war warning" that Hawaii itself could be attacked.

Whether or not Stark shared this conviction, he came to depend heavily on Turner, believed him to be one of the most efficient subordinates who had ever reported to him: "invaluable," as Stark recalled (to this writer). But that Turner dominated his soft-spoken superior, as had been suggested, was exceedingly doubtful.

On the other hand, Turner *did* dominate nearly every other officer of equal or even higher rank with whom he came in contact. His sense of competition had been developed to a degree which was, at the least, excessive. Trusted aides who could objectively admire, for the most part, the man's efficiency and courage, recognized an obsession in Turner's desire to lead—a desire which, in practice, transcended mere rivalry or competition to become a destructive force. In effect, he wished to beat down not only those who opposed him, or who he fancied opposed him, but even those who were charged with parallel planes of responsibility.

One of these was Admiral Leigh Noyes, the communications chief, undersized, witty Vermonter whom Turner disdained, as he did anyone he considered his inferior. Through the caprice of military orders, however, Noyes was in a position which made it inevitable that he would run afoul of the stormy Turner.

"That Noyes!" the bushy-browed Turner would rage in the hearing of his subordinates. "He and his God-damn secrets!"

Leigh Noyes was gentle and meticulous, a good tennis player, sought after socially, generally a "ladies' man." He graduated from the Naval Academy in 1906 and sailed around the world a year and a half later with President Roosevelt's white battle fleet. The cruise designed primarily to impress and, if possible, intimidate Japan. There, anti-American sentiment was mounting because of the nation's mediation in the Russo-Japanese War. When the President reviewed the returned warships in New York, Noyes was on board the *Missouri*.

For his service during World War I Noyes was awarded the Navy Cross. While commander of the destroyer *Biddle*, operating in the Black Sea and adjacent waters, he rescued hundreds of Russian refugees from a sinking tug. In 1936 he completed the course at Pensacola to become a naval aviator— which, aside from his innate courage, was about the only thing Noyes had in common with Kelly Turner. Taking command of the carrier *Lexington*, Noyes led the futile search, in June, 1932, for the aviatrix Amelia Earhart, whose plane vanished in the vicinity of Howland Island in the Pacific.

When Noyes came to Naval Operations in 1939, preceding Turner by six months, he faced a chaotic archaic communications set-up; its administrative structure needed a thorough shaking up, and even its command functions were not clear. Communications, for example, had in the past assumed both intelligence and advisory functions, irrespective of whether it ever possessed such prerogatives.

In 1941 the department was bridled especially by a lack of personnel who could work in "sensitive" areas—translating, decoding, encoding, and, in fact, simply handling top-secret material. In Washington, between the Army and Navy, no more than twelve Japanese-language translators and two dozen fully qualified cryptanalysts could be conjured up. All cryptanalysts were civil servant employees and thus could not work nights, Saturday afternoons or at any time on Sunday because there were no overtime provisions. Urgent work meant that the badly overburdened officers themselves had to put in nocturnal stints.

The result was a continual backlog of communications, with a week or two-week lag of those communications not clearly labelled "top priority-urgent." Nor would the mere decision to hire more specialists in the various branches of communications, assuming the appropriations, in itself have solved anything in 1941. The personnel were not available—it took months, possibly years, to train a first-class radioman, and far longer than that to convert, say, a file clerk into a cryptanalyst or a Japanese-language student.

What's more, Noyes, a famed "fusser" during his Annapolis undergraduate days, had a way of hoarding the dispatches that were ready for delivery and then allowing recipients only quick glimpses of them. Some, the addressee would merely initial before the message was whisked away and returned to the rat's nest of naval communications. Noyes was unquestionably overzealous in guarding his precious messages. On the other hand, hush-hush had become a military way of life, especially in the Navy.

"Secrecy meant so much," Stark recalls today. "Knowledge of confidential matter had to be confined to a minimum number of persons." This rule of thumb was seconded by tall, granite-faced Admiral Ernest J. King, then Commander-in-Chief of the Atlantic Fleet, slugging away at the German submarines in an odd, private kind of war. "Don't tell anybody anything he doesn't need to know!" was his succinct phrase. The lid was on.

The need for security, however, did not stem entirely from personal caprice. In the period commencing in 1935, traitorism and espionage seemed to flourish in the United States and its outposts. By the appraisal of Ladislas Farago, a naval intelligence operative, there existed "a swarm of Japanese spies."

Until his expulsion in 1936, Captain Tamon Yamaguchi, naval attaché at the Japanese Embassy, was kingpin of Tokyo's "American area." Perhaps his most spectacular coup was the purchase of a secret Navy document from a former lieutenant-commander, John Semer Farnsworth, Annapolis '15. He also bought similar material from a one-time yeoman, William Thompson. Both Farnsworth and Thompson served sentences in a federal penitentiary.

Apparently pay scales in the Army and Navy made Japanese offers attractive. Civil service personnel were tempted for the same reason. For example, "Eileen," a Japanese-American working in the Library of Congress, was discovered by the FBI to be in Tokyo's pay. A fine opportunity to probe the network behind Eileen, thus presented, was obstructed by an embarrassed Civil Service Commission.

In Panama, "Lola Osawa," the pseudonym of the attractive wife of a Japanese naval officer, operated a haberdashery shop as a blind. The flashily dressed young Lola was herself playing on the need or greed of American service personnel and government employees. All in all, there developed in the late thirties a certain distrust of its own by the Navy, those on duty in Washington as well as those on island stations.

The State Department was especially obstructive to the interchange of intelligence information. Certain of their dispatches were of "such a highly secret nature" that State Department officials simply would not give them to anyone in other government agencies. "Lower level" matter was bogged down in a morass of processing, authorization, reproduction and distribution which, by comparison, made the cumbersome, secretive Navy system seem forthright and efficient.

Whatever the reasons—absurd or logical—whatever the ultimate justification, secrecy had come to stay. Spies might be lurking behind every typewriter, and possibly in the "Top Secret" file cabinets themselves. With the Navy, an example of ultimate absurdity lay in the zealous guarding from the Press by some air station commanders of the old PBY aeroplane, previous models of which had already been sold on the international scrap metal junk heap.

In spite of the cumbersome machinery of his communications department, Admiral Noyes was not operating in a vacuum. In 1939 he had summoned his staffers to inform them that the nation's chances of being involved in the war just starting in Europe were "considerable." Noting with some alarm that "in twenty years" the entire Navy had "gotten very much on a peacetime basis," he demanded a fast course reversal to "a war basis." By May, 1941, he considered that Naval Communications was sailing ahead on a full "war status"—from well-staffed twenty-four-hour watches to an increasingly stringent emphasis upon utter secrecy. In June he was resigned to America's going to war. By the end of November he was certain "the last chance . . . of a peaceful settlement" had passed, since Japan would "not accept those terms" as outlined by Hull. Were we or were we not going to stand for it? he could wonder as Tokyo's southward push towards Siam, Malaya and the Dutch East Indies appeared increasingly certain.

Noyes himself had to stand for a great deal from Naval Operations, in the person of its war plans boss, Turner. Possibly because he felt communications slipping into a secondary "service" role (as opposed to an opinion-forming or policy-making one), he was determined to make as much of his department as he could, and to wring the utmost importance out of the delivery of every message.

While Turner regarded him with haughty contempt, Noyes reacted with far more violent spleen towards the officer whom his contemporaries knew as "Ping" Wilkinson. Rear-Admiral Theodore Stark Wilkinson—53 years old, scholarly, soft-spoken, No. 1 in the Academy Class of '09 and undisputed top cadet in all respects, military, scholastic, and athletic—was Chief of Naval Intelligence. The son of a Louisiana Confederate officer, the tall handsome Wilkinson won the Medal of Honour for bravery during the Veracruz occupation in April, 1914, only five years after he graduated from the Academy. Assigned to ordnance during World War I, he was commended for development of mines, depth charges and gas shells. Perhaps surprisingly, he held no major command until February, 1941, when he became skipper of the battleship *Mississippi.* When he arrived in mid-October of 1941 to head the Office of Naval Intelligence, Wilkinson was totally inexperienced in this highly specialized profession. He did not have a single day's acquaintanceship with the East. When he expressed any opinion at all it was to the effect that he personally did not believe the Japanese were likely to attack the United States.

Wilkinson's assignment was tragically indicative of the Navy's indifferent attitude towards ONI. He was the fourth director of the important department in little more than a year. In a branch of the nation's defence forces where spit-and-polish, form and formality and an almost maudlin allegiance to the old-school-tie principle were normally at premium, ONI was a plum especially reserved for "good fellows." Ability and experience obviously were not factors weighed in filling this post, which had degenerated into the equivalent of some political ward. Membership, too, in Washington's posh Chevy Chase Club, while not an official prerequisite for the Navy Department's stuffed chairs, was quite helpful.

The status of ONI and the misconceptions concerning it were simply another part of a broader, insidious fallacy that was found in the Navy even of 1941: "a good officer can perform *any* duty to which he is ordered." In the time of John Paul Jones, this philosophy might have been reasonable enough. With the coming of the steam warship—or certainly no later than the era of Admiral Farragut—the notion of specialization might have merited some polite attention.

The apogee of nonsense in the Navy's policy regarding intelligence—if indeed the existing chaos could be dignified by the term "policy"—was the useless assignment of Captain Ellis M. Zacharias, Class of '12. In November, 1940, he had been removed from the post of intelligence officer of the Eleventh Naval District, at San Diego, and ordered to command the heavy cruiser *Salt Lake City*. Zacharias easily out-ranked every intelligence or pseudo-intelligence officer in qualifications for the highest post in that field. With twenty-five years of intelligence experience, the lean, dark-haired, sharp-featured Zacharias spoke Japanese as fluently as any American was able. From duty in Japan he also knew the Orient intimately. But because he was an outspoken and often controversial figure and because of his ideas on the administration of the Office of Naval Intelligence, Zacharias had not served in the Navy Department since the early thirties. In fact, it was common gossip that the slogan among the ranking admirals was "Keep Zach out!"

When Nomura passed through San Francisco on his way to Washington in February of 1941, Zacharias was with his ship at the adjacent Mare Island Navy Yard. Zacharias had known the tall Japanese Ambassador since the days when he himself was a naval attaché in the United States Embassy in Tokyo. He did not think Nomura would be overly on guard if he paid him a social call at the Fairmont Hotel, smoked a cigarette and drank a glass of Scotch with him. Both indulgences were enjoyed by the newly appointed Ambassador.

For an intelligence officer who had once given a cocktail party in Washington so that his subordinates could ransack the momentarily unoccupied apartment of a guest—the Japanese naval attaché—Zacharias' approach to the Japanese Ambassador was comparatively direct. Nomura, gracious and apparently confident, told his old friend that Japan "regretted her partnership in the Axis," was "greatly concerned" over the China venture, and personally hoped to "prevent a resort to force in settling the difficulties existing between our two countries." Conversation revolved around these points for more than an hour. Afterwards "Zacharias-San" wrote a long letter about the meeting to Admiral Stark.

A month later, in March, Zacharias arrived with his cruiser in Pearl Harbour. He paid a call upon Admiral Kimmel, who was just raising CINCPAC's flag over Pearl. In spite of Nomura's placating words at the Fairmont, Zacharias was convinced that, *if* Japan decided to attack, she would do so from "the vacant sea," northwest of the Hawaiian Islands, far to the north of the Pacific sealanes. In these trackless wastes, the U.S. fleet formerly conducted manœuvres on the ironic supposition that a vast Japanese armada was sweeping in from this direction. Zacharias asserted that there need be no fear, tactically, from invading warships. But he assured Kimmel that hostilities would begin with "an air attack on our fleet on a week-end and probably a Sunday morning . . . downwind from the northward." It seemed to Zacharias that the immediate object of such an assault would be the elimination of exactly four battleships from the Pacific fleet. This would so weaken the U.S. Navy that Japan would be able to continue her "southern movement" without fear of intervention.

The captain concluded his warning with the suggestion that air patrols be extended "at least 500 miles" from Oahu. But he was told that "we have neither the personnel nor the material to carry out this patrol."

"Well, Admiral," countered Zacharias, "you better get them because that is what is coming!"

It was an outspoken comment even from an officer who was known for his bluntness. (In subsequent testimony, Kimmel said that Zacharias "may have expressed such sentiments—I do not know.")

In November, Tokyo's special trouble shooter, Saburo Kurusu, paused in Honolulu on his way eastward. Zacharias let it be known at CINCPAC headquarters that a tête-à-tête with Kurusu, whom he knew and had previously made it his business to know, might be profitable. Nevertheless, he was kept aboard his ship, engaged in "minor activities."

Thus, with Japanese-American relations at the lowest ebb in history, the Navy was deliberately, wilfully—and with myopic stupidity—depriving itself of the one man who quite possibly could have pried or cajoled information out of Kurusu, Nomura and other Tokyo representatives. And the trouble, as it had existed for two decades, all began on the "second deck."

While the position of ONI chief remained downgraded and the pronouncements of those filling it regarded in proportionate weight, the War Plans job, under Kelly Turner, grew in importance. For example, all dispatches from Naval Intelligence and Communications moving to Stark's office were to be cleared through Turner, thus imbuing him with the powers of supreme censor and arbiter. By the same token, he could volunteer only as much information as he pleased to the directors of intelligence and communications, and in the case of the war warning message of November 27 he did *not* please to tell Wilkinson, towards whom his resentment was ill-concealed.

Inescapably, the result of Turner's highhandedness and personal prejudices was a short circuit between the Chief of Naval Operations' three most vital sub-divisions. Noyes and the newcomer Wilkinson reciprocated the animosity of the War Plans officer; they would do nothing for him that was not absolutely necessary, certainly no favours.

Of all who guided the Navy's destinies in 1941, Turner himself seemed to fit most readily into that curious pattern of an officer born for war. As a Nelson or a Drake, a John Paul Jones or a Farragut, Turner chafed in peace, becoming worse than relatively worthless. Through his own aggressive instincts he became actually detrimental.

The conflict, confusion, jealousy and the cross-purposes rampant on the second deck were somewhat compensated for by the unusual ability of a certain few junior officers. Easily the most talented of these was Commander Arthur Howard McCollum, bespectacled, 43-year-old chief of the Far Eastern Section of Naval Intelligence. Born in Nagasaki, the one-time submariner not only understood the incredibly difficult Japanese language but also the minds and emotions of those who spoke it. Short of stature, with the keenness as well as nervousness of a terrier, McCollum was experienced in both intelligence and counter-intelligence. He had served on the West Coast in duties aimed at thwarting Japanese agents there.* Among his duties as chief of the Far Eastern Section was the preparation of a "daily digest" of highly secret matter, the audience being necessarily meagre. The amount of confidential material to which McCollum had access—including dispatches from the so-called ABCD powers (Britain, China and the Dutch, in addition to America)—afforded him an unusual, if alarming, perspective on the fast disintegrating situation in the Pacific.

Characteristically, McCollum was not welcomed into the confidence of the second deck. He had to scrape for most of what he gleaned and then, curiously enough, to pass it on for the enlightenment of those who made life difficult for him. No one, for example, had taken the trouble to discuss the "war warning" with him or even to inform him of the fact that it had been transmitted.

Repeated reports of southward Japanese troop convoy movements—especially from pilots of Admiral Hart's Manila-based PBYs—convinced McCollum that the Navy's Pacific admirals ought to be told "more." By the first of December he personally advised both Stark and Turner that "in my opinion war or rupture of diplomatic relations is imminent." He then asked if Hart, in particular, had been "adequately alerted." McCollum was given "categorical" assurances that he

*The FBI maintained a list of slightly more than 700 Japanese aliens on the West Coast believed to be spies or potential spies. All were arrested after the outbreak of hostilities.

had been. But that did not allay his fears. The more he pondered the more he believed that the Japanese "were going to jump us." Compounding his worries was the realization that, because of Turner's bullheaded antagonism and Noyes's innate secrecy, the Far Eastern desk was put "in the rather difficult position of not personally knowing what had been sent out to the fleet."

On Thursday, December 4, McCollum drafted "a rather brief dispatch . . . greatly condensed . . . we felt everything pointed to an imminent outbreak of hostilities between Japan and the United States." It was a further warning to all commanders, from the Caribbean and the Panama Canal to the far reaches of the Pacific. He took it to Admiral Wilkinson's office, knowing as he did so that naval intelligence had either surrendered its prerogatives to OP12, or that Turner, as the "know-it-all" of War Plans, had usurped them. As expected, he was directed to the War Plans chief.

When he was presented with McCollum's dispatch, Turner, adjusting his eyeglasses, began to work it over with a pencil. Scowling, he then showed McCollum the "war warning" message of the 27th—and this was the first time McCollum had ever seen the communication.

"Good gosh," McCollum said, abashed. "You put in the words 'war warning.' I do not know what could be plainer than that, but nevertheless I would like to see mine go, too."

"Well," barked Turner, "if you want to send it, you either send it the way I corrected it, or take it back to Wilkinson and we will argue about it."

Denuded of everything except some basic facts, the

heavily edited dispatch was returned to the intelligence chief's desk.

"Leave it here with me for a while," Wilkinson said.

The special warning, emasculated, died on Wilkinson's desk but not before Noyes happened by and remarked, "I think it is an insult to the intelligence of the Commander-in-Chief [of the Pacific Fleet]."

Across the ramp which, physically and ideologically, connected the Navy and Munitions Building so imperfectly, there was—with all the Army's own apathy, faltering purpose, and square pegs in round holes—no parallel to the second deck. Sherman Miles, 54, a tall, good-looking brigadier-general, was in charge of G2, Army Intelligence, and was Wilkinson's opposite number. He had been intelligence chief of the Army for three years, was conscientious, and generally knew his job, insofar as he was let in on highest level planning (or conceivably, scheming).

The Army War Plans officer, Brigadier-General Leonard T. Gerow, a 53-year-old Virginian, was, like his Chief of Staff, a V.M.I. graduate. He had been president of his class and the only graduate to be commissioned directly into the United States Army without an examination. He had distinguished himself as a field commander with the expedition against the Mexican bandit Villa and later under Pershing in France. Counterpart of Admiral Turner in title, Gerow was dynamic and able but tended to lose a measure of his battlefield aggressiveness behind a desk.

There were, however, in the Far Eastern Section of G2 two personalities and intellects who approximated the Navy's McCollum in both ability and experience. One was the tall chief of the Chinese desk, Lieutenant-Colonel Thomas J. Betts. The other was Colonel Rufus S. Bratton, nominally the chief of the Far Eastern Section but actually responsible for Japanese matters.

In the autumn of 1941 the genial Betts had been concerned with a matter transcending his immediate preoccupation with China and with the emissaries of that unhappy, invaded country. He was "finalizing," in the language of the services, long-discussed plans for a joint Army-Navy intelligence committee. A date for the first meeting of such a group had already been set: December 8.

Betts, who brought background insight, vision and a great measure of humour to his job, was an ideal choice for a task which to others would have been drudgery. He saw the military for what it was. He knew, for example, that the Army operated on conditioned reflexes, much like Pavlov's Russian dogs. Abruptly remove a pattern, a familiar set of causes and effects, and even the higher ranks tend to flounder. Betts watched the set routine of G2 with detachment and a certain amount of amusement. Dispatches, he was all too aware, had to be delivered in the regulation locked pouch, with one and sometimes two padlocks, for which the addressee possessed a key or keys. Something about the very mundane associations of this routine, the smell of leather, the click of the little brass locks and even the expectant expression of the messenger who held the repository of hush-hush, Nostradamus-like whisperings lent truth, reality and—certainty. Betts preferred to accept these procedures with good-natured resignation, or work to change them through the regular channels, rather than try to upset them overnight.

Bratton, 50 years old, was of an entirely different cut: serious, nervous, slower of thought, not known for a sense of humour. But insofar as service fetters permitted he was also an independent thinker. While Marshall, it was conceded, ran pretty much a one-man show in the War Department, Bratton was an officer who did not care to have his thoughts pretested for him and then run off on one of the department's myriad duplicating machines.

"Rufe," or "Togo," as his friends variously knew him, graduated from West Point in 1914. An expert rifleman and polo player in his military adolescence, the dour-faced native of Yorkville, South Carolina, spent the Great War first at Schofield Barracks in Hawaii, and later in the muddy disorganization of new Army camps that in 1917-1918 sprang up the length and breadth of the United States. In the early twenties and again in the thirties duty in Tokyo, including courses at the Imperial Japanese General Staff College, gave Bratton a rare and valuable skill: knowledge of the Japanese language. At the same time, however, it stamped him, along with the Navy's McCollum, as a member of the "language club." Older officers in intelligence duty, with no language ability, were inclined to band together in competition with this newer, linguistic group.

By December, 1941, Bratton had been on duty more than five years with the General Staff of the War Department and four years as top man in the increasingly important Far Eastern Section. This continuing assignment, in contrast to the Navy's affinity for separating officers from their specialities, in the event that they possessed one or more, was partly the result of the wisdom of his superior, Sherman Miles. And it was partly through necessity: there was an alarming lack of men who understood the Japanese language. The FBI itself depended heavily for its translation in Washington on Bratton's daughter, Leslie, who had learned the language while attending high school in Tokyo.

Thus Bratton, respected and trusted by Miles, who himself had prior Hawaiian duty, was in a unique position to observe the Far Eastern scene. Moreover, he kept unusually close to naval affairs by visiting with McCollum two or three times a day. And in his opinion the situation grew blacker every day. With a staff which could not approximate his knowledge or experience, Bratton worked long hours, from eight o'clock in the morning until seven in the evening or later. He gained weight, he became tired and sometimes irritable. At cost to his health and well-being, he carried on what appeared to be a one-man counter-intelligence war against the Japanese from the shaky citadel of the Munitions Building.

As November wore on, Bratton recognized the increasing danger signals from the East. He included, for example, in an intelligence bulletin for limited distribution within the War Department a statement from Koki Hirota, head of the militant, supernationalistic organization in Japan, the Black Dragon Society: "war with the United States would best begin December or February ... the new cabinet would likely start war within sixty days."

When, during the first week in December, he learned that the Japanese had ordered their consulates to burn code books, he became greatly disturbed over the implications. When Bratton was disturbed his jowels began to work, and this they doubtless did when he entered the office of the Army's War Plans Division to ask General Gerow if he did not think he should send additional warning overseas to commanders such as Short and MacArthur. Gerow thought, then decided that for the moment "sufficient" reminders had been transmitted.

"Time," Bratton was to testify later, "was running out . . . if they destroyed their codes and ciphers, a breach, at the least a breach in diplomatic relations and probably a war [was imminent].'"

Time was indeed running out.

5
"MAGIC"

The Navy had long been identified with a fetish for code names and abbreviations. COMDESRONO-NEDESLANT (Commander of Destroyer Squadron One of the Destroyers, Atlantic Fleet), for example, was more of a mouthful to a seasoned or even semi-seasoned Navy man that it was especially extraordinary.

Intelligence officers had to master this apparent gibberish merely as a part of their nautical three R's—and then often went on to devise their own hieroglyphics and passwords. In 1941 most officers of this classification were familiar with words such as "ultra" and "super," "khaki," "purple," and "magic." Most important, and bulwarked by the highest possible security classification, was the word "purple," with all its incalculable implications. It was applied to the current Japanese diplomatic code and cipher system, which, fortunately, was transmitted in Morse code or a variation, Imperial Japanese Kani. And because of the pagoda-like top-heaviness of the language, many Japanese messages went out in coded English.

As a second gift to counter-intelligence, the Japanese preferred cipher to code. Cipher, with antecedents predating Julius Caesar, substituted one letter for another, instead of the code system of using groups of letters or numbers to stand for a whole sentence, or thought. Therefore, cipher lent itself to rapid, mechanical encrypting, as well as decrypting by anyone with the key.

"Magic" was the general term applied to eavesdropping on anyone's code, friendly or otherwise. "Purple magic," decrypting the Japanese code, was therefore of the highest priority. And it was accomplished by a "purple" machine. This was a wondrous electrical device, run by a motor and replete with relays as well as inter-connecting circuits. It could be fed the endless garbles of code and after a reasonable amount of whirring—and, occasionally, spewing of sparks—come forth with a straight Japanese language version (assuming the message had been in Japanese). Any translator could then quickly reduce into plain English what minutes before had been cipher hash.

Development of the machine and the breaking of the code apparently had been a photo finish between the Navy and the Army. In August, 1940, William Friedman, chief cryptanalyst with the Signal Corps and a mathematical genius, reported his "first completely deciphered text" of the Japanese diplomatic code. His personal elation, however, was short-lived since he suffered a nervous collapse and was retired from active duty (although he later returned to similar work as a civilian).

At approximately the same time, a traitor in the Japanese consulate in New York (an attaché whose identity is protected by the Navy to this day) sold the books that provided the key to another, lesser code. When the purple machine and its operators were working at their best, they could, they were certain, "break" the Tokyo wireless traffic much faster than embassy staff communicators with the legitimate key. In fact, McCollum, from his desk in the Far Eastern Section of Naval Intelligence, often wished he could telephone the Japanese code room and advise that the sender had prefaced transmission with a wrong key.

Of all those who had midwifed the delivery of the Navy's purple machine the most devoted and assiduous was Commander Laurence F. Safford, 48-year-old head of the Security Intelligence Section of Naval Communications. The tall, blond Boston-born Safford had graduated from the Naval Academy in 1916, sailing through with "an air of utter detachment." A mathematical wizard and chess player, "Sappho" Safford, as he was known, was "eager and tense" behind a reserve and continual preoccupation. His superior was Admiral Noyes, but for the most part Safford had to exist and perform his duties in the limbo between Naval Intelligence and Naval Communications. And he was a member of the "nonlanguage club": he did not understand Japanese.

The magic that flowed from the wonderful purple machines was aptly named. It enabled, in a manner of speaking, the President and his Cabinet to read the cards in the hands of their opponents. In July, for example, purple unravelled this message from Tokyo which furnished the Japanese Embassy in Washington with the official reaction of Hitler's assault upon the Soviets:

> Needless to say, the Russo-German war has given us an excellent opportunity to settle the northern question, and it is a fact that we are proceeding with our preparations to take advantage of this occasion.

A few days later a far more revealing and inflammatory message between Tokyo and Japanese military headquarters in China was intercepted:

> The immediate purpose of our occupation of French Indo-China will be to achieve our purposes there. Secondly, its purpose is, when the international situation is suitable, to launch therefrom a rapid attack ... after the occupation of French Indo-China, next on our schedule is the sending of an ultimatum to the Netherlands Indies. In the seizing of Singapore, the Navy will play the principal part. As for the Army, in seizing Singapore it will need only one division and in seizing the Netherlands Indies, only two.

The meaning was not obscure.

International secrets continued to pour out of the Navy's purple machines, and they increased rather than decreased in excitement and implication. On September 24, Tokyo transmitted a request to its consul general in Honolulu, Nagao Kita, which gave counter-intelligence a great deal to ponder.

Strictly Secret

Henceforth, we would like to have you make reports concerning vessels along the following lines in so far as possible:

1. The waters [of Pearl Harbour] are to be divided roughly into five sub-areas. (We have no objections to your abbreviating as much as you like.)

Area A. Waters between Ford Island and the Arsenal.

Area B. Waters adjacent to the Island south and west of Ford Island. (This area is on the opposite side of the island from Area A.)

Area C. East Loch.

Area D. Middle Loch.

Area E. West Loch and the communication water routes.

2. With regard to warships and aircraft carriers, we would like to have you report on those at anchor (these are not so important), tied up at wharves, buoys, and in docks. (Designate types and classes briefly. If possible we would like to have you make mention of the fact when there are two or more vessels alongside the same wharf.)

The fact that this message sat in its "top secret" pigeonhole in Naval Communications for more than two weeks before it was deciphered (and even then was not passed on to Kimmel) not only underscored anew the critical shortage of specialists but hinted at something else of paramount importance. As one officer, then in communications, suggested (to this author): "That a message was not listed as translated does not mean necessarily that it had not been *partially* broken or, say, glanced at by some officer who at once realized the *gist* of the dispatch—even though on the log books it was not classed as 'processed' or distributed."

There were intercepts before December 7, not "translated," which clearly indicated that the Japanese were going to war, and that Hawaii was an objective. What the former communications officer was trying to say was that anyone in the Army or Navy code rooms—civilian or military—could have peeked at the intercepts and, ignoring the "chain of command," relayed priceless information to the highest personages.

Unless someone involved volunteers the evidence, there is no conceivable way to prove whether or not any of the crucial "untranslated" dispatches were relayed unofficially to higher-ups. It must, however, be assumed that the communications officer in question had some cause for suspicion or he would not have introduced so provocative a possibility.

On November 19 an especially meaningful message from Tokyo to Washington was intercepted on a short-wave receiving system designated as PA-K2. When deciphered, it read:

> Circular 2353
> Regarding the broadcast of a special message in an emergency.
> In case of emergency (danger of cutting off our diplomatic relations) and the cutting off of international communications, the following warnings will be added in the middle of the daily Japanese language short-wave news broadcast:
> 1. In case of Japan-U.S. relations in danger: *Higashi no kazeame* (East wind rain)
> 2. Japan-U.S.S.R. relations: *Kitanokaze kumori* (North wind cloudy)
> 3. Japan-British relations: *Nishi no kaze hare* (West wind cloudy)

This signal will be given in the middle and at the end as a weather forecast and each sentence will be repeated twice. When this is heard please destroy all code papers, etc. This is as yet to be a completely secret arrangement.

Forward as urgent intelligence.

Japan attached a considerable importance to this message; it was repeated several times in the ensuing two weeks. Transmitted on "systems" other than PA-K2 or purple, it was also picked up by the British and Dutch.

Thus three nations, with listening posts from London to Singapore, from Batavia to Washington, were monitoring every word from the big commercial station in Tokyo, JAP, waiting for the tell-tale "winds" message. Commander Safford himself "strained every nerve" to intercept the signal when and if it whispered in over the great reaches of the Pacific. Nervously, he asked McCollum at least once:

"Are you people in Naval Intelligence doing anything to get a warning out to the Pacific Fleet?"

"We are doing everything we can," the Far Eastern Section head assured him.

Safford, however, could not understand Japanese. To compensate for this lack he depended heavily on a fluent student, Lieutenant-Commander Alwin D. Kramer. An Academy graduate, class of '25, Kramer had distinguished himself as a rifleman. Tall, with a pencil moustache, sometimes known by the nickname "The Shadow," Kramer could evidence traits both of a dreamer and of one "possessed of a quick, incisive mind." His duties, through no fault of his own, accented once more the confusion and conflict rampant on the second deck of the Navy Department.

Assigned to the Far East Section of Naval Intelligence, he also had responsibilities in a "security" group of Naval Communications. For the most part he reported to Safford.

Thursday morning, December 4, at eight o'clock, the powerful Navy monitoring towers at nearby Cheltenham, Maryland, pulled a Tokyo news broadcast out of the air: About two hundred words long, it was tapped on the teletype to Kramer's office in the Navy Department for translation. From then on, however, exactly what was in this message became the source of much confusion and contradiction. (In fact, tens of thousands of words of testimony were consumed in wartime and postwar investigations without an absolutely definitive, unequivocal answer being found.)

When Safford read the translation of *some* message handed him by Kramer later that same morning, it seemed to him that a "winds execute" had been broadcast, signifying the deterioration of relations with England and with the United States, but not with Russia. In fact, he thought that Kramer had written his own interpretation on the paper as follows:

> War with England (including the Netherlands East Indies, etc.)
> War with the U.S.
> Peace with Russia.

Kramer later was to deny he had handled exactly such message, let alone pencilled any interpretation on it. However, a message bearing on the general winds subject was sent from Safford to Admiral

Noyes that Thursday. As Turner was to recall subsequently, Noyes called him on the office interphone.

"The weather message," he told the War Plans admiral, "the first weather message has come in."

"What did it say?" Turner asked.

"North wind clear," replied Noyes (who likely was mis-quoting the message).

"Well, there is something wrong about that," observed Turner.

"I think so, too," concluded Noyes, who then clicked off the intercom.

In later investigations as well as in converations with the author Safford has remained adamant that he read a "winds execute" specifying "east wind rain" or "U.S. relations in danger." But he could not produce the original piece of paper. Kramer first corroborated Safford's statement, then changed his own testimony to deny that he had decoded anything to mean "war with the United States," the interpretation Safford had placed on the intercept.

Safford was to make this formal evaluation before a Joint Congressional Investigating Committee early in 1946:

> The basic Japanese War Plan was divided into three categories or provided for three contingencies, any or all of which might be followed, namely:
> 1. War with the United States.
> 2. War with Russia.
> 3. War with England including the invasion of Thailand and the capture of Manila and the Dutch East Indies.

The winds message gave us the answer in all three cases:

Affirmative for the 1st and 3rd categories and negative for the 2nd.

The winds message was probably a "signal of execute" of some sort.

The "signal of execute" theory received strong confirmation from a secret message received from the Philippines in the early afternoon of December 4, 1941. This message informed us that the Japanese Navy had introduced a new cipher system for its so-called "Operations Code" at 0600 GCT that date. This time was seven and a half hours before the winds message was broadcast....

The Japanese were going to start the war on Saturday, December 6, 1941, or Sunday, December 7, 1941.

The Congressional committee pronounced the following opinion on this controversial message: "Based on the evidence it is concluded that no genuine 'winds' message in execution of the code and applying to the United States was received by the War or Navy Departments prior to the attack.... It appears, however, that messages were received which were initially thought possibly to be in execution of the code but were determined not to be execute messages."

However, in the middle of this same first week in December other messages were intercepted, decoded and translated which *were* unequivocal. Perhaps the most ominous were those concerning the destruction of Japanese code machines, the three most important of which read:

> Please discontinue the use of your code machine and dispose of it immediately.

In regard to the disposition of the machine please be very careful to carry out the instructions you have received regarding this. Pay particular attention to taking apart and breaking up the important parts of the machine.

As soon as you have received this telegram wire the one word SETUJU in plain language, and as soon as you have carried out the instructions, wire the one word HASSO in plain language.

Also at this time you will of course burn the machine codes and the YU GO No. 26 of my telegram [the rules for the use of the machine between head office and the Ambassador Resident in England].

These instructions were followed shortly by:

Urgent instructions were sent yesterday to Japanese diplomats and consular posts at Hong Kong, Singapore, Batavia, Manila, Washington and London to destroy most of their codes and ciphers at once and to burn all other important and confidential secret documents.

After a 5-minute interval, another dispatch from Tokyo read:

Ordered London, Hong Kong, Singapore and Manila to destroy machine. Batavia machine already sent to Tokyo. December 2 Washington also directed destroy all but one copy of other systems and all secret documents. British Admiralty London today reports Embassy London has complied.

These messages were known to Admiral Stark, although apparently not to General Marshall. However, the Chief of Naval Operations was so impressed with the obvious auguries of code destruction that he sent a confidential dispatch of his own to Admiral

Kimmel advising him of what was happening. In so doing, Stark inadvertently included the secret word "purple."

Understandably mystified, the Commander-in-Chief of the Pacific Fleet asked Lieutenant-Commander Edwin T. Layton, his intelligence officer, "*What* is a purple machine?"

Layton, Annapolis '24, admitted he had no idea. But he promised to seek out Lieutenant H. M. Coleman, new fleet security officer just reported "aboard" from Washington, and ask him if *he* knew.

The whole trouble was: Pearl Harbour was "purpleless." The closest approximation to such a decoder was a machine now discarded and relegated to a warehouse cellar on the submarine base. The code which it had been designed to "crack" had been scrapped by Japan in 1938.

The Pacific Fleet was dependent for its latest magic concerning American-Japanese relations on the Navy Department itself. And one message which was *not* relayed to Admiral Kimmel, even after it was finally decoded, was the suspicious Tokyo request for fleet anchorages. One reason why it was not relayed to Honolulu was Noyes's obsession for secrecy in general, and, in particular, that not a hint should trickle back to Tokyo that the United States had broken the diplomatic code. There was also another reason. Admiral Turner, mastiff of War Plans, was convinced in his own mind that Pearl Harbour, whatever else it might lack in armanent, *did* possess one of those purple machines. He thought he had been "assured" of that by his rival, Admiral Leigh Noyes. And Turner, presumably, was not alone in his misconception. Admiral Stark also believed that Pearl Harbour, along with Manila, owned a purple device. Even the British had been given one of the precious machines over the violent protests of one of Wilkinson's predecessors.

As the ultimate in confusion, officers of lesser rank—such as McCollum and Bratton, for example—*knew* that no purple machine had been allotted Pearl Harbour. McCollum figured that one reason for this signal lack lay in the Navy's distrust of its own. At the same time, he hoped that Naval Intelligence could keep sending paraphrases of enough of the purple intercepts to compensate for the total absence of so vital an instrument.

As for the code destruction message, it got no further than the Navy in Honolulu. Admiral Kimmel neglected to pass it along to General Short.

6
HONOLULU

Hawaii was a Mecca for foreign agents: observers on Japanese merchant ships and naval "training" vessels paying "courtesy" calls, even fishermen in their sampans who could taxi out to meet larger ships at sea delivering agents. To the average customs guard, one Oriental looked much like another. Identity cards, even those with photographs and measurements, were meaningless as Japanese crewmen sauntered ashore. Half a dozen sailors ostensibly bound for shore leave could as easily have been half a dozen agents who would not return aboard.

Not only did numbers of the 160,000 Japanese residents of the island seem to spend an abnormal amount of time with cameras and pads, if not binoculars, but the picture postcard business flourished. Excellent panoramic views of Pearl Harbour, "lying low under the surrounding hills" and clearly showing the fleet and its anchorages, could be bought by any tourist for five or ten cents. From the beautiful residential heights of Aiea, anyone could obtain a breath-taking view of the harbour, 1,000 feet below, of the airfields and all naval installations.

There was not a great deal of doubt that the Japanese had adopted a policy of all-out espionage. Their spiderweb covered Honolulu and was divided into military-like zones with block leaders and assistant block leaders. The latter were instructed to collect all scraps of information, especially the arrivals and departures of Americans. Major-General D. Herron, Short's predecessor, had himself made rough calculations as to the loyalty of the Japanese in the Hawaiian Islands:

"We were satisfied that at least 5 percent were committed to the American cause, either through conviction or by force of circumstances, such as being *persona non grata* to the Japanese government. Another 5 percent ... would be irreconcilable, hostile to the United States. The other 90 percent, like anybody else, would sit on the fence until they saw which way the cat was going to jump."

Zacharias estimated there were approximately 1,000 Japanese agents in the islands, of varying degrees of importance and menace. Certainly, the problem was a nightmare of counter-intelligence, since theoretically every Japanese in Hawaii *could* be an agent. Even the Buddhist priests on Maui Island were kept under surveillance and their temple studied for wireless antennae.

The Honolulu telephone directory was testament to the mushrooming Japanese population. It listed a spread of business activities including automobile dealers, an investment company, a hotel association, schools, a home for Japanese aged, a bazaar and, naturally, a crematory. There were eight major Japanese importing houses, while the majority of grocers as well as fruit and vegetable vendors on the islands were Japanese. The same racial representatives also operated more than 50 percent of the legal bars, and probably a large proportion of the clandestine, incense parlours operated primarily for the joy of sailors.

No conscientious counter-agent could afford to dismiss any one of these listings, not excluding the crematorium, as beyond the realm of a spy nest. Indeed, further suspicion might be aroused by the Japanese consulate's bland listing of but five assistant consuls.

On hand to meet Japan's determined "total espionage" was a numerically inadequate corps of American intelligence and counter-intelligence personnel. In their own modest consulate the British could count almost as many. In addition to Lieutenant-Commander Layton, there was Captain Irving H. Mayfield, the Fourteenth Naval District's intelligence officer, an assigned rather than "career man" post, and Commander John J. Rochefort, in charge of a complex of "snooper" and direction-finding stations spread out all the way north to Dutch Harbour, Alaska, and south to Samoa.

Rochefort, 41, tall and slender, was a skilled cryptologist, a Japanese-language expert and trained in intelligence as well as communications. With ten officers and twenty men attached to his "security unit" headquarters and seventy others in his far-flung outposts, his command was the most important intelligence operation in this part of the Pacific. Rochefort, from his proximity to Japanese and other tell-tale activities, including the daily gusher of information transmitted from Tokyo and her naval units, was certain "trouble" was "coming." The only question in his mind was "Where?" He was inclined to place the locale "along the China coast, possibly in the Philippines," reasoning that the warlords were too deeply committed in South-east Asia for adventures elsewhere.

The situation in the Army was not much better. General Short's quota was two G2 officers: Lieutenant-Colonel Kendall J. Fielder, and his assistant, Lieutenant-Colonel George W. Bicknell. While these two intelligence officers worked effectively as a team and were personal friends, Fielder, sought socially in Honolulu as a guitar player and raconteur, was more conservative in his approach to his profession. He tended to think Naval Intelligence over-dramatized its work. To Bicknell, on the other hand, it seemed that the top echelon of the Army, including Walter Short, should be a "a little bit more intelligence conscious."

Harmonious interchange of information between the two services was, unfortunately, hampered by seemingly arbitrary regulations. Titbits of intelligence were doled out to some while denied to others. Officers such as Mayfield, Layton and Rochefort could handle most highly secret gems, but their contents—or indeed their very tags—could not necessarily be discussed with Fielder or Bicknell. This was not considered at all unusual. The Army and the Navy had always gone their own separate ways. Why should they operate any differently now? It was only 1941 and to most—civilian and servicemen—there seemed plenty of time.

Rochefort himself was not happy about the mishmash that consumed so many of his hours, once observing that naval communicators were weighted with a mountain of messages "absolutely of no value ... wages, visas and that sort of thing." And since the Navy was the "big" service in the Hawaiian area, its share of responsibilities was always proportionately heavy, including this burdensome traffic.

Operating with considerably fewer fetters was a 21-year veteran of the FBI, Robert L. Shivers. The short, dark-haired, rather retiring Shivers possessed the supreme advantage of being allowed—in fact ordered—to confine his duties to those of the utmost priority and importance. He also co-ordinated his work with ONI and G2 officers in Hawaii and was on especially friendly terms with Bicknell.

For some months Shivers's attention had been focused on 1742 Nuuanu Avenue, the Japanese consulate, where Nagao Kita, the consul general, directed an inordinately swollen platoon of 217 assistant consuls. They were placed throughout the Hawaiian Islands as coastal look-outs and observers of industry and inland transport.

Captain Mayfield, aware that a dozen subordinates would have served the consul, suggested to General Short that the Military Police round up this dedicated shock force of espionage and charge the lot with failure to register as foreign agents. The commanding general, shaking his head, emphasized that the United States must continue "good relations" with the Japanese.

All during 1941 there had been a rising crescendo of Japanese activity. In July, for example, there had been a flurry of code burning at the consulate, then the incineration was abruptly ceased. For the rest of the summer the Japanese in Hawaii did not appear to American intelligence personnel to be acting any differently than they had been.

By November, however, the clouds of international relations grew darker. In his Weekly Intelligence Summary, at the end of the month, Bicknell wrote:

"From all information which had been gathered in our office in Hawaii it looks as though hostilities could be expected either by the end of November or, if not then, not until spring."

The "war warning" from Stark on November 27 had the expected effect of increasing military activity in Hawaii, even though no high officer, in either the Army or the Navy, seemed to think that the islands would really be harmed. Kimmel had summoned Bloch to his offices at the submarine base. His flagship, the *Pennsylvania*, was anchored in battleship row, off Ford Island along with seven other "heavies" of the fleet. Captain Charles H. McMorris, Kimmel's war plans officer, was himself certain that this was "just another warning," while the three agreed that if war *were* imminent, any initial attack would be directed against the Philippines, not Pearl.

Intelligence just arrived from the Far East tended to support such a rationalization: 30,000 Japanese troops aboard 70 transports were butting southward towards the Gulf of Siam and Malaya. The harbours of Kobe and Yokohama had been mined in late November. According to an Army Intelligence summary:

> The combined Air Force has assembled in Takao, Formosa, with some units believed in Hainan Island. The Third Fleet is believed moving in direction of Takao and Bako, Pescadores off the West Coast of Formosa from home waters in Japan. Units from the Second Fleet are at present possibly *en route* to South China as advance scouts. Strong concentration of submarines and air groups in the Marshalls.

The commander-in-chief of the Japanese Second Fleet was directing units into a task force of two sections: one to operate in the South China area; the other off Japan's mandated islands, the Marshalls, south of Wake, to mother several air groups and be in turn supported by perhaps as much as one-third of Japan's submarine force, or at least twenty-five submarines. The entire air carrier fleet, ten ships, was on the prowl, either near Sasebo, on the South-west coast of Japan, or in the Korea Strait—or, certainly, *somewhere*.

Of all the vexatious pieces in this mosaic of naval intelligence, however, the most disturbing was the revelation that radio call signs of Japanese warships had been changed as of December 1. This was not especially unusual, except that the procedure had been duplicated just a month before. It was unheard of for any navy to change these signals so frequently—unless major operations were contemplated.

The Fourteenth Naval District's own summary

of this phenomenon elaborated:

> This fact that service calls lasted only one month indicates an additional progressive step in preparing for active operations on a large scale. For a period of two to three days prior to the change of calls, the bulk of the radio traffic consisted of dispatches from one to four or five days old. It appears that the Japanese Navy is adopting more and more security provisions. A study of traffic prior to 0000, 1 December indicates that an effort was made to deliver all dispatches using old calls so that promptly with the change of calls, there would be a minimum of undelivered dispatches and consequent confusion and compromises. Either that or the large number of old messages may have been used to pad the total volume and make it appear as if nothing unusual was pending.

Already Kimmel had placed his submarines on "war patrol" in areas of the Pacific which included Wake and Midway islands. He had also reinforced the Marine garrisons of Wake, Palmyra and Johnston islands, which were included in the great sweep of the Fourteenth Naval District, while increasing the "readiness" of other fleet units. On his own responsibility, as a disciple of "shoot first and explain afterwards," he instructed the Pacific Fleet to depth-bomb all unidentified submarine contacts in Hawaiian waters. In doing so, he knew he risked committing an "overt act" against a very "touchy" Japan.

To send the Marines and also twenty-five additional Navy pursuit aircraft to Wake, located half-way between Hawaii and the Philippines, he dispatched Task Force 8, commanded by tough, able Admiral William F. ("Bull") Halsey. *En route* to this lonely excrescence of coral, especially naked to Japanese aggression, the force would conduct reconnaissance missions and other operations.

Halsey's flagship, the powerful, 30-knot carrier *Enterprise*, was already stripped down for such a sortie. Battleship linoleum had been ripped from her decking, paint had been scraped off bulkheads, all inflammable material and furniture, except for a piano or two, had been removed. Her colour was altered from light to a darker grey. Portholes were welded shut and cast-iron fittings replaced with forged, malleable metal.

Obviously being readied for one and only one condition—war—the "Big E" would be escorted by three heavy cruisers and seven destroyers. Bull Halsey, who had been briefed on the "war warning" from the Navy Department, asked Kimmel—for the record—what to do if he met Japanese units.

"Use your common sense!" snapped the Commander-in-Chief of the Pacific. Halsey, thinking it "the best order" he had ever received, promised that "even a Japanese sampan" that crossed his bows would be sunk. On November 28, the day after the war warning, the salty Admiral pulled his long-visored sea cap down just above his eyes, and leaned back in his red-cushioned "con" chair high up on the bridge of the *Enterprise*. Task Force 8 was standing out to sea.

In putting into the Pacific, Halsey left a Pearl Harbour that was haunted by several large question marks, even though the latest word from Washington may have sounded, to some, like "just another warning." Layton, the fleet intelligence officer, for example, soon became desperately afraid he had "lost" two entire Japanese carrier divisions.

His new "location sheet" of estimated positions of potentially opposing naval units showed Carrier Division 4, composed of two carriers and four destroyers, and Carrier Division 3, of two carriers and three destroyers as well as the converted carrier, *Kasuga Maru,* in the Bako-Takao area, Formosa; and the 10,000-ton *Koryu,* guarded by four destroyers, in the Marshalls. But Layton had concluded that both carrier divisions were leaving this area, headed into the South China Sea, menacing Singapore and all of Malaya. Division 3, not excessively formidable, was composed of the two smallest carriers, the *Hosyo* and *Ryuzyo,* each displacing but little more than 7,000 tons.

The trouble was, the fleet intelligence officer was unable even to speculate on the whereabouts of the other two divisions—which included four aircraft carriers.

"What!" exclaimed Admiral Kimmel on December 2, "you don't know where Carrier Division 1 and Carrier Division 2 are?"

"No, sir, I do not," Layton replied frankly. "I think they are in home waters, but I do not *know* where they are. As for the rest of these units, I feel pretty confident of their location."

Then Admiral Kimmel looked at him with a characteristically stern expression, but there was the hint of a twinkle in his eyes when he said, "Do you mean to say they could be rounding Diamond Head and you wouldn't know it?"

At the same time, Layton also revealed that for

more than a week Tokyo's battleships had not been located by radio direction finders (at various Pacific and Far East tracking stations) or by their own wireless transmissions.

"Do you think they could be off here or out at sea?" Kimmel asked, "without our knowing it?"

"Yes, if they maintain radio silence."

"Do you think they *are*?" the Admiral persisted.

"I estimate they are in port," replied Layton, "having completed two weeks' operations, and they are having overhaul for new operations."

On the first of December the Navy voluntarily closed off one channel of communications: a "wire tap" to the busy Japanese consulate on Nuuanu Avenue. The "stop" action, ordered by Captain Mayfield, came about very curiously.

A linesman for the Mutual Telephone Company of Hawaii, making a routine check on the poles, discovered two separate wire taps running to the Japanese consulate. One was traced to Naval Intelligence, the other to the FBI. Discreetly, the linesman went to the Navy and to Shivers but not to the consul general.

Mayfield's reaction was to discontinue the naval tap of 21-month standing, although Shivers continued the FBI snooping. His line, as a matter of fact, led to the cook's quarters. Reasoning that no Japanese cook received enough pay to afford his own phone, the FBI agent concluded that this set must be for the purpose of communication between intelligence operatives.

It was fortunate that Shivers stubbornly clung to his own channel into the consulate. Within twenty-four hours Mayfield called the FBI agent to ask if he could "verify" a report that the Japanese consul general was burning his papers and codes. Shivers replied that he had intercepted a conversation that very noon between the cook and someone unidentified in Honolulu, and the cook *did* mention that Consul Kita was destroying his important papers. Shivers observed that he had passed on this important bit to Bicknell. The Army assistant G2 chief had, in turn, thanked his FBI informant and promised to mention the matter at the Saturday staff meeting with General Short.

Genuinely concerned, Mayfield concluded his phone call to Shivers by saying, "If I suddenly call you and say I am moving to the east side of the island or north, south or west sides, it will mean that Japan is moving against the countries which lie in those directions from Japan."

All in all, the atmosphere in the Pacific became more explosively charged as the first week of December moved on. An increasingly vexed Layton, by Wednesday as he prepared his latest report for Kimmel, still did not know where those missing Japanese vessels were:

> Almost a complete blank of information on the carriers today. Lack of identification has somewhat promoted this lack of information. However, since over 200 service calls have been partially identified since the change on the 1st of December and not one carrier call has been recovered, it is evident that carrier traffic is at a low ebb.

However, straws still drifted in the sultry Pacific

winds. Army Signal Corps men had intercepted two messages in the past twenty-four hours, the first from Tokyo to Honolulu:

> In view of the present situation, the presence in port of warships, aeroplane carriers and cruisers is of utmost importance. Hereafter, to the utmost of your ability, let me know day by day. Wire me in each case whether or not there are any observation balloons above Pearl Harbour or if there are any indications that they will be sent up. Also advise me whether or not the warships are provided with anti-mine nets.

The second, from Honolulu, signed "Kita," concerned light signals to be flashed seaward from a house on Lanikai Beach which would reveal movements and anchorages of the Pacific Fleet. It also provided for ads in the Honolulu newspapers, tattling on the same subject, which involved Chinese rugs for sale, a farm for sale, beauty operator wanted, etc.

Neither served any immediate purpose to counter-espionage, however. Decoding and translating was so back-logged, even as in Washington, that the two reports sat at Fort Shafter in their initial gibberish until middle or late December.

More timely was a cable from Manila stamped "Urgent" and forwarded via British Army Intelligence officers in Honolulu, to Mayfield, Bicknell and Shivers:

> We have received considerable intelligence confirming following developments in Indo-China:
> A-1. Accelerated Japanese preparations of airfields and railways.
> 2. Arrival since November 10 of additional 100,000

repeat 100,000 troops and considerable quantities fighters, medium bombers, tanks and guns (75 mm.).

B. Estimate of specific quantities have already been telegraphed Washington November 21 by American military intelligence here.

C. Our considered opinion concludes that Japan envisages early hostilities with Britain and United States. Japan does not repeat not intend to attack Russia at present but will act in South.

Outnumbered and outgunned in the Pacific—on land, at sea and in the air—the United States, whatever might be brewing, had one crutch: the "Rainbow" plan, or WPL-46. At first this blueprint, "for use only in the event of war," was tagged "Yellow." Then, cryptographers in ONI objected that Japanese counter-intelligence operatives, if they happened across a "Yellow" message, would be certain it referred to their own race. "Orange" therefore became the code for a strategy that assumed a major offensive could be launched against the Marshalls and Gilberts within six months after hostilities began. An American victory was assumed—we never lose wars. This triumph would be consolidated by a sea battle possibly reminiscent of Jutland, and involving such classical Admiral Mahan concepts as "crossing the 'T' " in Japan's home waters. Nippon's fleet would, of course, be sunk to the last launch.

Orange, however, had to be altered to Rainbow as it was realized that a war would involve two oceans. But even Rainbow, which, in spite of its optimistic connotation, did not produce as self-assured a ring to its authors as Orange was based on the supposition that the Pacific Fleet would start out fresh, intact and full of fight.

General Short's responsibilities and his challenge were somewhat different. He must repel invasion, in the event an amphibious force battered its way past the U.S. Navy. And as a matter of fact he accomplished, in the opinion of subordinate officers such as Colonel Fielder, "more to prepare Hawaii for defence in a year than his predecessors did in ten." But in the Hawaiian Department's preoccupation with training and against the possibility of sabotage, there were unfortunate by-products, as well as some oversights. Telephones and switchboards, linking antiaircraft gun positions with command headquarters at Schofield, were locked up at night to prevent theft— and harm. A battle command post, in an underground location, in the process of being remodelled, also was without eyes, ears or voice. Cables and other essential equipment had temporarily been removed from this critical apex to a remote tunnel to guard against blast effects.

Alerts of any kind in Hawaii had been planned with solicitude for the nerves of the residents. As a consequence, there was a general feeling that as little show of armed might as possible should be evident in Honolulu and elsewhere in the island group. Such concern was not only heightened but officially sanctioned in General Marshall's own warning of November 27.

Part of the heavy coast artillery was in the middle of Honolulu. Fort de Russy itself, off Kalakaua Avenue, was adjacent to Waikiki Beach and the Royal Hawaiian Hotel. A full-dress invasion alert presupposed the removal of "live ammunition" from magazines and placing it at gun locations, whether or not the actual weapon was yet there. Any such procedure, even in practice, would certainly alarm the residents—and it would upset the meticulous condition of the Hawaiian Department's housekeeping. As Bicknell, for one, observed, "Any ammunition that was taken out of storage and put out on the field had to be cleaned before it was put back again."

General Short was deficient, however, in his understanding of what was going on down at the Submarine Base and the Navy Yard, with respect to the Pacific Fleet or the Fourteenth Naval District. Although he had discussed the "war warning" messages with Admiral Kimmel in general terms, he was unaware that the Navy was not instituting long-range reconnaissance. As for Kimmel, he laboured under the delusion that the Army had swung into an all-out state of readiness, rather than one limited to ferreting out sabotage.

Kimmel had already emphasized to Bloch, the Commander of the Fourteenth Naval District, that his small covey of PBYs, like great auks in a museum, was inadequate for the demands of sustained patrol. Short's tatterdemalion Air Corps was possibly worse. Of 227 planes based at Hickam, Wheeler and Bellows fields, nearly one-half were officially categorized as "obsolescent"; only twelve B-17's could merit the flattering designation, "long-range patrol." And six of these had been cannibalized for parts for the maintenance of Philippines-bound bombers.

The two air chiefs—Vice-Admiral Patrick N. L. Bellinger, Jr., senior aviator of both the Pacific Fleet and the district, a pioneer transatlantic flier, and

Major-General Frederick L. Martin, commanding the Hawaiian Air Force—were well aware of these shortcomings. Both endorsed what Admiral Kimmel had written months ago: "A surprise attack on Pearl Harbour is a possibility." The two aviators wanted continual long-range reconnaissance. But, with priority being accorded the Philippines, on one face of the globe, and the Atlantic Fleet, on the other, what could be done about it?

If, for the most part, Kimmel and Short's interchange of defence information and attempts jointly to rectify weaknesses were cursory, the two nonetheless remained in friendly, first-name accord. In tune with his regular habits, Short invited the Admiral to play golf every other Sunday, at which time they "talked of all kinds of things around the course." They usually chose the course beside the beautiful Palm Circle, at Fort Shafter, on the fringes of Honolulu, which was also a quartering or bedding post for senior officers.

On the first Wednesday in December, Short and Kimmel conferred. The General obtained the impression that the Navy "either knew the location of the Japanese carriers or had enough information so that they were not uneasy." In any case, the Hawaiian Department commander felt the Navy could "handle the situation." There was nothing more to say except to arrange the next meeting: Sunday morning, December 7, at the first tee.

Meanwhile, on CINCPAC's desk, or possibly in Layton's safe, was his latest radio intelligence summary:

"No information on submarines or carriers."

The next day the second of the Navy's two Honolulu-based carriers, the veteran *Lexington*, thumped out to sea, as the mother ship of Task Force 2, commanded by Rear-Admiral John Henry Newton. Three heavy cruisers and five destroyers shepherded the "Lex," bound for Midway, where twenty-five Marine-piloted aircraft would be flown ashore to reinforce the island's defences.

At the same time, Vice-Admiral Wilson Brown, on the cruiser *Indianapolis,* was leading another and smaller task force—No.3—to Johnston Island, 700 miles south-west of Oahu. This force would conduct bombardment, then landing exercises. Afterwards the two naval assault groups would rendezvous and steam for home base.

The cautious, snail-like gait with which fleet vessels moved out of Pearl Harbour afforded daily proof that the Hawaiian anchorage was indeed, as Admiral Richardson had heatedly labelled it, "a mousetrap." From Waipio Point, across the channel and to the south of Ford Island, and the remaining short sprint into the open sea, the channel funnelled down to 450 yards and was so shallow that the "fatties" of the fleet, the battleships, carriers and oilers, had to creep forward at a few knots. Their very mass, when combined with accleration, had a tendency to push away the water immediately beneath their keels and leave them sitting in the mud. Further, their wakes could cause damage ashore. These considerations meant that the fleet, once in the Pearl Harbour anchorage, could not be shunted elsewhere at a moment's notice.

Unlike the departure of Admiral Halsey, the previous week, with Task Force 8, Newton and Brown's groups left without any special briefings on the worsening crisis, the known movements of Japanese naval units off South-east Asia, or the missing carriers. The latest intelligence summary, for example, read: "No traffic from the commander carriers or submarine force has been seen." As to general Japanese radio transmission:

> Traffic volume heavy. All circuits overloaded with Tokyo broadcast going over full twenty-four hours.... It is noted that some traffic being broadcast is several days old which indicates the uncertainty of delivery existing in the radio organization. There were many messages of high precedence which appears to be caused by the jammed conditions of all circuits.

Neither Newton nor Brown had been advised of the war warning. Newton, moustached, distinguished Navy Cross winner for his convoy escort work in 1917-1918, admitted with bafflement that all he knew of the United States-Japan crisis was what he "read in the newspapers." Therefore, he had no reason to attach "unusual significance" to the present mission. And Newton was not alone. Admiral Bellinger, the naval air commander, himself had not been advised of the war warning.

Kimmel, like Short, felt "enjoined to preserve secrecy and not to alarm the people." He had been thoroughgoing in his briefing to Halsey because he considered that Task Force 8, bound for Wake, was headed for much more dangerous waters than was the case with either Newton or Brown's relatively close-to-home cruise.

Now, Thursday evening, there were no carriers in Pearl. The *Enterprise* and the "Lex" were at sea, the *Saratoga* was clearing Puget Sound, *en route* to Hawaii. At their moorings, however, were ninety-four assorted U.S. Navy vessels in the great Oahu anchorage, ranging from harbour tugs to eight battleships: the flagship *Pennsylvania,* and the *Arizona, California, Maryland, Nevada, Oklahoma, Tennessee,* and *West Virginia.* This preponderance of the heavies in one row, like monster clay ducks in a shooting gallery, was, Kimmel himself admitted, "purely coincidence."

Three of them would have joined Task Force 2 on Thursday morning had not their wallowing speed made them unwelcome company. The question had already been asked, with reason: What good *were* the battlewagons? Whatever their use, their uniformed populations now contemplated the humdrum of another week-end in port. Awnings were stretched across aft decks against the heat of afternoon; the sailors thought of "liberty" and the finer, tempting things of life from which they were separated by only a few yards of harbour water. Some 200 of their personnel—musicians—were practicing for the "Battle of the Bands" at the Receiving Station Saturday night. Every battleship rated a band of twenty-three members, including the leader. Also tooting up for the contest were the bands of two sizeable auxiliaries, the minelayer *Oglala* and the submarine tender *Argonne.*

The noisy affair would be held in Bloch Centre, a recreational area named in honour of the Fourteenth Naval District's commandant. Bloch himself would not be present since his wife was at home, convalescing from an operation. Kimmel, usually not a "party man," possessed even less heart these days for diversions. Although he had not given Admiral Newton or Admiral Brown any testaments of his concern, he nonetheless remained a worried man. Several times during the week he had pondered aloud in his intelligence chief's hearing:

"I wish I knew what we were going to do."

Layton was certain that his chief was vexed by naval policy in the Pacific—or lack of it—as to action after a likely attack on South-east Asia which did not directly involve the United States, its possessions or its armed forces. There was every reason Kimmel should be hard put merely to keep abreast of, let alone anticipate or interpret, the fluctuating and often contradictory international policies of a State Department and a White House willing to fight a war, not even declared, in the Atlantic Ocean.

Japan, on the other hand, was worried about neither moral scruples nor legality. Almost before the mast tips of the vanguard destroyers of Task Force 3 disappeared into the Pacific, Consul Kita was tapping out his latest gleanings to Tokyo:

> ... the *Lexington* and five heavy cruisers left port....
> The following ships were in port on the afternoon of the 5th: eight battleships, three light cruisers, sixteen destroyers.

As other recent intercepts, however, this one sat on a decrypter's desk in the Navy Department, its secrecy guarded by an unfortunate set of circumstances that included the lack of specialized

Army and Navy personnel, no overtime provisions for civil servants, and imperfectly masked contempt for "the little yellow people," a continually strengthening belief that the Philippines, as though they were unrelated islands on another planet, would become a target, if target there was to be, and—dominating all other factors, impressions and illusions—the robust conviction that time remained, that the midnight hour was yet comfortably distant.

7
"A BARE CHANCE OF PEACE...."

As the first week in December approached its end, there was every indication that the President of the United States, weary, sick from an infected sinus, and irritable, had resigned himself to a nearing outbreak of hostilities. He had also been something more than annoyed by the latest disclosure of his arch-enemy Colonel Robert McCormick's *Chicago Tribune*. A copyrighted story alleged that a joint Army-Navy board had called for a five-million-man army to fight against Germany by July 1, 1943.

Concerning his manifest war fears, Roosevelt wrote to Wendell Willkie, the man he had so soundly trounced in the previous year's election. It would "give me very great pleasure," he said, "if you would care to make a short trip to Australia" to talk with the prime minister of the land "down under" as well as New Zealand. "There is always the Japanese matter to consider," Roosevelt concluded. "The situation is definitely serious and there might be an armed clash at any moment if the Japanese continue their forward progress against the Philippines, Dutch East Indies or Malaya or Burma. Perhaps the next four or five days will decide the matter."

In a conference with Donald Nelson, 63-year-old director of priorities with the Office of Production Management, Roosevelt, "gravely" shaking his head, had confided, "I wouldn't be a bit surprised if we were at war with Japan by Thursday, December 4."

All week, reporters had been aware not only of the President's grim, tense mood, but of the air of mingled mystery and activity that pervaded the White House. Day after day the correspondents, watching congressmen and other callers "zip in and out," could only conclude that Roosevelt himself was as "busy as a family of beavers."

His own naval aide, Captain John R. Beardall, chosen for the duty partly because he could match Roosevelt's height, had become so concerned over the likely combustion of war that he established, by the end of the week a twenty-four hour officer-watch on the White House mail room. Its principal function was to handle "magic."

Roosevelt asked Beardall, "When do you think it will happen?" while reading some late dispatches. The captain replied without hesitating, "Most any time."

Estimates prepared by Naval Intelligence of Japanese concentrations bore out Beardall's words. Their assessment included 25,000 men in Tonkin Province in northern Indo-China and 80,000 men in southern Indo-China, plus 250 planes; in Camranh

Bay, or near, 1 heavy cruiser, 1 converted seaplane tender, 9 submarines, and 21 transports; 2 destroyers off Saigon; 1 light cruiser and 1 minelayer off the Indo-China coast; and in the broad Hainan-Formosa area 70 ships including 21 transports or supply vessels, 4 cruisers, 24 destroyers and 10 submarines. In "supporting distances" there were at least 95,000 more troops and 358 aircraft.

Now Roosevelt, in a formal note, demanded to know why the Japanese government was sending "so many military, naval, and air forces" into Indo-China, seemingly a jumping-off spot for Thailand, the Burma Road and almost all of Britain and the Netherlands' Far Eastern possessions.

The "very rapid and material increase in the forces of all arms stationed by Japan in Indo-China," his note asserted, "would seem to imply the utilization of these forces by Japan for purposes of further aggression. Such aggression could conceivably be against the Philippine Islands; against the many islands in the East Indies; against Burma; against Malaya; or, either through coercion or through the actual use of force, for the purpose of undertaking the occupation of Thailand."

The President concluded, "I should like to know the intention of the Japanese government."

The reply snapped back from Premier Tojo, was handed to Cordell Hull on Friday by Nomura and Kurusu, and read:

> As Chinese troops have recently shown frequent signs of movements along the northern frontier of French Indo-China bordering on China, Japanese troops, with the object of mainly taking precautionary measures,

have been reinforced to a certain extent, in the northern part of French Indo-China. As a natural sequence of this step, certain movements have been made among the troops stationed in the southern part of the said territory. It seems that an exaggerated report has been [made] of these movements. It should be added that no measure has been taken on the part of the Japanese government that may transgress the stipulations of the Protocol of Joint Defence between Japan and France.

Hull politely chided the Japanese for trying to create the impression that their troops in Indo-China were for defensive purposes. After diplomatic arguing back and forth, Nomura, who had already asserted that "there must be wise statesmanship to save the situation," bluntly observed, "This isn't getting us anywhere." Hull rejoined:

"We are not looking for trouble, but at the same time we are not running away from menaces."

When the two envoys left, Hull decided it was past time to tell his diplomats in Tokyo and other Eastern outposts to be prepared for the destruction of "codes, secret archives, passports and the like, the closing of offices and the severance of local employees in the event of a sudden emergency cutting off communications with the department."

In the Navy Department, Admiral Noyes was coming to much the same conclusions. "We had better," he announced, "destroy our own codes and ciphers in our most outlying stations." He was greatly relieved when Turner, from whom he had expected an argument, or at least a sharp growl, and Wilkinson, from whom he had not, readily concurred. At last he could get rid of those books.

This decision, for which there had probably been no parallel since Fort Sumter was evacuated in 1861, was quickly "implemented," in the jargon of the Navy and War departments. McCollum himself prepared and released for transmission a dispatch to the embassy, the military attaché and the naval attaché in Tokyo, ordering the destruction of the books. As he did so, he had reason to think that the admirals on the second deck at last were conceding that "war might break out any time," although he persisted in his concern over what he considered were insufficient warnings to the Pacific Fleet itself. War, he contended, "carried with it the possibility of an attack on the fleet wherever it might be."

Concurrently, Safford advised the naval station at Guam to destroy all confidential files—everything of the same nature that the Americans on official duty in Tokyo were commanded to destroy, "except that essential for current purposes. The latter must be in such shape as to be gotten rid of instantly, in event of emergency."

While an "information" copy of this dispatch was sent to Admiral Kimmel, there was no direct explanation as to why Guam, 3,000 miles west of the Hawaiian group, had been singled out among all the American-held Pacific islands. This low-lying extrusion in the Marianas was surrounded by glowering Japanese bases, presumed to be fortified like Pacific Gibraltars—but Wake and Midway, too, had reason for alarm, as did Johnston and Palmyra islands and Samoa, while all the Philippines might well be trembling for their existence.

Admiral Noyes, still not fully satisfied in his own

mind whether Safford was right or wrong or partially right about that earlier "winds execute" message, now called up Colonel Otis K. Sadtler, a senior intelligence officer with the Signal Corps, to advise him that the code word which "implied" a break between Japan and Great Britain had been monitored.

Sadtler hurried into General Miles's office, and he in turn summoned Bratton. The Far Eastern specialist rummaged in his coat pocket until he drew out a crumpled slip of paper. Reading a series of words from it, he asked Sadtler which one it was. The latter, who did not understand Japanese, said he would call Noyes back on his "secret" telephone.

Noyes, after listening to the phrase Bratton had written down for him—*"Nishi no kaze hare,"* or "West wind cloudy"—admitted he, too, understood no Japanese and could not verify if this was the phrase intercepted or not. Besides, he had an engagement "immediately" in the office of the Chief of Naval Operations.

Sadtler returned to Sherman Miles who, in spite of Noyes's inexact information or failure to advise him of the code destruction orders, decided he had better let Hawaii know what was going on. He dictated a dispatch for Fielder, at G2:

> Contact Commander Rochefort immediately through Commandant Fourteenth Naval District regarding broadcasts from Tokyo regarding weather.

Sadtler, coming to the conclusion that the "winds implement"—whatever it really meant—was "the most important message" he had ever received, next went into the office of General Gerow. Gerow seemed to think, as he had previously, that enough people in "various departments" had already been properly alerted as to what might be happening in the East.

Sadtler then determined to talk to dour, tough Colonel Walter Bedell Smith, 46-year-old secretary of the General Staff, an important officer who was known to "have Marshall's ear." Smith, who had served in World War I with the Indiana National Guard, asked Sadtler what he had done, listened, then snapped that he did not "wish to discuss it further."

Sadtler's concern mounted as he made the latest count of the *"Haruna"* messages acknowledging to Tokyo that consulates around the world were burning their secret files. Vancouver, Seattle and Hollywood had been the latest Japanese consulates to reply. Already intercepted had been the *"Harunas"* from distant stations such as Surabaya and Panama. Like *"Hasso,"* the name of a warship, or *"Setuju,"* a poet, *"Haruna,"* a mountain on Honshu and also a warship, was simply one of a number of compliance codes, chosen arbitrarily by Japanese cryptographers.

Sadtler, as a communications officer, was not expected to make policy, to issue orders or warnings, or to interpret unless instructed to do so. However, another dispatch, over Miles's signature and possibly at Sadtler's inspiration, was prepared this Friday, to the Army commander at the Panama Canal Zone:

> U.S.-Japanese relations strained. Will inform you if and when severance of Japanese relations imminent.

Since the message was not marked with a priority classification, it would not be transmitted until Sunday, December 7, two days hence.

Meanwhile, Turner himself had somehow concluded that the chances of a "heavy raid" on Hawaii were 50-50, and he decided to talk about it with Rear-Admiral Royal E. Ingersoll, quiet-mannered Assistant Chief of Naval Operations, balance wheel in the turbulence of the second deck. Turner asked Ingersoll: "What more ought to be done—should we send any more dispatches, or what?"

Ingersoll, who believed, among other things, that the Navy's aggressive operations in the Atlantic were "irregular" but not necessarily "illegal," reminded Turner that "everyone" in the Navy had expected war with Japan for the past twenty years. In itself the possibility was not new or surprising—merely more imminent. The burning of codes Ingersoll stressed as the latest and most positive indication that Japan "expected to be at war very shortly"—with Great Britain, the United States or Russia, or even all three simultaneously.

After an hour of sober discussion, the two admirals agreed that "everything had been done covering the entire situation that ought to be done." They then visited Admiral Stark, who in turn reiterated what he believed and had voiced before: that while he did not "expect" an attack he "knew" it could happen. Stark re-emphasized that "primarily" the Navy wanted to "gain time," as did General Marshall, and that he and the Chief of Staff "stood together on that." And he pointed out that 20,000 troops and 600 aeroplanes were bound for the Philippines that month to bolster the Pacific frontier.

Captain Charles Wellborn, administrative aide and flag secretary to the Chief of Naval Operations, suggested at this important conference that the department might be guilty of crying "wolf" if any more warnings were sent to the fleet or outlying stations. Though he personally believed war to be "awfully close," he had the feeling that additional word from Washington might have the perverse effect of relaxing instead of increasing vigilance.

To Turner the decision was "unanimous" that Kimmel's instructions as to a "defensive deployment" were fully "sufficient." The conference was at an end.

It appeared that Marshall and Stark still had the "time" they so desperately needed, but the supply was running short. The Federal Communications Commission, which had been asked to monitor specifically for the "winds execute" message through its own powerful receiving stations, made early this Friday evening a routine progress report to G2:

> Results negative but am pleased to receive the negative results as it means that we have that much more time.

Intercepted simultaneously by the Navy was a somewhat more positive communication from Peking to Tokyo:

> Concurrent with opening war on Britain and America we have considered Holland as a semi-belligerent and have exercised strict surveillance over her consulates and prohibited all communications between them and the enemy countries.

In the jam of wireless traffic, however, this intercept would not be translated for another six days, or December 11. Like other messages which came in through "purple," it could have been noticed and *partially* understood by some one.

However, on November 28, the day Roosevelt left for Warm Springs, this message, from the Foreign Office in Tokyo to the embassy in Washington, was intercepted and decoded:

> Well, you two ambassadors have exerted superhuman efforts, but in spite of this, the United States has gone ahead and presented this humiliating proposal [the Ten-Point Note]. This was quite unexpected and extremely regrettable. The Imperial government can by no means use it as a basis for negotiations. Therefore, with a report of the views of the Imperial government on this American proposal which I will send you in two or three days, the negotiations will be *de facto* ruptured.

Even more outspoken was another "magic" message, from Tokyo to Berlin, branding the American proposal "insulting," rendering it "impossible" for the Japanese government to find an acceptable basis for further rapprochement. Hitler was advised that the present negotiations were "ruptured-broken," then informed by way of postscript that "the time of the breaking out of this war may come quicker than anyone dreams."

Communications traffic from the Japanese Embassy continued. Tokyo was asked on Friday, December 5:

> We have completed destruction of codes, but since the U.S.-Japanese negotiations are still continuing I request

your approval of our desire to delay a while yet the destruction of the one code machine.

From Tokyo:

> Will you please re your No. 1245 have Terasaki, Takagi, Ando, Yamamoto and others leave by plane within the next couple of days?

Word at the same time was published in the Press that the Japanese minister, several officials of the legation and numerous members of the Japanese colony in Mexico were also packing for home. The decision followed the arrival of a courier from the United States, believed to have brought tidings of an impending Japanese-American rupture. The conclusion was that Mexico would follow whatever course her big northern neighbour charted.

From the Pacific and from the Far East other straws of at least equal portent were drifting on the wind. In Australia the War Cabinet had been in session all day and into the night to plan for "any emergency." Among the immediate measures: cancellation of all leaves for troops in the Darwin area, while men already on leave in the south were ordered to return "immediately"; one million gas masks to be distributed to civilians; full-time officers to be provided for the Volunteer Defence Corps; while, earlier, 650,000 Australian pounds had been authorized to improve inland roads, in the event the coast was blockaded. Australian planes and naval forces, it was also announced, would be made available for the defence of the Netherlands Indies.

In Singapore it was much the same situation;

troops were being recalled to their posts for a state of readiness. All non-Britons were forbidden to leave Malaya, and Japanese waiting to sail for Thailand were forced to disembark. "Well-informed sources" were speculating that Thailand was tagged for the next coup, conceivably by "peaceful penetration." An attack on Malaya or the Philippines was "not ruled out" by the same military seers, but it was believed that neither was a priority target.

In Manila, an unconvinced Cabinet requested all "non-essential" civilians to leave the city and other danger areas in the islands. Officials indicated that the next step might be compulsory evacuation.

While all this was going on, Tomokazu Hori, spokesman for the Cabinet Information Board in Tokyo, indicated that alarm by Japan's neighbouring countries was unwarranted. "Both sides," he asserted at a Press conference, "will continue to negotiate with sincerity to find a common formula to ease the situation in the Pacific. If there were no sincerity there would be no need to continue the negotiations."

As *Time* magazine noted in its issue then on the stands:

"A bare chance of peace remained."

8
THE FOURTEEN-PART MESSAGE

Before Saturday dawn had lighted the mists above Puget Sound, the Navy's wireless towers on Bainbridge Island overheard new secrets between Tokyo and the Ambassador in Washington. Radio operators at this important Pacific coast link in our chain of monitoring stations recorded the message which, when translated in the next six hours, would announce yet another communication:

> This separate message is a very long one. I will send it in fourteen parts and I imagine you will receive it tomorrow. However, I am not sure. The situation is extremely delicate, and when you receive it I want you to please keep it secret for the time being.
>
> Concerning the time of presenting this memorandum to the United States I will wire you in a separate message. However, I want you in the meantime to put it in nicely drafted form and make every preparation to present it to the Americans just as soon as you receive instructions.

And as Saturday, December 6, commenced in Washington, the Army's G2 was sending its own message to Honolulu:

> Word has just been received from ONI by telephone to the effect that the Japanese Embassy in Washington, D.C., was reliably reported to have burned a code book and ciphers last night.

In the adjacent Navy Building, Safford was manifesting concern of his own. Although the intelligence which had been recorded at the Puget Sound listening post had not yet reached Washington, much less been decoded or translated, Safford was disturbed by an increasing awareness that something was going to happen. Troubled about the potential perils facing isolated Wake Island, he drafted this message for CINCPAC, information Wake garrison:

> In view of the imminence of war destroy all registered publications on Wake except this system and current editions of aircraft code and direction-finding code.

Then Safford hurried it into Admiral Noyes's office. Noyes took issue with Safford's message and asked, in effect, "What do you mean by using such language as that?"

"Admiral," retorted his subordinate, "the war is just a matter of days if not hours!"

"You may think there is going to be a war," the communications chief said, "but I think they are bluffing."

"Well, Admiral," Safford persisted, "if all those publications on Wake are captured, we will never be able to explain."

Finally, the dispatch was reworded and sent for "deferred" handling, which meant it would languish a day or two in transmission.

About this time Saturday morning, the machinery of a somewhat parallel but more unusual and certainly significant drama was already in motion. Ferdinand L. Mayer, 54-year-old career diplomat who had retired the past year, had finished a leisurely breakfast at the beautiful Georgetown estate "Evermay" of Ferdinand Lammot Belin, former Ambassador to Poland and multi-millionaire industrialist. With them was James Dunn, one of Cordell Hull's immediate assistants.

Mayer, a native of Indianapolis who had served in Japan, China and Germany as well as South America, had been coaxed to Washington from retirement in Bennington, Vermont, through the efforts of his host, Belin, and an even more well-known American, Colonel William J. ("Wild Bill") Donovan. The New York lawyer, and in 1918 the hell-for-leather soldier of the "Fighting 69th," and his friend Belin had speculated earlier in the week that special envoy Kurusu probably had "something on his mind" which had by no means been extracted by the State Department, the Federal Bureau of Investigation, the Navy, or anyone else.

Such considerations were recently a part of the prerogatives of the perceptive Donovan, already establishing the Co-ordinator of Information's office, temporary "cover" for an embryo super cloak-and-dagger agency (the OSS). Donovan, who had often been chided by the 69th's famed regimental chaplain,

Father Duffy, for his recklessness before the enemy, was among those who decided by late autumn of 1941 that something fast had better be done by the United States.

Belin advised Donovan that Mayer had known Kurusu eleven years previously when both men were assigned to Peru. Because of his Chicago-born wife, Alice, and other affinities for the United States and its customs, Saburo Kurusu had gravitated easily towards the small American colony in Lima. A revolution brought the diplomatic corps even closer together. There was, therefore, every reason for Donovan to believe that if Kurusu would talk to anyone, it would be Mayer.

In the tapestried Japanese Embassy, where Mayer arrived shortly after 11 a.m. on this Saturday morning, he shook hands with "a most cordial" Saburo Kurusu. After brief allusions to Peru and Chicago, where the Japanese envoy had served for six years, Kurusu indicated that he was "extremely anxious" to discuss his mission to Washington. At the same time, it appeared obvious that the Japanese was "apprehensive" of being overheard by members of the embassy staff, as he kept "repeatedly turning his head to see if anyone were approaching." The two, however, were in a room by themselves.

"Fred," Kurusu finally confided, "we are in an awful mess. In the first place, I was delayed two months in coming on this mission through an attack of conjunctivitis when I could neither read nor write. This complicated the situation because time was running out, from the point of view of restraining the military element, and it had been planned that I should have left for the United States in August or September."

Kurusu then went on to say, "with the most courageous candour," in Mayer's estimation, that the remnants of Japan's "civil government" had weeks before decided that the best way to contain the militarists' "effervescence" was to allow the Army to plunge into Indo-China as a "least harmful alternative." By the envoy's interpretation, neither Russia nor Britain nor the United States should have felt unnecessarily menaced by the mere presence of Japanese troops in that South-east Asian country.

Kurusu then observed that Hull seemed "suspicious" of his motives. For this reason he hoped Mayer would intercede for him to second the "sincerity" of his mission, as well as to vouch for the "harmlessness" of troops in Indo-China. The principal difficulties, the envoy noted, appeared to be the State Department, the "national sentimentality" of the United States with respect to China, and, on the other side, the "lack of humour" of Japanese "militarists."

How to get the troops out of China, he admitted frankly, was the first major obstacle, although he conceded a "certain garrisoning" would remain necessary. Then he asserted that the "show was up" there, and Tojo obviously was only trying to save face. "So we must find a way out, and we believe that President Roosevelt as arbiter between ourselves and the Chinese is the best move from our point of view, as well as everyone's else's."

He had, Kurusu reaffirmed, talked with the "militarists" before he left Tokyo, and was convinced that their "bluster and roar" was but "normal face-saving." Further, pro-Axis sentiment was on the downgrade, most Japanese believing that a German victory would not be in Japan's best interests. He cited the "arrogance" of German officers in Tokyo as well as of those in the German refugee colony.

However, as the two professional diplomats—and old friends—continued to talk, Kurusu's tone became more sombre. It appeared increasingly certain that he wanted to say or at least convey, something of the most shocking import; but he feared that he had already been forthright "to the very extreme limits of a patriotic Japanese." Implanted deeply upon Kurusu's mind was the notion that the State Department obstructed his and Nomura's efforts every time the pair "seemed to make some progress in their talks with the President."

Although in the early portion of the conversation, which was to last one hour and a half, Kurusu had appeared to be holding out hope for settlement, he now proceeded to emphasize that the situation was "one of extreme danger of war." As Mayer himself was to report it, "that is to say of attack by the Japanese government, which was then largely dominated by the Army group to which Kurusu and his friends were violently opposed, since, as Kurusu said, war with the United States was suicide for Japan." But the "hotheads," in the opinion of Kurusu, could "upset the applecart ... at any time."

These sentiments were expressed with what sounded to Mayer like "such extraordinary honesty and courage" that he "begged" Kurusu to dine with Belin that night at eight o'clock. "I felt," the retired diplomat was to recall to this author, "I really needed a witness for this most extraordinary expression of view which, if understood by our government, must surely at the least provide it with a most urgent reason to alert all possible military establishments in the Far East."

It was past noon when Mayer walked out onto Massachusetts Avenue, convinced that Kurusu was desperately trying to warn of an impending attack. He hurried back to "Evermay" where his first act was to pick up the telephone to report his "extraordinary" interview to James Dunn at the State Department.

There, Hull had been in "frequent contact" all morning with Knox and Stimson, discussing the "triple priority and most urgent" cable received at 10.40 from Ambassador John G. Winant in London:

> British Admiralty reports that at 3 a.m. London time this morning two parties seen off Cambodia Point, sailing slowly westward towards Kra fourteen hours distant in time. First party, twenty-five transports, six cruisers, ten destroyers. Second party, ten transports, two cruisers, ten destroyers.

Much the same intelligence had been flashed to the Navy shortly before by Admiral Hart from Manila. To Hull it was "manifest" that "the long-threatened Japanese movement of expansion by force to the south was under way. We and our friends were in imminent danger." Stimson thought so too, since he had shaken up his week-end engagements in order to remain in Washington and close to the telephone.

At the White House, Roosevelt, conferring with

Budget Director Harold Smith, commented (from a diary entry made available for this book): "We might be at war with Japan although no one knew."

Before Smith left, the President observed that he was going to send a personal message to the Emperor of Japan. He considered his step a last resort. Roosevelt then told most of his staff to take advantage of the good weather to start Christmas shopping. He ate a light lunch with Harry Hopkins and his secretary, Grace Tully.

After that, the Chief Executive was faced with a full afternoon of appointments, not customary for Saturday, nor recommended by Dr. McIntire, who was concerned about his patient's continuing sinus infection. On his calendar were the names of Hull; Attorney-General Francis Biddle, leaving for Detroit to make a speech Sunday for Defence Bonds; Lord Halifax, the British Ambassador; then, around cocktail time, a more relaxed meeting with his friend and Dutchess County neighbour, Vincent Astor. In the evening he would drop in on a dinner party for thirty-four which his wife was giving. There were a number of house guests this week-end, including cousins of the President and a friend from Albany, Mrs. Charles S. Hamlin.

To Mrs. Roosevelt, her husband had appeared "increasingly worried" of late, with a habit of skipping her many social functions at the last minute. On the other hand, the First Lady was fully aware that he "carried so many secrets in his head" that he had to be always careful of what he said in social gatherings.

Saturday in the Navy and Munitions buildings was

just another working day. And there was little cause for concern on the part of most who worked there other than the annual bother of Christmas shopping. Unlike the White House employees, they would have to wait until later in the afternoon to visit the stores.

Officers such as Admiral Stark, nonetheless, remained worried. He asked Ingersoll to send a fresh message to Kimmel:

> In view of the international situation and the exposed position of our outlying Pacific islands, you may authorize the destruction by them of secret and confidential documents now or under later conditions of greater emergency. Means of communication to support our current operations and special intelligence should, of course, be maintained until the last moment.

Thus code destruction was dominating the attention of several high-placed officers in the Navy Department, reacting along closely parallel lines. The early-morning "pilot" dispatch, intercepted by Bainbridge Island, announcing the Fourteen-Part Message to come, had not, however, been seen or even appreciated by many persons as Saturday morning dragged into afternoon.

Bratton was the first to handle it. After discussing its implications with General Miles of G2 and General Gerow of War Plans, he distributed copies of it to the offices of the Secretary of War, the Secretary of State, and to the Chief of Staff through Colonel Smith.

It was obvious from the so-called pilot message that a flood of intercept material would be coming into the SIS, the Signal Intelligence Service, this afternoon—too much for the Army, which had no twenty-four hour watch, to handle. Accordingly, Bratton called on Safford for Navy help. The latter agreed.

The worried Bratton had made his request none too soon. The eighth part of the message, the first to arrive through communications, started coming in during mid-afternoon. Although encoded, the text was in English, thereby vastly speeding up the processing. In itself this one part was lengthy, assertive and oblique. It commenced:

> Of the various principles put forward by the American government as a basis of the Japanese-American agreement, there are some which the Japanese government is ready to accept in principle, but in view of the world's actual conditions, it seems only a Utopian ideal, on the part of the American government, to attempt to force their immediate adoption.*

---

*See Appendix for complete text of the Fourteen-Part Message.

9
THE MORI MESSAGE

In Honolulu on December 6, the Fourteenth Naval District was winding up a week's routine with its daily intelligence summary:

> General—Traffic volume very heavy with a great deal of old traffic being transmitted. Messages as far back as 1 December were seen in the traffic. This is not believed an attempt to maintain a high traffic level but is the result of confusion in traffic routing with uncertainty of delivery. The stations now holding broadcasts are TOKYO (with three distinct and separate broadcasts), SAIPAN, OMINATO and TAKAO.
>
> Yesterday's high level of traffic from TOKYO originators was maintained with the Intelligence activity still sending periodic messages. Practically all of TOKYO'S messages carry prefixes of high priority.
>
> Combined Fleet—Still no traffic from the Second and Third Fleet Commanders. These units are sending their traffic via the TAKAO and TOKYO broadcasts. The Commander-in-Chief Combined Fleet originated several

messages to the Carriers, Fourth Fleet and the Major Commanders.

At Fort Shafter the Army's Saturday morning staff conference was brief. A possibly provocative subject was introduced by Colonel Fielder's G2 assistant, George Bicknell, who was concerned over the increasingly brisk bonfire of Japanese consulate papers on Nuuanu Avenue. This had, Bicknell insisted, "a very serious intent." He could not escape the conviction that "something warlike was about to happen somewhere."

General Short was not present. In his stead was Chief of Staff Walter C. Phillips. Bicknell and Fielder assumed that the proceedings would be conveyed by Colonel Phillips to the commanding general.

On Saturday afternoon of this half working day, Willamette University of Salem, Oregon, would meet the University of Hawaii in the Shriners' eleventh annual football classic. Those not Christmas shopping were already thronging towards the stadium even before the noon hour had been mutely proclaimed by the great clock hands on Aloha Tower, at the harbour's edge.

In the week-end's all-consuming preoccupations, little notice was paid Saturday's newspaper headlines. The Honolulu *Advertiser* started the day with an eight-column banner: AMERICA EXPECTED TO REJECT JAPAN'S REPLY ON INDO-CHINA. On Page 6 there were two short articles, with single-column heads: "Japanese Navy Moving South" and "British Told to Quit

Thailand." With less length, as well as in smaller type, the afternoon *Star-Bulletin* proclaimed: JAPANESE LEADER OFFERS NEW U.S. PEACE PLAN. There was beneath it a sub story: "Singapore's Forces Called to Station."

And on the same page one was a picture of a sentry beside the American flag, above the caption, "Army on Alert."

That afternoon, however, Consul Kita advised Tokyo to the contrary:

> ... at the present time there are no signs of barrage balloon equipment. In addition, it is difficult to imagine that they actually have any. However, even though they have actually made preparations, because they must control the air over the water and land runways of the airports in the vicinity of Pearl Harbour, Hickman, Ford and Ewa, there are limits to the balloon defence of Pearl Harbour. I imagine in all probability there is considerable opportunity left to take advantage for a surprise attack against these places.
>
> In my opinion the battleships do not have torpedo nets.

Slightly later, adding to the previous details he had forwarded on ship movements and berthing plans, the Japanese emissary postscripted, "It appears that no air reconnaissance is being conducted by the fleet air arm."

Although this was not a diplomatic message, and therefore encoded in a lesser system than "purple," the still pyramiding accumulation of traffic and the lack of personnel over the weekend deferred the intercept for decoding at least until Monday morning, December 8. Whether it had been partially decoded and scanned by someone in intelligence was, as with earlier messages, not satisfactorily established. It was, unquestionably, the most revealing message yet transmitted.

While many of the Army and Navy families were stadium-bound, there were others who preferred to spend this Saturday afternoon in the ease and comfort of their porches. George Bicknell was among them, but his afternoon of leisure did not last long. First, the junior intelligence officer was disturbed at his Black Point residence, Aiea Heights, by a phone call from Hickam Field.

"George," rasped the voice on the other end of the line, "can you arrange to have KGMB stay on the air all night tonight?" The caller was Lieutenant-Colonel Clay I. Hoppough, signal officer for General Martin's Hawaiian Air Force. He explained that a flight of B-17's was winging in from the mainland, *en route* to the Philippines, and their navigators could home on the commercial radio station.

This expedient had been employed before, but Bicknell still did not like it. "It annoys me no end, Clay," he retorted, "to have these radio stations going on the air for a twenty-four hour period only on the days on which aeroplanes are flying from the coast. It would be much more sensible to put the station on twenty-fours a day for a period of a month, then there would be no special significance as to when aeroplanes were flying."

Hoppough promised to "take that up later." Tonight, however, he had no choice but to "make the arrangements as requested," and General Martin would take the responsibility.

Against his better judgement, Bicknell asked the manager at KGMB to keep the station transmitting. Obligingly, KGMB agreed. Instead of the normal sign-off following the 11 to 12 p.m. Night Owl programme, the same "owl" would "spin platters" all night until the regular Sunday sign-on time.

Before four o'clock, Bicknell was interrupted once more by the jangling of the telephone. This time it was his friend Robert Shivers of the FBI.

"You better come right down here, George," Shivers said. "I want you to see something which I think is a matter of great importance."

Bicknell drove down frond-lined Kamehameha Avenue from the spectacular elevations of Aiea Heights past Tripler Hospital to the centre of Honolulu. In the Dillingham Building, at Merchant and Bishop streets, one of the city's five major office structures, he found an unusually excited agent.

"This thing," said Shivers, "looks very significant to me. I think something is going to happen."

The "thing" was the transcript of a lengthy telephone call between Mrs. Motokazu Mori, wife of a local dentist, and the Tokyo newspaper *Yomiuri Shimbun*. Both Dr. Mori, whose office at 1481 Nuuanu Avenue was only three blocks from the Japanese consulate, and his wife had merited the "suspicious" lists of G2 and the FBI for some months, with the result that telephone lines both to the office and to the dentist's home, on Wylie Street, had been tapped.

The present call had been recorded on a wax cylinder the evening before and "unscrambled" Saturday morning. Mrs. Mori listed herself as a bona fide correspondent for the Japanese newspaper, but Shivers was struck by the non-reportorial nature of this conversation. Further, the controlled Press of Nippon was not known for its generosity in expenses. At $15 for three minutes, the prevailing long-distance rates to Tokyo, this call—devoted to what editors would call "boiler plate" or filler material—would have cost upward of $200. It was an unheard-of extravagance.

The conversation commenced:

> (from Japan) Hello, is this Mori?
> (from Honolulu) Hello, this is Mori.
> I am sorry to have troubled you. Thank you very much.
> Not at all.
> I received your telegram and was able to grasp the essential points. I would like to have your impressions on the conditions you are observing at present. Are aeroplanes flying daily?
> Yes, lots of them fly around.
> Are they large planes?
> Yes, they are quite big.
> Are they flying from morning till night?
> Well, not to that extent, but last week they were quite active in the air.
> I hear there are many sailors, there, is that right?
> There aren't so many now. There were more in the beginning part of this year and the ending part of last year.

Is that so?

I do not know why this is so, but it appears that there are very few sailors here at present.

Are any Japanese people there holding meetings to discuss U.S.-Japanese negotiations being conducted presently?

No, not particularly. The minds of the Japanese here appear calmer than expected. They are getting along harmoniously ... we are not hated or despised. The soldiers here and we get along very well. All races are living in harmony....

Although there is no munitions industry here engaged in by the Army, civilian workers are building houses for the Army personnel. Most of the work here is directed towards building houses of various sorts. There are not enough carpenters, electricians and plumbers. ...

Are there many big factories there?

No, there are no factories but a lot of small buildings of various kinds are being constructed.

The trans-Pacific telephone conversation then touched upon several topics including a population increase of from 150,000 in Honolulu to possibly as much as 240,000, and next the unrelated fact that there "seem to be precautionary measures taken" at nighttime.

What about searchlights?

Well, not much to talk about.

Do they put searchlights on when planes fly about at night?

No.

Bicknell's interest was intensified when he listened to this portion of the recording. He was well aware of the Army and Navy procedure of switching *on* searchlights when the long-range reconnaissance planes were groping their way home after night patrol.

As the conversation continued, Mrs. Mori volunteered that the Honolulu newspapers were "pretty bad ... opposite to the atmosphere pervading the city." Asked about the impression Kurusu made when he was in Hawaii, the dentist's wife responded:

> A very good one. Mr. Kurusu understands the American mind, and he was very adept at answering queries of the Press.

This in itself was indicative to Bicknell and Shivers that Mori and the party in the *Yomiuri Shimbun* office talked most infrequently on the phone, if indeed they ever had previously. Kurusu had passed through Honolulu more than three weeks before.

> Are there any Japanese people there who are planning to evacuate Hawaii?
> There are almost none wishing to do that.
> What is the climate there now?
> These last few days have been very cold with occasional rainfall, a phenomenon very rare in Hawaii. Today the wind is blowing very strongly, a very unusual climate.

Bicknell did not have to be a strategist to understand the importance of weather intelligence to any military commander. To the junior G2 officer the information about the winds sounded "very helpful" to a potential enemy. The conversation continued from Hawaii:

> Here is something interesting. Litvinov, the Russian Ambassador to the United States, arrived here yesterday.

I believe he enplaned for the mainland today. He made no statements on any problems. . . .

Do you know anything about the United States fleet?

No, I don't know anything about the fleet. Since we try to avoid talking about such matters, we do not know much about the fleet. At any rate the fleet here seems small. I don't know if all of the fleet has done this, but it seems that the fleet has left here.

Is that so? What kind of flowers are in bloom in Hawaii at present?

Presently the flowers in bloom are fewest out of the whole year. However, the hibiscus and the poinsettia are in bloom now.

In some ways, the two intelligence experts considered this talk of flowers—obviously a special code—the crux of the telephone conversation, with other statements minor if not actual padding and false scents to an eavesdropper. Why should the *Yomiuri Shimbun* pay $15 every three minutes to obtain horticultural knowledge that could be found in any gardener's guide?

Do you feel an inconvenience there due to the suspension of importation of Japanese goods?

Yes, we feel the inconvenience very much. There are no Japanese soy, and many other foodstuffs which come from Japan.

Once again the conversation trailed back to flowers as Mrs. Mori explained:

Japanese chrysanthemums are in full bloom here, and there are no herring roe for this year's New Year's celebration.

How many first-generation Japanese are there in Hawaii according to last surveys made?

About 50,000....

Any first-generation Japanese in the Army?

No, they do not draw any first-generation Japanese.

Is it right, that there are 1,500 [second generation] in the Army?

Yes, this is true up to the present, but may increase since more will be inducted in January.

Thank you very much.

Not at all. I'm sorry I couldn't be of much use.

Oh, no, that was fine. Best regards to your wife.

Mrs. Mori then said: "Wait a moment please." But somewhat abruptly, as if belatedly the Tokyo caller suspected a tap, the phone was clicked off. Neither Bicknell nor Shivers could determine whether Tokyo actually thought Dr. Mori was on the Honolulu end or whether "best regards to your wife" was simply calculated to obscure. In any case, "in view of all the things that had transpired," this conversation seemed to Bicknell "of special interest." He telephoned his superior, Kendall Fielder.

"I have a matter of great importance," he said, "that should be taken up with the General right away."

It was now about 5.30 in the afternoon.

General Short, Fielder explained, was going out to Schofield Barracks for dinner—an Army Relief benefit—and would have no time for a conference that afternoon. Perhaps it would be better to wait until morning?

Bicknell, thoroughly alarmed, persisted. "It *cannot* wait until morning," he said, reiterating that the matter was of "such importance that it would not carry over to the next day."

Fielder paused, then said he would talk it over with

Short and call Bicknell back. The two officers, Walter Short and Kendall Fielder, lived next door to each other at Fort Shafter and were good friends. They and their wives visited back and forth, and entertained frequently. In fact, the two couples were going together this evening to the Schofield Barracks benefit.

In a few minutes Fielder, true to his word, called his assistant.

"If you can get out to Shafter in ten minutes," he said, "General Short says he will wait that long."

Bicknell assured Fielder he could do it. He took the transcript from Shivers and headed for the street. Outside he was greeted by a scene of tumultuous discord—the songs, the shouts, the screams of victory. The University of Hawaii had just defeated Willamette 20-6. Merchant Street was choked with celebrating fans, as well as brassy fragments of the fourteen bands which had played at the stadium. Christmas shoppers, infected by the hysteria of the moment, added to the traffic snarl as Bicknell headed for Fort Shafter.

10
PROPERLY ALERTED

At 4.30 p.m. the Navy and Munitions Buildings were emptied of their last Saturday workers. Momentarily, the pavements along Constitution Avenue were thick with people, then just as abruptly empty again.

On the second deck, Commander Safford reached for his hat. "There is nothing I can do but get in your way and make you nervous," he said to his colleagues. "I'm going home."

Thirteen parts of the wordy Fourteen-Part Message were now on the decoders' desks. There was a lot of work ahead this Saturday night, and Safford, who had an evening engagement, left "his best man on the watch side," Lieutenant (jg) George W. Lynn, on duty. He had every confidence in Lynn.

Lamps in other offices were winking off as their occupants prepared to move out into the gathering dusk of December. Before he left, Admiral Turner looked up and saw Wilkinson.

"You are mistaken, Kelly," said the soft-spoken intelligence chief, pausing before Turner's desk.

"Mistaken in what?" Turner asked.

"Mistaken that Japan would attack the United States."

Turner shrugged, and that was all there was to the conversation. No argument ensued. The quick, curious interchange was not uncommon in the Army or the Navy, whose members often wanted to be on record for stating even an unofficial opinion.

Turner and Wilkinson walked down the corridor together towards the stairway. Admiral Stark was hurrying home from the Naval Operation's office to greet familiar dinner guests, Captain and Mrs. Harold D. Krick. Krick had been flag lieutenant when the Admiral was commander of cruisers. The two couples had tickets to see *The Student Prince* at the National Theatre that evening.

Among the last to leave the Navy Department were Captain Charles Wellborn, Captain John McCrea, and Stark's flag lieutenant, Commander William R. Smedberg. Before they dispersed to their various evening ways, Smedberg was to recall that one of the trio observed:

"Tomorrow ought to be the day the Japs land on Kra."

The tone was peculiarly flat and matter-of-fact, although Smedberg could not remember which of the three had uttered the prophecy. Another of their colleagues—Captain Joseph R. Redman, Noyes's assistant—had made an even stronger prediction several days before. Returning on the train the previous Saturday from the Army-Navy game in Philadelphia, Redman had categorically asserted, "If the Japs don't strike us this week-end, I'll eat my shirt!"

So far, the captain had not started chewing on his shirt. At 4.20 p.m., this Saturday, further substantiation for the morning advisories was stringing into the War Department's Communications Centre from an observer in Singapore:

> At one o'clock in the afternoon, following a course due west, were seen a battleship, five cruisers, seven destroyers and twenty-five merchant ships; these were seen at 106° 8′ E 8° N; this was the first report.
> Ten merchant ships, two cruisers and ten destroyers were seen following the same course at 106° 20′ E 7° 35′ N.
> Both of the above reports came from patrols of the Royal Air Force.

In other words, the first convoy was in the South China Sea, forty miles south of Soctrang, on the south coast of Indo-China, and about 365 miles from the nearest landfall on the Malay Peninsula, across the Gulf of Siam. The second was approximately fifty miles south of the first. If they maintained the same course and speed, both forces could be expected to raise the Malaya coast the following afternoon—Sunday, in the United States time zone; Monday, across the international dateline.

A statement in the Press from Tokyo, attributed to Lieutenant-General Teiichi Suzuki, president of the Cabinet Planning Board, imbued these military movements with magnified menace: "Japan's patience will no longer be necessary in event the countries hostile to peace in East Asia—countries whose identity now is becoming absolutely clear—attempt to continue and increase Far Eastern disturbances."

"Purple" itself, like an impassive hand of doom, kept coming in:

> Re my No. 902. There is really no need to tell you this, but in the preparation of the *aide-mémoire* be absolutely sure not to use a typist or other person.
> Be most extremely cautious in preserving secrecy.

A handful of communicators, intelligence people and decoders, struggling to keep up with such messages, were all who remained in the now echoing yellow halls of the two old Constitution Avenue buildings. Kramer had held his translators until midafternoon, well past the Saturday closing. When he saw that the floodgates of Japanese intercepts remained wide open, he requested the personnel to stay on still longer, even though he was embarrassed to make such demands on the civil service employees whom he could not reward with overtime pay.

Up on Massachusetts Avenue, the Japanese Embassy staffers also were overworked. H. R. Baukhage, a commentator for the ABC radio network, had obtained an interview with Kurusu "just to have some filler material for my Monday broadcast." The envoy, far less communicative than he had been in the presence of his friend "Fred" Mayer, was politely oblique.

Feeling a reporter's frustration when an anticipated story has not materialized, the knowledgeable "Buck" Baukhage started out through the front hall of the spacious building. As he did so his attention focused on hurrying employees laden with wastebaskets and cartons obviously heavy with paper.

"Aren't you rather busy for Saturday afternoon?" he asked.

"Very busy, so very busy" was all he could elicit from any of them. The answer was truthful. Baukhage did not grasp the significance of what was happening, nor would he unless he had followed the pigmy battalions to the backyard incinerator where they were burning codes and secret papers.

At the White House, Roosevelt had hurled himself into a series of afternoon appointments and problems which would have taxed the physical and nervous energies of a well man. No report was made of the twenty-minute conference with Lord Halifax. But it was a reasonable assumption that the call had been sparked by the "Naval Person," Churchill himself, whose cable of the past Sunday had thus far been ignored at least officially by the American Commander-in-Chief:

> It seems to me that one important method remains unused in averting war between Japan and our two countries—namely, a plain declaration, secret or public as may be thought best, that any further act of aggression by Japan will lead ultimately to the gravest consequence.... I am convinced that it might make all the difference and prevent a melancholy extension of the war.

Another hint of the afternoon's talk with Halifax was contained in a memorandum received by the Australian Minister of External Affairs from the

Australian Minister in Washington, Richard G. Casey, who relayed intelligence obtained "orally" from President Roosevelt this same day:

> 1. President has decided to send message to Emperor.
> 2. President's subsequent procedure is that if no answer is received by him from the Emperor by Monday evening,
> a. he will issue his warning on Tuesday afternoon or evening.
> b. warning or equivalent by British or others will not follow until Wednesday morning, i.e., after his own warning has been delivered repeatedly to Tokyo and Washington.

Roosevelt, just as he had forecast earlier to Budget Director Harold Smith, and as Minister Casey had learned or guessed, was attempting to communicate directly with the Emperor. Late in the afternoon he summoned Miss Tully. She was about to leave for the Mayflower Hotel where Richard Harkness, a radio newsman, was giving a cocktail party.

The note he dictated was substantially the same as the one Hull had prepared at least a week earlier. The "unprecedented approach," in Grace Tully's private evaluation, read:

> Almost a century ago the President of the United States addressed to the Emperor of Japan a message extending an offer of friendship of the people of the United States to the people of Japan. That offer was accepted, and in the long period of unbroken peace and friendship which has followed, our respective nations, through the virtues of their peoples and wisdom of their rulers, have prospered and have substantially helped humanity.

> Only in situations of extraordinary importance to our two countries need I address to Your Majesty messages on matters of state. I feel I should now so address you because of the deep and far-reaching emergency which appears to be in formation. . . .
>
> During the past few weeks it has become clear to the world that Japanese military, naval and air forces have been sent to southern Indo-China in such large numbers as to create a reasonable doubt on the part of other nations that this continuing concentration in Indo-China is not defensive in its character. . . . It is only reasonable that the people of the Philippines, of the hundreds of islands of the East Indies, of Malaya and of Thailand itself are asking themselves whether these forces of Japan are preparing or intending to make attack on one or more of these many directions. . . .
>
> It is clear that a continuance of such a situation is unthinkable.
>
> None of these peoples whom I have spoken of above can sit either indefinitely or permanently on a keg of dynamite.
>
> There is absolutely no thought on the part of the United States of invading Indo-China if every Japanese soldier or sailor were withdrawn therefrom.

The Chief Executive attached a memorandum to this appeal, before speeding it to Cordell Hull: "Shoot this to Grew. I think can go in grey code—saves time—I don't mind if it gets picked up."

(The President, however, had no way of foreseeing that the appeal to the Emperor would be stalled at the Tokyo cable office by Japanese authorities for ten and a half hours after receipt—far too late for Ambassador Grew to make any practical use of it.)

Now, suffering from sinus pains, Roosevelt was wheeled to Dr. McIntire's office for treatment, another one of the punishing ordeals so dreaded by his wife Eleanor. Returning to the Oval Room forty-five minutes later, he greeted his tall, reticent neighbour from Rhinebeck, Vincent Astor. It was cocktail time. Roosevelt had nearly an hour before he would have to excuse himself and dress for his wife's dinner.

There was in Washington the usual assortment of Saturday evening functions: formal, informal or, like that at Belin's mansion, calculated. One of the largest was the one to be held at the Washington Navy Yard in honour of former Secretary of the Navy Charles Edison, son of the late inventor. Among the smaller and more typical was that of Admiral Wilkinson and his wife, Catherine, at their North Uhle Street residence in nearby Arlington, Virginia. His guest list crossed interservice lines to include his Army opposite, General Miles. Navy guests were Captain and Mrs. John Beardall and Captain and Mrs. Schuirmann. A man who believed in extending hospitality to the guests of his country, Wilkinson had invited two officer attachés from the French Embassy. Since the United States recognized the Vichy government, with retired Admiral William D. Leahy as ambassador to it, Wilkinson was aware that the two representatives of France were potential channels of information back to their captive land and thence to Nazi Germany. In other words, he and Sherman Miles would have to be as careful of their conversation as they should be attentive to that of their French guests.

Beardall had left the White House at 5.30 p.m. after advising Lieutenant Lester Schulz, standing the confidential mail watch, that he could expect an important pouch during the evening. Schulz, Annapolis '34, with two days' experience in the new post, was still literally trying to find his way around the Executive Mansion. That he was reticent of nature did not ease his problem.

At the Wardman Park Hotel, Secretary and Mrs. Knox, plain and quiet-living people, would entertain just one couple at dinner: Mr. and Mrs. John O'Keith. O'Keith, after brief service in the Navy Department, was returning to Chicago to become vice-president of the *Daily News*.

The Otis K. Sadtlers were already engaged in preliminaries to a supper for Army acquaintances. The talk, turning to the incineration of Japanese codes, swung in a familiar, troubled direction: war. All present agreed "it" was coming; Mrs. Sadtler was certain that her husband indicated it would be "probably the next day." But the battlegrounds the Army group conjectured were remote from any American-held territories: Indo-China, Thailand, Malaya. . . .

In the hushed red-brick amplitude of Quarters "No. 1" at Fort Myer, the George Catlett Marshalls were beginning another "monastic" evening. Mrs. Marshall had fallen in October and broken four ribs causing cancellation of the social engagements which the quiet-loving pair normally would have accepted. Since her accident, the Marshalls had been out to dinner but once—Wednesday of this week; they spent all other evenings at home reading.

The General had a predilection for motion pictures, even as President Roosevelt had for detective stories, and would have attended the post theatre tonight if he had not already seen the film. He told his chauffeur, burly Sergeant John Semanko, that he would not be needing him, although he should stand by to drive him to the office late next morning for a routine look-around. This would, naturally, follow his Sunday horseback ride, accompanied only by his Dalmatian. The Chief of Staff was a man of die-stamped, regular habits, and simple pleasures.

Others in Washington would view an assorted offering of theatre fare, including Abbott and Costello in *Keep 'Em Flying*, and *They Died with Their Boots On* starring Errol Flynn as General Custer. Some, not at the theatre or at entertainment of any sort, were preparing for Sunday. The Rev. Theodore P. Fricke, of St. Matthew's Lutheran Church, was among that number. He was finishing his next morning's sermon, "Looking Towards a Better Day."

At his estate, "Woodley," however, Secretary Stimson saw few prospects for a better day. Something in particular was bothering him this Saturday, although it was not strictly a concern of the War Department. Nonetheless, he had to know. Telephoning his aide, Major E. L. Harrison, he requested these naval statistics: "Compilation of men-of-war in Far East: British, American, Japanese, Dutch, Russian. Also compilation of American men-of-war in Pacific Fleet, with locations and a list of American men-of-war in the Atlantic without locations."

This request—actually an order since it came from the Secretary of War—was forwarded by telephone at 8 p.m. to the Navy Operations duty officer. A time limit was set for obtaining the statistics: 9 a.m. Sunday for the Pacific figures, 10 a.m. for the Atlantic.

Certainly, Roosevelt knew the statistics generally. But the way the Royal Navy was being shunted around the Empire's far-flung fighting fronts, there was no telling exactly the strength of any given place or moment of the Admiralty's scattered seaborne sluggers. He knew that the *Prince of Wales*, the site of the Atlantic Charter Conference, had just dropped anchor in Singapore together with the *Repulse*.

The Netherlands East Indies fleet, while bravely manned, was inconsequential. It included not one capital ship. With the Netherlands in German hands, the Dutch government-in-exile nonetheless had commitments in home waters and to its other possessions throughout the world. To fulfil them it maintained a Navy comprised primarily of destroyers, minesweepers, a few submarines, tugboats—a seagoing hodgepodge, of which its five cruisers were relatively the mightiest. In fact, two of Japan's battleships of the *Yamato* class, with the aid of an aircraft carrier or two, could easily carry the bulk of the Netherlands' naval complement, approximately 11,000 men.

The President understood these international naval measurements as well as he appreciated that the United States Navy, committed to battle in the North Atlantic, was out-numbered two to one in the Pacific by Japan, and that the carrier disadvantage was at least five to one.

Yet, if Stimson was uncertain as to the location of the United States fleet and even if Roosevelt, perhaps, was not fully informed, these intelligence gaps in high places were not surprising. Apparently there was no firmer certainty at the Navy Department.

For example, Bratton, still on duty in the Army's Far Eastern section, and struggling now with the incoming Fourteen-Part Message from Tokyo to the Washington Embassy, had asked his naval opposite:

"Are you sure these people are properly alerted? Are they on the job? Have they been properly warned?"

McCollum had answered "Yes." But he did not know that the draft of his own warning of Thursday had never been sent. And he had added, thinking probably of the three task forces that had put out from Pearl Harbour, "The fleet has gone or is going to sea."

Bratton was further assured by McCollum, with whom he was in close daily contact, that "when the emergency arises the fleet is not going to be there." Thus Bratton was confident that "no major element of the fleet" was in Honolulu this Saturday night. He also believed that others in G2 and ONI were under the same impression.

However, the question of where all or part of the fleet was or *ought* to be was far from elementary. There were those who believed that, since the basing of the ships in Hawaii was an accomplished fact, they should stay there, or in the area. Ambassador Grew, for example, well aware of the dilemma, believed that "to withdraw the fleet from Pearl Harbour would be a complete confession of weakness."

In any case, irrespective of who knew it or did not

know it, the preponderance of the fleet's heavy units had *not* been withdrawn, although the swift, scrappy welterweights of the battle line, the carriers and the cruisers, were—providentially?—at sea.

The last moments of the *U.S.S. Arizona* are shrouded in smoke

A pall of smoke filled the sky over Pearl Harbour after the Japanese bombs fell

Pearl Harbour in 1941, before the attack

The *West Virginia* and the *Tennessee* afire

U.S.S. Shaw exploding

The White House, December 1941

Frequent visitors to the White House were Secretary of War Henry L. Stimson (*left*) and Chief of Staff George C. Marshall

President Roosevelt signs the Declaration of War with Japan, 8 December 1941

Frank Knox, Secretary of the Navy—a Republican from Chicago

Cordell Hull, Secretary of State, accompanied by (*left*) Ambassador Kichisaburo Nomura and Japan's special envoy, Saburo Kurusu

Admiral Harold R. Stark, Chief of Naval Operations

Japanese fishermen could taxi out of Hawaii in their sampans to meet larger ships, well at sea, delivering agents. Here the fleet is moored near the Kalakaua Avenue Bridge in the Ala Wai Canal

General Walter C. Short

Admiral Husband E. Kimmel

Admiral Richmond Kelly Turner

Admiral Leigh Noyes

11
SATURDAY NIGHT IN THE PACIFIC

Bicknell succeeded in bucking the traffic and arriving at Fort Shafter in ten minutes. He found General Short at his residence, together with Fielder and their wives. All appeared ready to start for the dinner at Schofield Barracks, half an hour's drive distant.

Short read the Mori manuscript "very carefully," in Bicknell's estimation, as Fielder peered across his shoulder. Then the General and his G2 aide discussed it for a minute or two before turning towards Bicknell and asking if he knew the Moris. Bicknell said he did, and that he also "suspected" them.

The commander of the Hawaiian Department concluded that the Mori transcript presented "a very good picture of the situation in Hawaii." Bicknell, he was later to recall, thought bitterly, that was just the trouble with it; it was too accurate a picture. But he told Short that he had not "had time thoroughly to analyse and evaluate the message." Just the same he considered it "very significant and an indication of something in the wind." What otherwise would have compounded his concern was the comforting illusion that Short "knew all the other things that had been transpiring," including the burning of the codes at the Japanese consulate.

Quite the opposite was the case, however. In contradiction of testimony by both Fielder and Phillips, Short was to testify that he had never been informed of the code destruction.

Colonel Fielder, however, did not share Bicknell's concern. Observing that the phone conversation sounded "silly from our Western mind's point of view," he considered it "a more or less typical reporter's approach to a story that would sell a paper."

Short settled the brief discussion by observing that "no one of us could figure out what it possibly meant." He suggested to Bicknell that perhaps he was "a little too intelligence conscious." Then the Shorts and Fielders said good night to Bicknell and drove off for Schofield Barracks. Frustrated, the G2 officer started for Aiea Heights and home.

Elsewhere in Honolulu, others continued their Saturday evenings. Admiral Kimmel was on his way to dine with a classmate, Vice-Admiral Herbert Fairfax Leary, who commanded Heavy Cruiser Division 9. Like his Army counterpart, Admiral Kimmel was abstemious and a man of conservative, retiring habits. Both officers would leave their respective social functions two hours or more before midnight. Besides, they had a golf date in the morning.

Layton, the fleet's intelligence officer, was taking life easy at his home located on the east side of Honolulu when he received a phone call.

"Are you going to the office tomorrow?" inquired Mayfield, his opposite in the naval district.

"I expect to," replied Layton. He had felt some "concern" in the last few days, although he refused to acknowledge that code burning or lack of contact with the Japanese carriers in themselves hinted at war.

He would appreciate it, Mayfield said, if Layton would stop at his office on Sunday. Although the former was at his office when he made the phone call, he told Layton that no useful purpose would be served if he came down now.

"There is nothing you can do here," he explained, "because I haven't got the material, and I won't have it until tomorrow morning, but I would like to have you stop in here because I have something that I want your opinion on." Mayfield did not care to mention over the telephone that Shivers wanted to show him the transcript of a long-distance conversation between someone named "Mori" and a newspaper office in Tokyo.

In downtown Honolulu, Fort Street was ablaze with Christmas lights. There were many football dances, and the likelihood that they would continue well into the night. At the McKinley High School auditorium the *National Defence Talent Review* was in full swing, and "Campbell and Wild," a black-face dancing team from the Army, appeared capable of swinging off with all the honours.

From the Naval Receiving Station, the "Battle of the Bands" was hurling metallic notes across the dark harbour waters. The contest featured all the latest dance hits: "There'll Be Bluebirds over the White Cliffs of Dover," "Chattanooga Choo-Choo," "I Don't Want to Set the World on Fire," "Maria Elena," "The Hut-Sut Song," "The Shepherd's Serenade," and the very popular "Take the 'A' Train."

From the harbour were visible only the dim anchor lights of vessels of the fleet, led in avoirdupois and grandeur by the battleships, the flagship *Pennsylvania* and her brood: the *Arizona, California, Maryland, Nevada, Oklahoma, Tennessee* and *West Virginia*. They were neatly in line off the east shore of Ford Island, half their number moored side by side like so many barges in the back waters of any large port.

In Washington there might have been those who did not know for certain where the fleet was. In Honolulu, almost everyone knew or could easily find out, including Consul Kita.

West of Hawaii, 4,130 interminable miles to Manila, it was already past the Sunday noon hour. From the Philippine Islands, in the official Washington view a less consequential target than Hawaii, General Douglas MacArthur, commanding the Army Forces in the Far East, had advised General Marshall:

> All Air Corps stations here on alert. Aeroplanes dispersed and each under guard.

Earlier in 1941, MacArthur had commented to Admiral Stark's aide, Captain John McCrea who was there on a special mission, that "war is inevitable." However, in later years MacArthur was to note his satisfaction that, at least, he was supplied "ample and complete information" from the War Department "for the purpose of alerting the Army Command of the Philippines on a war basis."

Admiral Hart, Asiatic Fleet commander, himself believed the "war warning" of late November was "quite simple." He commented. "We were told that we were to await the blow, in dispositions such as to minimize the damage from it, and it was left to the commanders on the spot to decide all the details."

Ready or not, neither MacArthur nor Hart possessed even the minimum tools of war needed to fend off the military juggernaut, Japan, only 1,000 miles to the north-east. The 130,000 troops which served under MacArthur were not all that their numbers would seem to indicate. All but 30,000 of his soldiers were poorly equipped and partially trained Filipinos—brave, sturdy fighters, but far from ready to come up against an army which was hard, professional and field-proved from the long China "venture."

His air force, commanded by 51-year-old energetic Major-General Lewis H. Brereton, was proportionately slim and shaky. While the balance sheet proclaimed 277 aeroplanes, only about half of that total were modern and trimmed for combat. These included thirty-five Flying Fortresses and approximately a hundred P-40 fighters. It had, in fact, been determined after the North Atlantic Conference in August to build-up the Far East air squadrons as part of a deterrent policy.

"We decided," Stimson was to explain, "that if a sufficient number of our bombing planes, which would be able to proceed to the Philippine Islands under their own power, could be gathered there this would present a very effective nucleus of a defence against the advance of the Japanese Navy or convoys in South Asiatic waters."

The flight of B-17's, for which KGMB, Honolulu, would broadcast all Saturday night, was Manila-bound. Yet there was only so much assistance that could be given the Far East air arm. Brereton, when he had left Washington a few weeks previously to assume his new command, had checked on Army Air Corps totals. There were only sixty-four fully qualified four-engine pilots and 171 pursuit or fighter pilots available in the Combat Command. Thus the Army had to make-do with half-trained flying personnel, and hope that the fledglings, through a kindly Providence, would acquire skill before they destroyed themselves along with their valuable machines.

"We were definitely a third-rate air power" was Brereton's opinion, and "the situation seemed hopeless."

On Sunday night, he was guest of honour at a party given at the Manila Hotel by the 27th Bombardment Group. This was a unit which as yet had been allotted no aeroplanes. In the course of the evening Brereton talked with Rear-Admiral William R. Purnell, Admiral Hart's Chief of Staff.

Purnell, whom Brereton knew well enough to call

"Speck," mentioned that Hart had received messages from the Navy Department which could be interpreted as further war warnings. He understood, also, that the commanding officer of the Asiatic Fleet was even at this hour conferring with General MacArthur and Francis B. Sayre, the High Commissioner of the Philippines. It was but a question of days, Purnell said, "perhaps hours" before "the shooting" was liable to start.

MacArthur, Hart and Brereton, while they knew they would be on the front lines of any Pacific war, also possessed the advantages of such an advanced position. Navy PBYs were continuing their close shadowing of Japanese convoys. Liaison with Australian and Netherlands East Indies intelligence sources was close and effective. And, certainly most important of all, MacArthur held a trump denied Short or Kimmel in Honolulu: the wonderful "purple" machine. United States commanders in the Philippines knew about the code burnings, the deteriorating diplomatic negotiations and other telltale matters of import that Washington had snooped out. On the other hand, with nowhere near the combined staffs of G2 and ONI in the Munitions Building and the Navy Department, less intercepts could be processed in Manila than in Washington.

Brereton was not particularly interested in corroborating the sources of Purnell's information. Nor was he surprised that MacArthur and Hart might be in conversations with Sayre. This was quite common. But Purnell's comment, coming on top of all the other dire pieces of information he had been mentally assembling, was enough to send him to a lobby telephone. He rang up his operations duty officer and ordered a "combat alert" commencing at daylight. At Clark, Nichols, Nielson and the incompleted Del Monte fields, crews would be briefed and ready, their aircraft warmed up, fuelled and armed, as if an army were actually *en route* to attack the islands.

Shortly after he gave this order Brereton talked with Brigadier-General Richard K. Sutherland, MacArthur's chief of staff, who confirmed what Purnell had said earlier.

Admiral Hart, with a fleet comprised of two cruisers, thirteen World War I four-stack destroyers and twenty-nine submarines generally ready for action, had no more reason for complacency than Brereton. Recently, his PBY flying boats, slow and tempting targets, had become valuable assets: they had been shadowing Tokyo's Malaya-bound convoys.

Hart, although in possession of no fresh war warning as such, had earlier in the day received a communication from Captain John M. Creighton, a U.S. naval attaché in Singapore, quoting a dispatch just in from the London War Office:

> We have now received assurance of American armed support in cases as follows: "Afirm" [if] we are obliged execute our plans to forestall Japs landing Isthmus of Kra or take action in reply to Nips invasion any other part of Siam; "Baker" if Dutch Indies are attacked and we go to their defence; "Cast" if Japs attack us. Therefore without reference to London put plan in action if first you have good info Jap expedition advancing with the apparent intention of landing in Kra, second if Nips violate any part of Thailand. Para: if NEI are attacked put into operation plans agreed upon between British and Dutch.

Hart had hurried off a cable to the Chief of Naval Operations asking, in effect, exactly *what* he was supposed to do when and if Washington decided to lend "armed support" to Britain.

As MacArthur, Hart and Brereton in their various ways and capabilities awaited "something" in the Philippines, Singapore, some 1,500 miles to the south-west, was braced for what its commanders believed an imminent blow. Sunday evening, the bosuns' whistles piped along the waterfront, echoing the length of Collier Key and Raffles Key, up Connaught Drive and Clyde Street, recalling men to their ships. All shore leaves had been cancelled. Bars and brothels were emptied of their sailor customers.

It would not again be like old times in Singapore for a long while.

12
"THIS MEANS WAR"

Roosevelt did not appear to enjoy his wife's dinner party. To his friend, Mrs. Charles S. Hamlin of Albany, he seemed "very quiet and looked disturbed... very worn." He mentioned that he would take it easy Sunday, working on his stamp collection in the morning, then "get in an afternoon snooze and drive in the Virginia countryside." Another, more informal dinner was planned for Sunday evening.

Long before the violin concert that was scheduled after dinner, in fact just after the meat course, Roosevelt excused himself and was assisted from the room. His face continued to haunt his Albany neighbour: "unusually solemn."

At the ex-ambassador's estate in Georgetown, Belin was entertaining the Japanese envoy whom he had never previously met. Belin was "astonished beyond measure" at Kurusu's "frankness." The Japanese diplomat repeated in substance what he had already confided that morning to Mayer, who now became all the more certain their guest was "trying in the most desperate fashion to warn us of a momentary attack somewhere."

His hosts, Mayer was to record, were bending every effort "to try to find out whether Kurusu knew where this impending attack most likely would take place and, if so, to assess it. At about 8.30 p.m. the telephone rang. It was the Japanese Embassy informing Kurusu that Roosevelt had transmitted a personal appeal to Hirohito, although all that was known about it was the State Department's curt announcement to the Press. The contents of the note had not been published.

This, Kurusu observed, brightening, was "a clever move on the part of the United States." Since the Emperor, by the envoy's reasoning, could hardly say flatly "no" or even "yes," it was bound to cause "headaches in Tokyo and more thinking."

Headaches, however, were in fashion this first Saturday of December. Bratton and Kramer both had cause for such an affliction. By keeping personnel on through the afternoon and even into the dinner hour, the Army and Navy decrypting staffs between them had converted, shortly before 8.30, the first thirteen parts of the Fourteen-Part Message to the Japanese Ambassador.

"The government of Japan," Part 1 commenced, "prompted by a genuine desire to come to an amicable understanding with the government of the United States in order that the two countries by their joint efforts may secure the peace of the Pacific area and thereby contribute towards the realization of world peace, has continued negotiations with the utmost sincerity since April last."

Insisting it had been "the immutable policy" of Japan to "ensure the stability of East Asia," the message lashed out at alleged interference by America and Great Britain in Japan's efforts towards "a general peace" with China as well as with Japan's "joint defence," along with France, of French Indo-China; it reviewed Japanese-United States negotiations and restated Japan's "equitable solution" to mutual differences, reducible largely to the premise that America keep wholly out of the Far East, restore commercial relations with Japan, supply her oil, and also aid her in "the acquisition in the Netherlands East Indies of those goods and commodities of which the two countries are in need"; then went on to Nippon's "spirit of conciliation" while denouncing "the American government, obsessed with its own views and options... scheming for the extension of the war."

Part 10 was exceptionally blunt. Denouncing Anglo-American "collusion" in the East, it warned that "the Japanese government cannot tolerate the perpetuation of such a situation."

Part 13 came closest to new information when, with reference to the American suggestions of November 26, it noted, "therefore, viewed in its entirety, the Japanese government regrets that it cannot accept the proposal as a basis of negotiations."

In these earlier parts, although Tojo's War Cabinet rejected the American proposals, nothing so radical as a diplomatic rupture was implied. The verbose truculence, however, clearly indicated that the message was working up to some climax in the still missing fourteenth part.

Bratton read the thirteenth part. Then he telephoned Signal Corps intelligence to ascertain if the fourteenth might possibly be coming through shortly.

"No, there is very little likelihood of that part coming in this evening," replied the duty officer. "We think we have gotten all of that message that we are going to get tonight."

Bratton was tired. He decided to go home. First, however, he gathered up Secretary Hull's folder, containing his set of the thirteen parts, and locked it in the State Department pouch. He planned to deliver it in person without delay. For the remainder of the evening he left his office in charge of Lieutenant-Colonel Carlisle C. Dusenbury, his immediate assistant. The soldierly-appearing Dusenbury, described by another associate as "a typical good infantry officer," had once won a medal for saving a drowning man.

"It was my impression," Dusenbury was to recall, "that he felt the thirteen parts had not enough significance to justify distribution and that until the message was completed no action was indicated. Therefore my purpose in staying at the office was to wait for the remainder and in case of its receipt, I would have notified Colonel Bratton for instructions."

At the State Department, Bratton explained to the night duty officer that the pouch contained "a highly important message" which he wished sent at once to

Hull's quarters, the Carlton Hotel, on 16th Street, less than ten minutes' walk distant. Bratton then returned to his own home on 36th Place, in Georgetown, where he telephoned General Miles, who lived in a similar row house on nearby N Street. "Someone" replied that the General was out to dinner but would be returning shortly.

At the Navy Department, Kramer, ticking off his own list, was unable to reach either Admiral Stark or Admiral Turner. He was told that Stark was at the National Theatre. But the phone in Turner's residence on Western Avenue, in the Chevy Chase section, rang unanswered. However, he was able to talk with both Wilkinson and McCollum, whom he told "in cryptic terms" of the general sense of the thirteen parts. It was agreed that Kramer should take copies to the White House and to Secretary Knox, and finally to Wilkinson's residence.

Although the White House was only ten minutes' walk from the Navy Department and the Wardman Park Hotel, Knox's residence, only another ten minutes by taxi, Kramer would then have to cross the river to Arlington for his third stop, Admiral Wilkinson's house. Kramer who also lived in that Virginia suburb, decided to have his wife chauffeur him on his nocturnal rounds.

Shortly before 9.30, with Mrs. Kramer driving, he arrived at the White House, where he told Lieutenant Schulz on watch, there was something in the folder "that the President should see as quickly as possible." In company with an usher, Schulz went directly to the Oval Room, where he found Roosevelt seated at his desk. Harry Hopkins was the only other person in the room.

For "perhaps ten minutes" Roosevelt read and re-read the thirteen parts, while Hopkins paced "back and forth slowly, not more than ten feet away." Schulz was impressed by the President's calm manner, although he was not prepared for his subsequent remark to Hopkins after the White House confidant had himself glanced over the intercept.

"This means war," Roosevelt said to Hopkins, in substance, if not in those actual words.

The words were uttered in matter-of-fact, almost resigned tones (Schulz was to recount to this writer). It did not seem to Schulz that the President was predicting that war would come "tonight, or tomorrow necessarily, or even in a few days," but that the thirteen parts plainly signified the end of negotiations, with armed conflict the only future alternative.

For five minutes, just as though Schulz were not in the room, the two men discussed "the situation of the Japanese forces . . . their deployment." Hopkins expressed the opinion that "since war was imminent," the Japanese intended "to strike when they were ready, at a moment when all was most opportune for them." He said that it was "too bad" the United States "could not strike the first blow."

Schulz saw Roosevelt nodding his head while countering, "No, you can't do that. We are a democracy and a peaceful people [Schulz now believed the President raised his voice slightly to conclude] . . . but we have a good record." The young naval officer interpreted this to mean that America would "have to stand on that record—we could not make the first overt move. We would have to wait until it came."

Roosevelt's apparent reluctance to do anything that might antagonize the Japanese had, as a matter of fact, long frustrated men of action in the Navy Department, such as Admiral Turner. Not until December 1 had he sanctioned the use of small "spy vessels" in Asiatic waters. On that date Admiral Hart had been ordered, at the President's request, to charter "three small vessels... to observe and report by radio Japanese movements in west China Sea and Gulf of Siam."

(There were those, including a few naval officers, who read provocation into the ultimate employment of these coastal, sail-motor ships. Whatever the reasons that led to their hire, none was ready to sail by December 7.)

At approximately 10 p.m., by Schulz's recollection, Roosevelt said he "believed" he would talk with Admiral Stark, whom he referred to, as always, as "Betty." The President placed a telephone call only to be informed that the Chief of Naval Operations was at the theatre. Roosevelt did not wish him paged, fearing that might cause "undue alarm." Instead, he left word at Quarters "A" for Stark to call the White House.

Then Roosevelt returned the dispatch to Schulz, and the young lieutenant left the study. He immediately telephoned Captain Beardall, Roosevelt's naval aide, at Wilkinson's home, and reported that he had shown the papers to the Chief Executive and "carried out my instructions." Beardall informed him that he was free to leave. Schulz put on his cap and bridge coat and "secured" his duty for the night, the last Army or Navy officer in the White House this Saturday—so far as he himself could determine. (Nor was he to tell anyone of the comments he overheard in the Oval Room until four years later.)

Meanwhile, Kramer made his second stop, at the Wardman Park, at about 9.45. The Secretary of the Navy consumed about twenty minutes in reading the thirteen parts, while Kramer "engaged in general conversation" with Mrs. Knox and her guests, the O'Keiths.

Knox, impressed with both the thirteen parts and the portent of the fourteenth to come, got on the telephone—to Stimson and Hull—and arranged a special conference between the three at 10 a.m. Sunday at the State Department. He asked Kramer to be there at that time, bringing back the Japanese message, together with the fourteenth part, if it had arrived.

Although few words were exchanged between the Secretary of the Navy and the communications officer, Kramer did express his "construction" that the thirteen parts "aimed towards a conclusion of negotiations." It seemed to Kramer that Knox "agreed."

Mrs. Kramer then drove her busy husband through the Saturday night streets of Washington and over the bridge, facing the Lincoln Memorial, to Arlington. At 2301 North Uhle Street, he was greeted by Admiral Wilkinson, who took the message. After glancing over it, he discussed it with his guests, Sherman Miles and Beardall. His third American guest, Schuirmann, was left out of the impromptu conference and became increasingly annoyed, as well as hotly curious. He assumed that Kramer had brought an item of great importance; yet, since a captain did not ask an admiral, if the Admiral did not volunteer, Schuirmann was compelled to contain his impatience. He resolved to be at the Navy Department as early as possible the next morning to find out why Wilkinson had become visibly "most concerned."

Wilkinson did not "consider it a military paper," rather a "a diplomatic paper ... a justification of the position of Japan." Nevertheless, he excused himself and rang up Admiral Stark, only to be advised, as the President had been before him, that the Chief of Naval Operations was at the theatre. But Wilkinson did talk to Turner, who said, in spite of Kramer's inability to reach him, that he had been at home all evening—perhaps he had been momentarily walking one of his many Lhasa terriers along the open lots of Western Avenue. Wilkinson expressed doubt to Turner that "diplomatic relations would be broken." Turner, however, suggested he would like to have a personal look at the thirteen parts.

Sherman Miles, seconding his host's reaction, observed there was "little military significance" to the transmission from Tokyo, filled as it was with "falsehoods and lies." Miles saw "no reason for alerting or waking up the Chief of Staff ... or certainly Secretary Hull."

As Kramer started on his way once more to Washington, across the Potomac, the gathering at Admiral Wilkinson's house began to break up. Miles, among the first to arrive home, found Bratton's message and telephoned him. Bratton explained he had delivered the first thirteen parts to the Secretary of State's night duty officer and that the fourteenth, "the most important," was yet to come in. Miles told Bratton that he himself had just read the dispatch. But since he had decided there was no reason for "waking up" General Marshall, Miles gave no further instructions to Bratton for delivery of the intercept, neither to the Chief of Staff or to his secretary, Colonel Walter Bedell Smith, or to General Gerow of War Plans. After all, "alerting" officers of the stature of Marshall and Gerow to something of "little military significance" and, too, ridden with "falsehoods and lies" did not appear to be an act that would normally reflect good soldierly judgement.

At 11.30 the headlights of the official limousine bearing Admiral Stark, his wife and the Kricks lit up the winding gravel driveway of Quarters "A," Observatory Circle. As soon as he entered his comfortable old brick mansion, the Chief of Naval Operations was advised of the White House call. He excused himself and walked up the carpeted stairs to the second floor where the direct telephone to the Executive Mansion was located. In "five to ten minutes" he returned, his manner "apparently not disturbed." Judging by Stark's expression, Krick observed, it was likely that "nothing unusual" had happened.

As Admiral Stark was to recall to this author he *did* spend those minutes talking with Roosevelt, but the President "didn't go into the message." However, the contents were discussed in at least a general way since, by Schulz's witness, the thirteen parts were the original inspiration for the President's telephone call.

Stark returned from his White House call with the

impression that the Japanese note was a "rehash," an opinion that was to be strengthened in his mind when he read the communication itself. It must be assumed, then, that Roosevelt created the feeling in "Betty" Stark's mind that the thirteen parts constituted merely old material. But this would become the night's greatest enigma: how could the very man, who about an hour and a half earlier had declared "this means war," so shortly afterwards indicate or even imply that the same message was only a "rehash"?

Kramer continued to cover so much ground and to deliver the intercept to so many people that he remained uncertain, later, of just whom he had seen or where he had been. He did stop, however, on Klingle Road, near the Wardman Park Hotel, to visit, and awaken, Rear-Admiral Ingersoll, Assistant Chief of Naval Operations. Ingersoll, who by virtue of his position should have been Stark's *alter ego*, was not on the routing list for many dispatches. Wilkinson himself had in all probability suggested the stop-off. Ingersoll would logically have been the one to determine whether the Chief of Naval Operations should be notified.

Ingersoll asked Kramer if Stark had seen the message. He was sure that Kramer replied "yes," which convinced him that he might as well go back to bed. In any case, he was certain that Stark "assumed patrols had been initiated." It appeared that no action was called for. Ingersoll closed the door, gathered his nightgown closer about him and turned off the light. (Both Ingersoll and Stark shared a predilection for the old-fashioned nightgown in preference to pyjamas.)

Midnight was at hand when Kramer reached Turner's doorstep, half-way across the District of Columbia from Wilkinson's home in Arlington. The War Plans Chief adjusted his eyeglasses and scrutinized the thirteen parts, which he assessed subsequently to be "very important." He questioned Kramer sharply as to exactly who had read the communication. When his earlier understanding, gleaned presumably from his telephone conversation, was confirmed that Wilkinson and Ingersoll, as well as the Secretary of the Navy, had received and read the thirteen parts, Turner concluded he did not "believe it was my function to take any action." Seeming to reverse his own policy of being, next to Stark, arbiter and spokesman for the second deck, Turner decided that it "was the duty of the Office of Naval Intelligence" to bring such matters "to the Chief of Naval Operations' attention." He removed his eyeglasses, returned the sheaf to Kramer and said good night.

Now the Kramers could go home. As the couple drove back towards Arlington a second time, there was "no doubt" in Kramer's mind that the Japanese would strike at the Kra Peninsula in the morning "and start war with Great Britain." He said as much to his wife.

Past the accepted hour of protocol and despite further telephone calls from the embassy, Kurusu lingered at Ferdinand Belin's home. Mayer and Belin persisted in their joint belief that the envoy was attempting to warn them of an "impending attack," although he probably did not know "the exact point of attack." But when Mayer telephoned Dunn, who had helped arrange the meeting, once more at the State Department (either that same evening or in the morning, Mayer recalled to the author), he still could not say that definite information had been elicited from Kurusu. He could only surmise. Thus, since Mayer did not have positive intelligence to convey and since he was not even certain that he reported back to Hull's assistant that same night, the chances were that the proceedings at Belin's house had not been communicated to Hull.

It was a few minutes after midnight and the Secretary of State was doubtless asleep in the Carlton Hotel. Indeed, he had not even been given a copy of the thirteen parts which had been left at the State Department. And for this singular omission there was no explanation. All Hull could know was whatever Knox may have told him by telephone when he requested the special Sunday meeting.

Others were asleep or preparing to go to sleep, while yet others were undoubtedly in bed but unable to sleep. The Fourteen-Part Message, with one part still to come, had evoked broadly conflicting reactions, ranging from alarm to total apathy. In the Army, two officers in particular were charged with recognizing matters of unusual significance and then communicating them to General Marshall. They were the War Plans officer, General Gerow, and the Secretary of the General Staff, Colonel Smith. Both officers were shown the "pilot" message, which heralded the fourteen parts to come. Neither—insofar as could ever be ascertained—saw any one of those parts until Sunday. Walter Bedell Smith, as the most direct liaison with the Chief of Staff, evinced the least reaction to the pilot. Those who served under him, with him or even above him, however, were united in their belief that Smith was an "obstructionist," a man who ran interference for his "boss." Furthermore, Smith nursed an ulcer, and it did not improve his outlook, or even his judgement.

A number of men were not quite so indifferent. The President's reaction had been relatively instantaneous, by Schulz's testimony: "This means war." Beardall, Bratton, McCollum and Kramer were convinced that the thirteen parts were, at the very least, "highly important." Secretary Knox was impressed sufficiently to call Stimson and Hull for an extraordinary morning conference.

On the other hand, Wilkinson, who did not discern military significance in the thirteen parts, seemingly was seconded by Sherman Miles. As for Admiral Stark, there was unfortunately no clear barometer of his concern. Apparently no one but Roosevelt had suggested that Stark be advised of the message, and the extent to which the President alluded to the thirteen parts in his conversation with Stark on the private line from the White House is without positive documentation.

Between Ingersoll and Kramer confusion had arisen as to whether Stark had read the communication. Either Ingersoll, being freshly awakened, and still sleepy, misunderstood Kramer or the latter, himself weary and perturbed, did not properly hear Ingersoll's question.

And since November 27 there had been so *many* misunderstandings. . . .

Wilkinson remained the only other possible inspiration for the message being delivered to Admiral Stark. But the intelligence chief saw no military import in the document. It was an honest evaluation. New on the job, the fourth officer to hold the post within two years, Wilkinson remained an amateur in intelligence. A man of a high degree of mental ability, he was, however, floundering in a specialized field into which he had been abruptly projected, without qualifications other than that, like Noyes, he was a good tennis player and popular with the Navy's "Chevy Chase Club clique."

Wilkinson was bound to make mistakes. And he had.

Turner, whom some classed as "the most hated officer in the Navy," was guilty of one of the oldest gambits in the history of the military: passing the buck. However, considering the appalling lack of harmony between Turner, Wilkinson, and Noyes, as well as Stark's apparent unawareness of this situation, Saturday night's total absence of any semblance of teamwork, while catastrophic for the nation and for the crews of the battleships in Pearl Harbour, was not wholly surprising.

Compounding the false sense of security was the illusion that Honolulu had access to "magic," the ignorance in Washington that the battleships were lined up off Ford Island, easy targets for even a myopic hunter, and the distracting focus of attention on the Japanese feints, if feints they were, against the Kra Peninsula, as well no doubt as some false Japanese naval radio messages. "Supersecrecy," as McCollum later put it, was the final ingredient which made impending disaster certain.

There was, as had been generally conceded, a lack of everything in both the Army and the Navy: not enough funds, not enough guns, ships or aeroplanes, not enough sailors or soldiers, or code machines, translators and, especially, not enough brains.

"Where was the good old Navy initiative?" one vice-admiral has rhetorically asked this writer. "Why, on the night of December 6, didn't some captain or commander send a message to Kimmel from the Navy Department?"

Why indeed? Because, perhaps, the lights this Saturday night were going out on an era. The curtain was coming down on yesterday. And tomorrow? What of tomorrow?

Washington, and a nation, slept.

13
FOR DELIVERY AT ONE O'CLOCK

America awoke on Sunday to reassurances from Secretary Knox. The New York *Times* quoted the former Chicago publisher's state-of-the-Navy message on page one:

"I am proud to report that the American people may feel fully confident in the Navy. In my opinion the loyalty, morale and technical ability of the personnel are without superior. On any comparable basis, the United States Navy is second to none."

Nor was Knox alone in his faith. Other papers were carrying, datelined San Juan, Puerto Rico, a dispatch from Senator Ralph Owen Brewster, Republican of Maine, one of a group inspecting naval bases: "The United States Navy can defeat the Japanese Navy any place and at any time!"

Still other newspapers, although with inside-page restraint, were seconding the Navy's material preparedness with excerpts from a Supply Corps announcement. Cushioned among weighty totals, which included 4½ million pounds of wool, was the item that the Navy had just purchased 336,000 pounds of chicken feathers.

There was a liberal splash of international news in the Sunday papers: 125,000 Japanese troops were probably in Indo-China, next door to Thailand, with 82,000 of them in southern Indo-China; two convoys were reported "just outside the Gulf of Siam," menacing Malaya and Singapore, the Kra Peninsula and even Borneo; general mobilization, according to an Italian source in Rome, had been ordered in Japan. On the Russian front, Nazi armies had been bogged down by winter and illogically over-extended supply lines, and by the increasingly ferocious resistance of soldiers whose homeland had been ravished. Although Moscow still remained hotly contested, the Germans were reported in retreat west of Rostov, in the Ukraine, and near encirclement at Taganrog.

Sunday morning was clear and beautiful in Washington. The air was mildly crisp, inspiring afternoon motor trips into the Maryland or Virginia countryside or picnics in the Blue Ridge. Perfect football weather: in fact, that afternoon there was going to be a sell-out contest at Griffith Stadium between the Washington Redskins and the Philadelphia Eagles.

The day would begin at various hours and in various ways for different people. Captain Schuirmann had slept fitfully, troubled by the message that had come to Wilkinson's home during the dinner party of the evening before. Although he had no set duties on Sunday, he arose at a far earlier hour than usual, breakfasted and then hastened to the Navy Department, hoping to learn, at last, what was in that secret dispatch.

Both Bratton and Kramer were up early in order to arrive at the department ahead of their superiors. Being specialists, they had forgotten what days-off were. There were so few people in the entire United States, men or women, officers or civilians, who understood the Japanese language.

Stimson, while the sun slanted through the long, multi-paned windows of his dining-room at "Woodley," either inscribed the first entry of December 7 in his diary, or roughed out a draft of what it would read in final form:

> Today is the day that the Japanese are going to bring their answer to Hull and everything in Magic indicated they had been keeping the time back until now in order to accomplish something hanging in the air.

Like Knox and Hull, he had his eye on the clock, mindful of the ten o'clock meeting called unexpectedly over the telephone by the Secretary of the Navy.

Stark used to tell his friends about his "lazy" Sunday mornings. He would walk around the sloping grounds of Quarters "A," potter in the greenhouse and perhaps reach his office—often afoot—at 10.30 for a casual check of overnight mail and dispatches before returning home for noon dinner.

This morning, contrary to habit, he thought he'd better have his chauffeur drive him down Massachusetts Avenue, past the Japanese Embassy, in order to be at his desk by 9 a.m. For one thing he wanted to get on with the mountainous ramifications of "re-distribution"—the constant shuffling of ships and personnel between Pacific and Atlantic—and in the process obtain the guidance of Kelly Turner, upon whom he depended. And, too, last night's late call from the White House impelled the Chief of Naval Operations to accelerate his Sunday timetable.

At Fort Myer, across the Potomac River, another officer *did* remain faithful to his Sunday routine. George Marshall ate a relatively late breakfast with his wife. "After breakfast," Katherine Marshall was to recall, "he ordered his horse and said he would take his usual Sunday morning ride before going to the office."

At the White House, Roosevelt, if he followed his usual Sunday pattern, would be in bed, swamped by the newspapers of several major cities, including sometimes his especial anathema, the Chicago *Tribune*. Afterwards, there was every indication that he would put on lounge clothes and work, just as he had promised, on his stamp collection until, at least, lunchtime.

Bratton, McCollum and Kramer arrived at their offices at about the same time: 7.30. Since the overworked Navy decoders had long since gone home, the Army was processing this morning. On his desk Bratton found the awaited fourteenth part, concluding just as he had expected it would:

> The Japanese government regrets to have to notify hereby the American government that in view of the attitude of the American government it cannot but

consider that it is impossible to reach an agreement through further negotiations.

Bratton now handed copies of the complete message to his assistant, Colonel Dusenbury, with instructions to distribute them, as usual, to the Chief of Staff, War Plans, G2 and the State Department. Copies were also forwarded to the Navy.

McCollum realized at once that the message was "so important" that, in addition to its distribution on the second deck, he would risk duplication of the Army's prerogative and send Kramer, while *en route* to the White House, to the State Department with a copy. Dusenbury, however, was already loping across the Mall towards the curious old building that housed American foreign policy.

While the Army and Navy officer-messengers were bearing, unaware, the same message to the same destination, Bratton signed in two more intercepts from Tokyo before nine o'clock:

> Will the ambassador please submit to the United States government (if possible to the Secretary of State) our reply to the United States at 1 p.m. on the 7th, your time.
> After deciphering part fourteen of my 902 and also 907, 908, and 909, please destroy at once the remaining cipher machine and all machine codes. Dispose in like manner also secret documents.

There was also this "thank you" note from Tokyo:

> I, together with the members of the bureau, deeply appreciate and heartily thank you for your great effort which you have been making for many months in behalf

of our country despite all difficulties in coping with the unprecedented crisis. We pray that you will continue to be in good health.

Bratton reacted to the "one o'clock" message like a man struck over the head. "Stunned," he nonetheless seemed to understand what was all too likely to happen. As he confided to Colonel Betts (who in turn recently told this writer), "I tried to figure *where it would be dawn* when it was one o'clock in Washington, Then, without looking at a time-date chart of the Pacific, I guessed it would be about 2 a.m. the next day—or Monday—in Manila and 3 a.m. in Tokyo, but it would be *just about sunrise,* or 7.30 a.m., in Hawaii!"

He was not far off. Sunrise at Oahu was at 6.26 on Sunday. It would be 7.30 a.m. farther west at, approximately, Johnston Island. The "implications," which admittedly inspired Bratton to "frenzied activity," were overwhelming, knowing, as he did, Japan's history for attacking without warning, especially in the early hours of morning. He turned "all other matters" over to Dusenbury and raced off towards the Chief of Staff's office.

From Bratton's very furor, if not from knowledge of the incoming dispatches, word spread around the Munitions Building that something was "up." Arriving in his office at about this time, Betts was greeted by his own immediate superior, Colonel Hayes A. Kroner.

"Rufe's got something hot," Kroner told him.

Like so many others in the War and Navy departments this week-end, Betts was certain that the Japs were coiled to strike, but somewhere around the Gulf of Siam. Besides, the soft-spoken Chinese expert had no time for rumour or speculation. The joint intelligence committee, on which he had worked so painstakingly, was supposed to be in operation tomorrow, Monday morning.

Colonel Thomas T. Handy, on duty in General Gerow's War Plans section, read the fourteen parts and felt, as did Betts, that "this means war"—but not against the United States.

When Bratton could not find Marshall in his office, he telephoned—a few minutes after 9 a.m.—his quarters at Fort Myer. There an orderly, possibly Master Sergeant James Powder, answered the phone and explained that the General was out riding.

"Get assistance," Bratton said. "Find General Marshall, ask him—tell him—who I am and tell him to go to the nearest telephone, that it is vitally important that I communicate with him at the earliest possible moment!"

Bratton hung up, with no assurance that the extreme urgency of the situation had been conveyed to the orderly. However, he telephoned General Miles at his home. Miles was impressed by Bratton's tone, and said to tell Marshall, if word *could* be conveyed to him, that he would go "right out" to Fort Myer should the Chief of Staff so desire. Bratton asserted that would not be necessary, but urged his superior to come to the Munitions Building "at once."

The quiet Sunday routine had not, thus far, been interrupted in the Navy Building. Admiral Stark was at his desk working on redistribution, occasionally calling on Ingersoll for suggestions and wishing that

Turner were "aboard." In the back of his mind (he later told this author) was one concern: he was "afraid" that "Guam might be attacked." Unlike Bratton, he was not thinking of Pearl Harbour. As for the Far East, he had already sent several dispatches in that direction—dispatches which, since November 27, he considered "sufficient" for the entire menaced Pacific area.

At the same hour, a few minutes past nine o'clock, a British officer entered Admiral Noyes's office, "in connection with the actual sighting that we had made of this Japanese convoy heading either for Thailand, Malay Peninsula or the Philippines. It was abreast the Philippines."

The two men swapped information. Then the Briton said he would like to have an appointment with the Secretary of State. Noyes obligingly telephoned Hull's office, to be informed that the Secretary was preparing for a meeting at ten, and also "the Japanese representative had asked for an appointment at one o'clock."

Meanwhile, Bratton kept telephoning Quarters "No. 1" with no success. Marshall was somewhere near the Potomac River, riding, as he was to recall, "at a pretty lively gait," his Dalmatian loping just behind the horse's hooves.

At ten o'clock, a worried Sherman Miles, proving he could take orders from a subordinate, arrived in Bratton's office. The two officers then hurried into Marshall's suite to find General Gerow seated there.

"General Miles and I stated," Bratton was to testify, "that we believed there was important significance in the time of the delivery of the reply, 1 p.m., an indication that some military action would be undertaken by the Japanese at that time. We thought it probable that the Japanese line of action would be into Thailand but that it might be into any one or more of a number of other areas. General Miles urged the Philippines, Hawaii, Panama and the West Coast be informed immediately that the Japanese reply would be delivered at one that afternoon, Washington time, and that they, the commanders in the areas indicated, should be on the alert."

However, decision and action would inevitably await Marshall's return from his horseback ride. Miles and Gerow, nonetheless, both possessed sufficient rank and authority to initiate any message they wished, especially if it were not operational in subject.

Decision did not *have* to wait on Marshall. But it would. This was the Army in 1941.

At a few minutes past ten o'clock, the "one o'clock message," word about it or the reactions of Colonel Bratton and General Miles still had not arrived in the Navy Department. The message itself had, physically, to be conveyed by officer-messenger down the long hall on the second floor of the Munitions Building, across the covered wooden ramp and onto the second deck of the adjoining structure. The total distance was equivalent to three city blocks.

Just before 10.30, Admiral Stark decided to telephone Turner to make sure he would be in. He told his War Plans chief that he wanted him to reply to a letter from Hart, the one requesting further clarification of the Asiatic's Fleet's duties in the event of a war not involving the United States. Hart could have no idea how potentially academic his question was. Turner promised he would be in the CNO's office by 11.30 at the latest. Stark thanked him and returned to the concerns of redistribution.

14
A "LAST EFFORT FOR PEACE"

At 10 a.m. Captain Beardall delivered the last part of the Fourteen-Part Message to the President. Roosevelt, still in bed, studied it briefly, then observed, "It looks like the Japanese are going to break off negotiations."

Later, to Admiral Stark, Beardall commented that the President was "not perturbed," indeed he was "not sure what *they* meant." This was, of course, the same man whom Lieutenant Schulz had quoted the evening before as observing "This means war," after he had read thirteen parts of the message; the same man who, just after Schulz's visit, had talked on the private telephone with Stark, causing the Chief of Naval Operations to conclude that the intercept was a "rehash"; the same man who, for the past week, had been telling assorted listeners, from his friends in Warm Springs to Budget Director Smith, that the nation might be at war with Japan in a few days.

Then, what *did* Roosevelt really mean? What *was* on his mind?

Since Beardall was alone on the White House military watch this morning, he locked the confidential pouch and started back to the Navy Department to return it in person. To a conscientious naval officer, away from his intelligence duty offices, a confidential pouch with its brass padlocks was roughly as disturbing as a bundle of bank notes or a ticking bomb. It was a relief to get it out of the way.

Admiral McIntire arrived about the time of Beardall's departure to spend the next two hours with the President. Since Charles K. Claunch, a White House usher, has, along with others, attested to the sinus treatments "almost every day," the assumption is that at least a portion of Sunday morning was consumed in medication. McIntire, the nose and throat specialist, was subsequently criticized by another physician practising in the same field.

"In all likelihood," Dr. Noah Fabricant, of Chicago, was to write, "Franklin D. Roosevelt was the most overtreated sinus patient in the history of the White House . . . over-medication of the nasal and sinus passages is a medically recognized shortcoming." Fabricant noted that relief tends to become "successively diminished" after each treatment.

Roosevelt's whole presidential career was characterized by power, emotion and impatience, among the other driving qualities associated with a man of action. His apparent apathy on Sunday morning was peculiarly out of character. Why did he just sit back and wait for something to happen? Did his sinus condition or the treatment of it have any conceivable bearing on his mood and reactions to major developments?

Dr. McIntire's own memoirs dismissed these two hours in one paragraph. He alluded to the "tenseness" of the President. Speculating briefly, he noted that "an attack on any American possession did not enter his [Roosevelt's] thoughts," although the possibility seemed to have been aired that the Japanese might "take advantage of Great Britain's extremity and strike at Singapore or some other point in the Far East."

McIntire suggested further that the tenseness probably was caused by apprehension as Roosevelt awaited the outcome of Hull's one o'clock meeting with the Japanese envoys. Actually, Nomura was not to call requesting this appointment until about noon. However, both the White House and the State Department had received the "one o'clock message" along with the last of the fourteen parts, and thus the Ambassador's very belated call did not come as any surprise.

"Tense" or not, there is no record that Roosevelt telephoned Hull, Stimson, Knox, Stark, Marshall or lesser leaders during Sunday morning either for additional information or for clarification of the facts in hand. Hull was to re-emphasize that Roosevelt had not been in communication with him at any time between Saturday evening and Sunday afternoon.

At Fort Myer, General Marshall returned to his home at 10.15 and took a shower. About 10.25, by Marshall's calculations, he returned Bratton's calls. The colonel dared only report, over the telephone, that he "had a most important message" which the Chief of Staff "must see at once." He added that if the General would stay at his quarters he would personally bring the message over, "in ten minutes."

"No, don't bother to do that," Marshall replied. "I am coming down to my office. You can give it to me then."

While Bratton did not mention his all-consuming fears about an attack on Pearl Harbour, or elsewhere, there was something in his tone of voice which galvanized the Chief of Staff, a deliberate man, into unusual acceleration. First, he ordered his official car to start over for him. It was presumably in the lot behind the Munitions Building, where it was normally parked. But as Marshall completed dressing he decided his automobile would not arrive at "Officers' Row," Fort Myer, soon enough.

"Get the roadster!" he ordered Sergeant Semanko, his orderly. He referred to the flashy red car of his stepson, Clifton Brown.

Semanko, a man of at least as regular habits as his superior, was dumbfounded. The Chief of Staff had never done such a thing before, starting off in one car, hoping to encounter a second one—somewhat like the Pony Express of the old days, it occurred to the sergeant.

The two roared away from Quarters "A," shattering the Sunday tranquillity of the old Army post, turned right and raced through deserted Arlington National Cemetery. They tore past the Amphitheatre, the Tomb of the Unknown Soldier, down the winding road of the eastern slope and through the main gates, facing Memorial Bridge across the Potomac. Just before driving onto the approaches of the bridge itself, they met the khaki-painted sedan.

Marshall, a belatedly worried Chief of Staff, jumped out of the roadster and into his official car. At a more leisurely rate, Semanko started back while the General's chauffeur sped across the broad stone span toward the marble splendour of the Lincoln Memorial.

At about the same time, a curious drama was unfolding in Admiral Stark's blue-green suite in the Navy Building. Kramer, back from the White House and the Department of State, found the one o'clock message, sent over from G2. He worked out the comparative time zones on a navigator's plotting circle, and came to much the same conclusion as Bratton had. He hurried down the hall to Stark's office, where he was met at the door by McCollum. Kramer showed him the message and pointed out the "probable tie-up of the time . . . with the scheme that had been developing for the past week or so in the South-west Pacific with reference to Malaya and the Kra Peninsula." McCollum, Kramer noted as the two men talked in the corridor, "grasped that point instantaneously."

Kramer, with previous destroyer duty out of Honolulu, knew that 7.30 Sunday morning in Pearl Harbour was "a quiet time of the week," as well as "a normal time to institute amphibious operations." Even so, he theorized in terms of Kota Bharu and Thailand, the Gulf of Siam and a sudden blow against the British and the Dutch, reasonably certain the former would be attacked. In other words, his thinking, like that of the Navy and War departments, was focused geographically nearly 6,000 miles west of the Hawaiian Islands. McCollum agreed that "if the Japanese intended to have war with us they would strike at or near one o'clock Washington time." He did not, however, link the time with Pearl Harbour.

Kramer left to make this second delivery to the White House and to the State Department, where he would briefly tell the duty officer much of what he had just confided to McCollum. McCollum returned to Stark's office, where Wilkinson, Ingersoll, Schuirmann and Beardall were present. Noyes was absent, "quite involved with a Japanese convoy" (sighting messages from Manila).

Now, with the one o'clock message in hand, the discussion switched from what had been rather unproductive speculation on the significance of the fourteen parts. Wilkinson, labelling the fourteenth part as "very serious" and comprised of "fighting words," wondered aloud if the fleet and especially the Philippines should be notified of the "imminence of hostilities in the South China Sea."

After the newest dispatch had been shown to the officers, McCollum had the impression that Admiral Stark's reaction to the one o'clock time was "so what?"—in meaning if not in those actual words. This was rather surprising since Stark's concern had been growing all week, largely because of the burning of Japanese codes: "a most telling thing" (he has told this writer).

Wilkinson, according to McCollum, had a concrete suggestion. "Why don't you pick up the telephone and call Kimmel?"

Schuirmann, for one, did not recall seeing Stark,

Turner, Noyes or anyone else telephone Honolulu. It would have been easy, but the mania for "super-secrecy" was so overwhelming that even low-classification restricted matters were communicated by coded dispatches, mail, cable or radio, rather than by telephone. Therefore, McCollum was all the more surprised when Stark lifted the telephone and gave every indication that he *was* actually about to put through a long-distance call to Admiral Kimmel.

This moment, sometime between 10.30 and 11 a.m. on Sunday morning, was possibly the most portentous of all. Destiny hung on Admiral Stark's elbow as he lifted the instrument. But then, with a slight shake of his head, he replaced it and said, in effect, "No, I think I will call the President."

When Stark reached the White House switchboard, he was informed that the President was busy. This may have meant that McIntire was at the moment engaged in a phase of the sinus draining operation, which could not be interrupted. Stark put the phone back in the cradle. The moment had come—and gone.

(Stark has said that he does not recall starting to phone Kimmel in Honolulu. But McCollum, who has an encyclopedic memory, even to total recall, is quite certain that the Chief of Naval Operations not only picked up the telephone but tried, on second thought, to get through to the President.)

The meeting had disbanded by the time Turner arrived in the Chief of Naval Operations' office—about 11.15. Surprisingly enough, he was not informed of the "one o'clock message." Instead Stark wanted to go over that Hart letter with his War Plans officer.

Over in the Munitions Building, Miles and Bratton who had not contacted their Navy opposites, Wilkinson and McCollum, even though they all were thinking along parallel lines, arrived at Marshall's office at 11.25. They found the General reading the fourteen parts aloud. They attempted several times to interrupt him so that Bratton could show him the "one o'clock message." But even though Miles considered his superior "approachable" he could not penetrate Marshall's deep concentration.

After perhaps fifteen minutes, Marshall finished the long document, and summoned Gerow on the intercom. Only then did he look at the message. He admitted there could be "some definite significance" to the message; that "something was going to happen at one o'clock"; but "when they specified a day, that, of course, had significance, but not comparable to an hour." Further, he deemed it to be "a new item of information of a peculiar character."

Miles and Bratton then said they were "convinced it meant Japanese hostile action against some American installation in the Pacific at or shortly after one o'clock." Miles repeated what he had told Gerow earlier in the morning: that new warnings should be sent to all area commanders, from Panama to the Philippines.

"It was at this point," Bratton was to testify, "after we had all concurred in urging that our outlying possessions be given an additional alert at once by the fastest possible means, General Marshall drew a piece of scratch paper towards him and picked up a pencil and wrote out in longhand a message to be sent to our overseas commanders. When he reached the bottom of the page he picked up the telephone and called the Chief of Naval Operations.... General Marshall in a guarded way told Admiral Stark what he had in front of him and what he proposed to do, in effect that he was going to send a warning to Hawaii, Panama, the Philippines and so on.

"After some conversation with the Chief of Naval Operations he put down the phone and said, 'Admiral Stark doesn't think that any additional warning is necessary.'"

Marshall then showed his officers what he had written:

> The Japanese are presenting at 1 p.m. Eastern Standard Time today what amounts to be an ultimatum. Also they are under orders to destroy their code machine immediately.
> Just what significance the hour set may have we do not know, but be on alert accordingly.

This message would go not only to Hawaii, but to the Western Defence Command on the Pacific coast, the Panama Command and the Philippine Command.

In a moment, the telephone rang again. It was Admiral Stark who requested that a line be added to Marshall's message: "Inform the Navy." He was fearful, among other considerations, that a further warning "might create the story of 'wolf!'" since he had already sent "so much." As Stark testified:

"I put the phone up... and stopped, and in a matter of seconds or certainly in a few minutes thought, well, it can't do any harm, there may be something unusual about it. General Marshall states he doesn't know what the significance is, but there might be something, and I turned back and picked up the phone. He had not yet sent the message, and I said, perhaps you are right. I think you had better go ahead and I would like to have you make sure that it goes to the naval opposites where this message was going, which was throughout the commands in the broad Pacific.

"I also asked General Marshall, knowing that the time was rather short, whether or not he would get it out quickly. I told him our own system under pressure was very fast. And he said, no, that he was sure he could get it out quickly also."

Marshall handed the dispatch to Bratton to take to the Signal Corps for transmission. As the colonel hurried away, Gerow called out, "Tell them to give first priority to the Philippines." The time was 11.50 a.m.

"The Chief of Staff," Bratton advised Colonel Edward T. French, on duty at the message centre, "wants this sent at once by the fastest safe means." French, looking it over, promised to accord it his "personal attention," but also asked for help in transforming the scrawl into "readable script." He could not decipher Marshall's handwriting, as indeed very few people could.

Bratton stood beside a typist and dictated the contents, then returned to Marshall's office.

"Go back," ordered Marshall, "and find out how long it is going to take for this message to be delivered to the addressees." The Chief of Staff could have telephoned the message to the various Pacific outposts. A "scrambler" device was attached to his telephone, but he did not often use it, fearful that an eavesdropper between Washington and Honolulu might have a "descrambler." Like the Navy, the Army was obsessed with apprehensions that it was being spied upon—both from without and from within.

Bratton relayed Marshall's question to French, who "did a little figuring mentally." After the encoding, the Signal officer estimated it would "take about thirty or forty minutes for it to be delivered to the persons to whom it is addressed."

French had his problems. For approximately the last hour and a half, the War Department radio, because of technical difficulties, had been out of contact with Honolulu. But French maintained a teletype wire direct to the Western Union office in Washington. He knew from past experience that Western Union would move the message to San Francisco rapidly. Then RCA would radio it to Honolulu from its 40-kilowatt trans-Pacific towers, which had four times the power of the Army's transmitters.

There was no question of the Signal Centre's employing telephonic relays for, as French noted, "that was up to the individuals themselves, the Chief of Staff, or whoever the individual concerned." Besides, like Marshall, he felt that the telephone was unsuited for classified messages. Sometimes the Navy, which used more powerful transmitters than the Army, was called on to help with an overload of radio traffic. French, nonetheless, did not check with the Navy since he knew time would be consumed in ascertaining whether its circuits were normal or experiencing the same trouble as the Army's.

French made a final test of the static-ridden circuits before commencing the transmission of Marshall's dispatch via commercial telegraph and radio. He did not, however, advise Bratton of his decision, or the reasoning behind it.

A number of persons were keeping thoughts and reports of known facts to themselves this Sunday. Bratton, for one, was so alarmed that his very voice had been infectious to the Chief of Staff. Fresh from his shower, Marshall was impelled from Sunday morning lethargy into feverish motion, involving even a relay of automobiles. Yet Bratton did not confide in Marshall, Gerow or Miles that he believed Pearl Harbour itself might be attacked.

Turner did not learn of the "one o'clock message" until a second stop in Stark's office. It was his opinion, too late for his judgement to be a factor, that this message's implications "would have been exceedingly important." However, the Navy Department operations and planning people were busy juggling the Atlantic and Pacific fleets this Sunday morning. Redistribution, a real thing, had to be tackled. It occupied the forefront of many minds. In a way, the Fourteen-Part Message and the "one o'clock message" were abstractions, certainly distractions.

What did either *really* mean?

It was relatively easy to switch a flotilla of destroyers between San Juan and San Diego. There was the Panama Canal. To divine the intentions of a potential enemy was something else again, even when you had peeked at his messages and snooped on his conversations.

At the State Department all this while Hull, Knox and Stimson were meeting as planned. The Secretary of State, observing that "the faces of my visitors were grim," was to record, "from all our reports it appeared that zero hour was a matter of hours, perhaps minutes." Again, he obtained a certain inner release by denouncing the "fire-eaters" in Tokyo, but seemingly the fourteen parts did not evoke much response from him other than the opinion that they were "little more than an insult."

Stimson reported of the session:

"Hull is very certain that the Japs were planning some deviltry and we are all wondering where the blow will strike. We three stayed together in conference until lunchtime, going over the plans for what should be said or done. The main thing is to hold the main people who are interested in the Far East together—the British, ourselves, the Dutch, the Australian, the Chinese. Hull expressed his views, giving the broad pictures of it, and I made him dictate it to a stenographer. . . . Knox also had his views on the importance of showing immediately how these different nations must stand together . . . the messages we were now receiving indicated that the Japanese force was continuing on in the Gulf of Siam and again we discussed whether we would not have to fight if Malaya or the Netherlands were attacked and the British or Dutch fought. We all three thought that we must fight if those nations fought. We realized that if Britain were eliminated it might well result in the destruction or capture of the British fleet. Such a result would give the Nazi allies overwhelming power in the Atlantic Ocean and would make the defence of the American republics enormously difficult if not impossible."

Before adjourning, Hull and Knox roughed out a note which they planned to send to Roosevelt for comment. It would warn Japan that the United States, Britain and the Netherlands would "be ready jointly to act together."

Now the morning had spent itself. For the moment, there seemed to be nothing more to do. Stimson was chauffeured to "Woodley" for lunch. Marshall would return to Quarters "A" at Fort Myer. First, however, he informed Colonel John R. Deane, assistant to Bedell Smith, of a curious engagement. He "expected" to see the President at 3 p.m. (an appointment neither then nor subsequently a matter of record). Marshall requested Deane "to arrange to keep the office open and have some of the commissioned and civilian personnel report for duty."

Why? and *when* had he been in communication with the President?

Knox had a choice of his apartment at the Wardman Park or a more formal Sunday dinner on his yacht *Sequoia,* berthed at the Navy Yard. He elected neither. About 12.30 he summoned Stark and Turner to his office. There were matters he wished to discuss through the meal hour—matters which manifestly could not wait.

At the White House, Dr. McIntire had completed his visit and gone home. Roosevelt kept one unusual Sunday morning appointment before his own lunch: with Dr. Hu Shih, the literary Chinese Ambassador. The only positive comment on this meeting was given by Dr. Hu later to Herbert Feis, a State Department official and a fellow author. Apparently the President had wished the Ambassador's reaction to the message he had sent to Hirohito the evening before.

"This," Roosevelt was quoted as saying, "is my last effort for peace. I am afraid it may fail."

At 1.10 Dr. Hu left. Roosevelt was first taken to his bedroom to change into loose-fitting clothes. Waiting for him in the Oval Room were Harry Hopkins, in a V-necked sweater and slacks, Fala, the President's Scottie, two tray lunches and—the President's stamp collection. It looked as though, at last, Roosevelt would put in a few hours at his favourite hobby before taking a drive into Rock Creek Park or nearby Virginia, where he had been watching the preliminaries to constructing a huge new War Department. There was no indication, however, whether Roosevelt planned to confer with Marshall before or after his ride.

In the Blue Parlour an unusually sombre Mrs. Roosevelt had just asked her luncheon guests to be seated. "Eleanor was a few minutes late and a bit flustered," recalled her friend Mrs. Hamlin of Albany, just back from Sunday services at historic St. John's Church, across Lafayette Park from the White House. "She said she was extremely sorry but the news from Japan was very bad and the President would be unable to have lunch with us."

And so Sunday morning passed. Those who should have been aware that the hands of the clock were moving toward the zero hour and who held the power to turn them back or, at least, to halt their progress, had not effectively reacted. Those who *did* react were not so empowered. Yet there was to be still another warning, even though the minutes were almost squandered. America, as the last hour was about to sound, was accorded one more chance. It was almost as though fate, on America's side, paused, hoping—hoping the right people would stir, like somnambulists suddenly shaken into consciousness, and do something.

15
SUNRISE AT PEARL HARBOUR

In the predawn hours, a wet, easterly wind moistened the Hawaiian Islands, presaging worse weather to come. Many residents awoke, half by instinct, half by experience, to lower their windows before returning to their beds and sleep. Honolulu was at long last dark and silent. All the victory dances and other celebrations had finally stilled. The Battle of the Bands had concluded with musicians from the *Pennsylvania* winners, those from the *Arizona* second. The bandsmen were back on their ships.

Newsboys were astir in the city's darkened streets, although even their activity had been delayed by a breakdown in the *Advertiser's* presses. The issues which lay beside milk bottles on Honolulu's doorsteps, to be flicked open and shut by the rising wind, warned mutely of danger. A streamer on page one announced: FDR WILL SEND MESSAGE TO

EMPEROR ON WAR CRISIS—Japanese Deny Massing Troops For Thai War. Below it, in one column: HIROHITO HOLDS POWER TO STOP JAPANESE ARMY.

Of far less menace, but of seasonal note, another front-page article advised, "Santa dressing to be in *Advertiser* Lobby at 9."

Other stories on inside pages were headed: P.I. CABINET URGES EVACUATION OF DANGER AREAS—Residents Jittery as War Approaches; SINGAPORE FORCES RECALLED TO WAR STATIONS—Bases Ready to Act in Any Emergency.

George Bicknell, the Hawaiian Department's assistant G2, did not have to put on his slippers and pick up the papers to be made aware of the approaching peril. He had "spent a very restless and nervous night with all of these things on my mind and and wondering what would happen next." Not only did the Mori message profoundly bother and puzzle him, but he continued to be distressed and somewhat offended by Short's remark that he was "a little too intelligence conscious." Something else, too, had been hammering away at his subconscious: that small army of agents Consul General Kita had marshalled. Apparently Bicknell, Shivers of the FBI, and Captain Mayfield were among the few Americans in Honolulu who seriously questioned whether Nagao Kita's 217 assistant consuls were scattered among the islands for purposes other than acquainting visiting countrymen with the splendours of Hawaii.

During these early hours the old four-stack destroyer *Ward*, 1,000 tons and capable of 35 knots, had been knifing back and forth in a two-mile expanse of ocean beyond Buoy 1, at the channel entrance to Pearl Harbour. At 3.50 a.m., Lieutenant William W. Outerbridge, her commanding officer, had been advised by the *Condor*, a mine-sweeper, that a periscope had been sighted. A search of more than two hours had failed to confirm the *Condor*'s report. Outerbridge, Annapolis '27, lay down, clothed, for a nap. At exactly 6.37, eleven minutes after sunrise, he was awakened by his executive officer, Lieutenant (jg) Oscar Goepner, a newly commissioned reservist.

"Come on the bridge, Captain!" Goepner shouted. "Come on the bridge!"

What Outerbridge saw was the small conning tower of a moving, half-submerged submarine, seventy-five yards distant.

"Go to general quarters! Go to general quarters!" the *Ward*'s captain ordered.

Point-blank, too close for effective use of the range finders, the World War I vessel opened fire. The second salvo scored a direct hit on the little black conning tower; the submarine at once vanished in an eruption of smoke and spray. Over the swirling waters where her target had been seconds before, the *Ward* criss-crossed to and fro, dropping depth charges.

At 6.54 a.m. Outerbridge, breaking off the action, notified the commandant of the Fourteenth Naval District, by voice transmission on his ship-to-shore radio: "We have attacked, fired upon, and dropped depth charges upon submarine operating in defensive area."

The naval radio station at Bishop's Point acknowledged. In a few minutes, the report was conveyed from the district to the Pacific Fleet communications watch. However, the spoken message from the *Ward* was heard by most of the battleships at anchor off Ford Island and by other fleet vessels, maintaining their routine radio "guard" in port as well as at sea.

Eight minutes later, at 7.02 a.m., "blips" were observed at the Opana radar station on Kahuku Point, twenty-eight miles north of Honolulu, one of the Signal Corps's five such experimental detection stations, recently placed in operation. The two young privates manning this radar (known as SCR 270B), George Elliott and Joseph L. Lockard, had kept their screen in reception after the normal 7 a.m. shutdown largely because the breakfast truck was late in chugging up to this isolated promontory and there was nothing else to do.

Now, two minutes after the time when the set should have been switched off, the screen came alive with a tell-tale shower of electronic shadows, or blips, indicating to Lockard that a large "flight of some sort" must be approaching, and from a direction which was only three degrees east of true north.

Since the maximum range of this set was 132 miles, and the images had just traced onto the cathode tube, it could be assumed that a quantity of something was winging towards Oahu from that distance. Lockard telephoned the radar information centre at Fort Shafter. The watch officer, Lieutenant Kermit A. Tyler, of the Hawaiian Air Force, thought about the report, then advised, "It's all right ... don't worry about it," or words which, he recalled, were to that effect.

Nevertheless, it was "the largest group" Lockard

had ever seen. For thirty minutes both he and Elliott continued fascinated, to watch it growing more distinct. When they heard the breakfast truck grinding up through the sugar-cane fields to Opana, they turned off the instrument.

About 7.15 Admiral Bloch was informed of the *Ward*'s action. He was already awake, concerned over his wife's convalescence. His reaction was identical with that of all the officers on the anchored ships whose radiomen had advised them of the *Ward*'s skirmish with the submarine. There had been so many similar sightings and even depth chargings of what had turned out to be nothing at all that Bloch was inclined to believe the *Ward* had been mistaken.

Kimmel, looking forward to his golf date, also was up. He was told of the action a few minutes after 7.30 a.m. Somewhat more concerned than the Fourteenth Naval District's commander, he said he would finish dressing and come to his offices on the Submarine Base. However, he too desired "verification... in view of the number of such contacts which had not been verified in the past."

And nobody—nobody informed General Short, or any of his staff.

Thus in a fleeting three-quarters of an hour—which was approximately from noon to 12.45 Washington time—there had been two distinct warnings off the shores of Oahu. The presumed destruction of the submarine was, at the very least, a broad hint of trouble. The blips on the radar were the flickering shadows of the actual fury sweeping in upon the island.

Time had run out. The hands of the clock had all but stopped. Yet no one of reason, of any position, anywhere, could ever use the phrase "without warning" and expect it to be more than a mockery of the facts, and of the truth.

16
"... THAT WAS AN EXCITEMENT, INDEED"

A few minutes after 1 p.m. (while Elliott and Lockard in Hawaii were still staring at the radar), Nomura called the State Department to say he and Kurusu could not make their appointment until 1.45. Hull, patiently, agreed. He had already cancelled a luncheon engagement. Or perhaps, half-sick and especially nervous since Nomura's noon phone request confirmed what he had been expecting, Hull had no appetite. And so the Secretary of State waited in the heavy, formal splendour of the Victorian building.

Across West Executive Avenue, Roosevelt and Hopkins ate their lunch from trays, whilst Fala sat up to beg tit-bits. The President's shirt sleeves were rolled up; he was about to start on his stamp album. Hopkins, lounging on a couch, was to recall that the two were chatting about matters "far removed from war."

At the Navy Department Admiral Noyes had finally

found an opportunity to study the fourteenth part. He had been distracted the past two days, in the midst of the avalanche of both routine and decidedly non-routine dispatches, by orders to ferret out, if possible, the Chicago *Tribune*'s informant. G2 was similarly and ill-advisedly belaboured—a "scramble to find out who-done-it," as General Miles put it. The intemperate command of course originated in the White House from a President whose fury could be as complete as his poise when he slightly raised his head, tilted up his cigarette holder and—smiled.

Now, as the overworked Noyes was reading the last part and wondering what its significance was, the inter-office phone rang. The time was between 1.25 and 1.40 (the exact minute was not logged). A radioman from communications watch was calling. Crisply, but with a note in his voice of one who has plainly been staggered, he reported to Admiral Noyes that another radioman at the Mare Island Navy Station in San Francisco Bay had picked up a strictly local transmission across the Pacific between the Navy Yard in Honolulu and the headquarters of the Commander-in-Chief, Pacific Fleet:

ENEMY AIR RAID—NOT DRILL

From that moment on, indecision, restraint, apathy and, for the most part, personal and administrative conflicts vanished with the suddenness of this stunning news itself. Noyes knew what to do. He ran down the corridor of the second deck to the Chief of Naval Operations' suite. Not finding him in, he started into the next office—the Secretary of the

Navy's—to encounter Knox, Stark and Turner on their way out.

Noyes gave them the message. Knox, visibly shocked and incredulous, adjusted his pince-nez. He blurted out in the hearing of his Marine aide, Captain John H. Dillon: "My God, this can't be true! This must mean the Philippines!"

"No, sir," Stark replied unhesitatingly, "this is Pearl."

Turner, Dillon recalled, said nothing.

Knox moved back to his desk as rapidly as his bulky frame would take him. He picked up the direct telephone to the White House. The difficulty Stark apparently had experienced in getting through to the President that morning was not to be repeated.

Roosevelt's reactions were, as in the past few days, various. Hopkins himself observed, after the President had replaced the phone, that there must have been "some mistake." Roosevelt thought the news was "probably true," and the kind of "unexpected thing" that the Japanese might do. In a curious paradox, he seemed to be expecting the "unexpected thing."

In rapid succession the President telephoned a number of people, apparently Stimson first.

"At just about two o'clock," the Secretary of War wrote, "while I was sitting at lunch, the President called me on the phone and told me in a rather excited voice that the Japanese were bombing Hawaii.

" 'Well, I have heard the telegrams which have come in about the Japanese advances in the Gulf of Siam. . . .'

" 'Oh, no, I don't mean that. They have attacked Hawaii. They are now bombing Hawaii.' "

Then, putting down the phone and returning to the lunch table, the elderly Stimson thought to himself, "Well, that was an excitement, indeed."

At approximately 2.05 Roosevelt telephoned Hull, just as Nomura and Kurusu were being ushered into the diplomatic waiting room. In a voice "steady but clipped" he informed his ailing Secretary of State: "There's a report that the Japanese have attacked Pearl Harbour." Hull asked if it had been confirmed. The Chief Executive replied, "No." But the President and the Secretary of State agreed the report was "probably" true.

Hull said he was "rather inclined not to see" the waiting envoys. But, he conceded there was "one chance out of a hundred" that the news might *not* be true. He would go ahead and let the two deliver their message.

Stephen T. Early, the presidential Press secretary, was at home, in pyjamas, reading the Sunday papers when his "boss" called.

"Have you got a pencil handy, Steve?" Roosevelt asked.

"Do I need it?" the secretary asked. He suspected the Chief Executive harboured some little joke.

"Yes, I have a pretty important statement here..." and he began dictating an announcement of the raid. It was to be held up only a few minutes for final confirmation.

Among the next to be called by the President was his son James, a Marine Corps captain, recuperating at his suburban home from a stomach operation.

"Hello, Jimmy, it's happened," Roosevelt said. His eldest son was impressed with his father's "extreme calmness—almost a sad, fatalistic but courageous acceptance."

When the President returned to his lunch there was, according to observations in Hopkins's diary, implied relief, judging from the tone and substance of his subsequent conversation. He seemed thankful that the matter was now "entirely out of his own hands," the nation's new enemy having "made the decision for him."

Telephone circuits to Honolulu were good paradoxically enough—far better obviously than commercial cable or telegraph, since General Marshall's warning was still hours away from delivery. While the White House operator was working on a call to Governor Joseph B. Poindexter, of Hawaii, other long-distance calls to the Pacific territory under attack were crackling through.

Stark had confirmed by telephone, the same instrument that he had reportedly been loath to use only that morning, the truth of the first intercepted radio message. He had reached Admiral Bloch himself. A "calm" Bloch told him that even now the planes were swooping overhead, black smoke was boiling upward from the fleet anchorage, there were many explosions. At first, Bloch said he thought the noise was from "blasting in a quarry," just to the rear of his residence. Bloch, like nearly everyone else in the islands, was in no way prepared for a bombing attack.

As Stark hung up he reflected momentarily on a private conversation he had held with Nomura several months back. If Japan should "start anything" in the Pacific, the American Admiral had warned the

Ambassador, "We'll break your empire." This was an extraordinary remark for a naval officer to make to a representative of a foreign power. But, as Stark recalled to the author, he did not utter it with any particular passion. It was a blunt statement between two professional men. Nomura, as Stark remembered the conversation, agreed with his American friend. Now at last, Stark thought, it was time to make good his assertion.

Washington switchboards were busy with calls from both directions. Shivers, the FBI agent in Honolulu, was fortunate in his own phone connection. His call was transferred through headquarters in Washington to New York City, where J. Edgar Hoover was spending the week-end. "The Japanese are bombing Pearl Harbour," Shivers said unemotional as always. "There is no doubt about it—those planes are Japanese. It's war. You may be able to hear the explosions yourself. Listen. . . ." And he held the mouthpiece to the open window of his office.

Listening in on the call at his box in Griffith Stadium, where he was watching the Redskins-Eagles football game, was Edward A. Tamm, assistant director of the FBI. There, increasingly curious spectators heard the loudspeakers paging a succession of generals and admirals.

Others were caught away from Washington on this Sunday. Brigadier-General Edwin M. ("Pa") Watson, Roosevelt's military aide and "crony," was in Charlottesville, Virginia. Attorney-General Biddle was about to speak at the Defence Bond rally in Detroit. Secretary of Labour Frances Perkins was at her home in New York, Judge Samuel I. Rosenman, a presidential adviser and speech writer, was in the same city, as were also Colonel Donovan, Vice-President Henry A. Wallace and Postmaster General Frank Walker. Walker, an international lawyer with experience in the Far East, had doubled in his official duties as White House confidant on Japan. He was supposed to have recently conveyed a warning to Tokyo through his own channels that expansion towards South-east Asia would almost surely provoke American intervention.

For the New Yorkers, a special plane was warmed-up at La Guardia Airport to rush them to Washington. Since there seemed extra space, Rosenman decided to bring along his young son.

While the alert spread through the government, Nomura and Kurusu continued to wait in the State Department anteroom. Not until 2.20 did Hull ask that the envoys be shown into his office. He did not invite them to be seated; they had to stand, stiff and at a disadvantage, in front of his broad, mahogany desk, their backs to a steel engraving of President Andrew Jackson, in a fiery mood, hanging on the opposite wall.

First, the Secretary of State asked Nomura why he had been instructed to deliver the note at one o'clock. Explaining "diffidently" that decoding the message had delayed his departure, the Japanese Ambassador was interrupted by Hull, the hill boy from Tennessee, old campaigner in the Spanish-American war, who could no longer mask his fury.

"I must say," he raged, "that in all my conversations with you during the last nine months I have never uttered one word of untruth. This is borne out absolutely by the record. In all my fifty years of public service I have never seen a document that was more crowded with infamous falsehoods and distortions—infamous falsehoods and distortions on a scale so huge that I never imagined until today that any government on this planet was capable of uttering them."

Nomura, "impassive but . . . under great emotional strain," was about to say something when Hull held up his hand and coldly waved the pair towards the door. The two walked out, "heads down." The episode in the Secretary of State's office had lasted twelve minutes. It was now 2.32 p.m., about five minutes after a numbed Steve Early had announced the President's bulletin to the three wire services.

Since Hull had made no reference to the attack on Pearl Harbour, Nomura and Kurusu in all likelihood first heard about it from the reporters and photographers milling about the State Department steps. The latter were to record only "non-committal phrases" from the retreating envoys.

"I'm afraid," Hull commented a few minutes later to Sumner Welles, "I was pretty rough on those Japs."

He put on his hat and coat and, shortly after three o'clock, arrived at the White House, where he found the President "very solemn in demeanour and conversation." Hull told him of the tongue-lashing he had just administered to the envoys. Roosevelt brightened, then congratulated his Secretary of State:

"Good for you!"

Knox, Stimson, and Marshall arrived within

minutes, while Stark stayed at the Navy Department to phone in bulletins. The circuit to Poindexter was now clear, and the President spoke with him. At one time his visitors heard Roosevelt exclaim: "My God, there's another wave of Jap planes over Hawaii right this minute!"

Downstairs, in the Blue Parlour, Mrs. Roosevelt's luncheon was breaking up. "As we came out into the hall," Mrs. Hamlin recalled, "the news seemed to flash instantaneously around the guests... [we] stood about in stupefied lots... there was nothing to say. Everyone seemed to melt away."

Eleanor Roosevelt entered her husband's study, realized he was "concentrating," and so did not stay. It did seem to her, however, that "in spite of his anxiety, Franklin was in a way more serene than he had appeared in a long time."

McIntire and then Beardall joined the gathering conference in the Oval Room. "Stunned and incredulous at first," McIntire observed, "[the President] quickly regained the poise that always marked him in moments of crisis." Next to arrive was a small group of Congressional leaders.

Many government executives hastened to their own offices after hearing news of the attack on the radio. Donald Nelson had been lunching with Harold Ickes at his farm in Olney, Maryland, together with Supreme Court Justice Hugo Black and Senator Tom Connally, chairman of the Senate Foreign Relations Committee. During a conversation about Japan the consensus among the guests, Nelson recalled, was that there seemed no likelihood of war "in the foreseeable future." Nelson was listening to the New York

Philharmonic on his car radio as he drove home, when "a harsh voice trembling with excitement" broke in:

"In ten minutes H.V. Kaltenborn is going to give you more information on the bombing of Pearl Harbour."

At 3 p.m. the two armed service warrens, the Navy Department and the Munitions Building, were virtually deserted. Nobody was there this Sunday afternoon,* and not many would return until late in the evening when the street lamps came on in yellow, semi-black-out, and soldiers, wearing incongruous World War I "tin" helmets, carrying rifles of the same vintage, were brought in by trucks from Fort Belvoir, Virginia, and Fort Myer to take up guard around the White House, the Capitol and other federal structures.

In the public relations office of the Navy Department, the Press officer on duty, Ensign Frank Rounds, was told: "All information will come from the White House." Beardall, who had relayed these instructions, explained that public relations information must be limited to simple geography. While the standard English reference book on the world's navies, *Jane's Fighting Ships*, contained complete specifications of everything that floated (and, now, some that did not) in the United States Navy, the

---

* The author, then an ensign in the Naval Reserve, was an exception. He heard of the attack on his car radio as he returned from a suburban inn *en route* to the afternoon watch in the public relations office of the Navy Department. On the way, he swung past the Japanese Embassy on Massachusetts Avenue and saw smoke still curling upward from the back yard and a mildly curious knot of spectators on the pavement.

same intelligence must not emanate from public relations.

No one seemed to expect war on a Sunday. In the Chief of Naval Personnel's office, the timeclock on the safe, containing secret mobilization plans, had been set for Monday morning.

The White House was jammed with reporters, photographers, newsreelmen and radio newscasters, all endeavouring to crowd into a Press room in which a dozen persons normally fought for meagre space.

Clusters of people formed outside the White House gates and in Lafayette Park, across Pennsylvania Avenue. Some attempted to raise their voices in "God Bless America," "My Country, 'Tis of Thee" and "The Star-Spangled Banner." All these men and women, and some children, reflected the dazed incredulity moving across the nation far beyond the city limits of Washington, D.C. The actual expressions of anger were to come later, well after the initial shock had passed. This December afternoon the only manifestations of revenge in Washington were exemplified best, or worst, by the chopping down of several Japanese cherry trees along the Tidal Basin.

Many young Army and Navy officers, caught at home by the news, stirred up impromptu cocktail parties. Many became quite drunk. They knew that tomorrow they would be wearing the uniforms hitherto forbidden in Washington through a curious concern over "alarming" the populace. And the day *after* tomorrow . . . ?

Roosevelt himself could well speculate on tomorrow. He was, in fact, already telling members of his Cabinet that the struggle would be "long, hard."

When Churchill was switched through to him on the transatlantic telephone, the President remarked that the United States and Britain were "in the same boat" now.

After adjourning the meeting with his Cabinet and military advisers—shortly before 5 p.m.—the Chief Executive called Grace Tully into his study. She found him wearing a grey sack jacket and smoking "deeply." He started dictating, his tone "a little different" than usual, the message he would deliver to Congress in the morning:

"Yesterday comma December 7 comma 1941 dash a day which will live in infamy dash the United States of America was suddenly and deliberately attacked by naval and air forces of the Empire of Japan period paragraph . . . "

EPILOGUE

The "unexpected thing," by President Roosevelt's definition, resulted in a staggering victory for Japan. Within less than two hours our military and naval forces suffered 3,435 casualties and the loss of or severe damage to 188 planes, eight battleships, three light cruisers and four other fleet vessels. The Hawaiian attack was conceded by those who received it to have been "well planned and skilfully executed," as were co-ordinated assaults against the Philippines, Singapore and the Netherlands East Indies.

The War Department itself was to admit that "the Japanese caught the United States Army about three months short of completing what had been planned as the most intensive phase of its rearmament."

It required incalculable effort and sacrifice before the United States would win redress for that Sunday morning in 1941. But the memory of the humiliation caused by a minor power to a vauntedly great one could not—and cannot—be erased. At best, it may be dimmed as the years accumulate.

Eight separate, official investigations were held during the ensuing four years. The Joint Committee of Congress, conducting the most exhaustive hearings, left a record of forty fat volumes of small print. Admiral Wilkinson, before the Joint Committee, pronounced the most tragic understatement and post-mortem of the decade, if not the century:

"We did not, perhaps erroneously, recognize . . . an inordinate interest in Hawaii."

Memoirs and other historical studies continue to probe the same subject. Yet, after tens of millions of words, the circumstances of our surprise are still far from crystal clear.

The findings of the several investigating committees were inconclusive and, often contradictory. They frequently found their own reasons for criticizing men in high places, including the President of the United States, his War and Navy Cabinet members, his Army Chief of Staff and Chief of Naval Operations, as well as lesser officers. The Navy Court of Inquiry was "of the opinion that Admiral Harold R. Stark, U.S.N., Chief of Naval Operations and responsible for the operations of the Fleet, failed to display the sound judgement expected of him in that he did not transmit to Admiral Kimmel . . . important information which he had regarding the Japanese situation and especially, in that on the morning of December 7, 1941, he did not transmit immediately information which appeared to indicate that a break in diplomatic relations was imminent and that an attack in the Hawaiian areas might be expected soon."

Kimmel emerged from all the same scrutiny not uncriticized. Short, as well as his Chief of Staff, Colonel Phillips, and General Gerow, of War Plans, also came in for their share of blame by the Army Pearl Harbour Board, which charged that the Commanding General of the Hawaiian Department:

"... failed in his duties in the following particulars: (a) to place in a state of readiness for war in the face of a war warning by adopting an alert against sabotage only ... (b) to reach or attempt to reach an agreement with the Admiral commanding the Pacific Fleet and the Admiral commanding the Fourteenth Naval District for implementing the joint Army and Navy plans and agreements then in existence which provided for joint action by the two services."

General Gerow was rebuked for showing "a lack of imagination in failing to make the proper deductions from the Japanese intercepts" and for "failing to keep the Commanding General, Hawaiian Department, adequately informed on the impending war situation." Whatever may have been his responsibility for the disaster of December 7, Gerow, as Commanding General of the Fifth Corps, distinguished himself in the fierce fighting from the Normandy beachhead to the Siegfried Line. And Admiral Stark was awarded a Distinguished Service Medal for his contributions as Commander of U.S. Naval Forces in European Waters.

Relieved of their commands, General Short and Admiral Kimmel suffered the most. In a shameful handling of their cases, in which the White House was at least as guilty as the War and Navy Departments, the two officers were unmercifully pressured to request retirement; then, the subsequent announcement made it appear as though Short and Kimmel were tacitly admitting guilt by wishing to withdraw under fire.

"The record," it was noted in the Joint Congressional investigation, "of the high military and civilian officials of the War and Navy Departments in dealing with the Pearl Harbour disaster from beginning to end does them no credit. It will have a permanent bad effect on the morale and integrity of the armed services."

Admiral Halsey himself rose to the defence of the Hawaiian commanders, as he wrote: "I have always considered Admiral Kimmel and General Short to be splendid officers who were thrown to the wolves as scapegoats for something over which they had no control."

In retirement in Groton, Connecticut, Kimmel seeks vindication to this day. His own suffering was intensified by the loss of a son, Lieutenant-Commander Manning M. Kimmel, whose submarine, the *Robalo*, was destroyed in a minefield off Java in the summer of 1944. It was believed that young Kimmel was one of a group of survivors who came ashore only to be tortured and executed by the Japanese. It is the conviction of intelligence officers such as McCollum that the *Robalo* would have been forewarned of the minefield had it not been for the Navy's continuing and even intensified policy of withholding information from its own. Admiral King as COMINCH—Commander-in-Chief of all U.S. fleets, of Naval Operations, of, in truth, the *entire* Navy, with authority never before vested in one officer—adamantly and ruthlessly perpetuated this policy, even after the lesson of Pearl Harbour.

"There is only one answer," Kimmel has written the author, "that makes sense to me. Admiral Stark had orders from Mr. Roosevelt not to send me a message of warning."

The Admiral has made similar charges in the past, in his memoirs and in a book by his Navy counsel, the late Admiral Robert A. Theobald, who was commander of destroyers in the Pacific at the time of the Pearl Harbour attack. He confined his defence before the Joint Congressional Committee, however, to charges that Naval Operations had inadequately supplied him with vital intelligence.

Admiral Stark, as might be expected, has categorically denied Kimmel's accusation, noting "he [Kimmel] must have some axe to grind." Thus far no evidence has been produced to support Kimmel's contention.

Joseph C. Harsch, correspondent for the *Christian Science Monitor,* has himself provided a postscript as to what may have figured in the background of Kimmel's judgement. Fresh from covering the fighting in Europe, Harsch, *en route* to Russia, was accorded an off-the-record interview with the Pacific Fleet commander on Saturday morning, December 6.

"Is there going to be a war in the Pacific?" Harsch asked Kimmel.

"No" was Kimmel's flat reply. He thereupon explained his reasoning, which was predicated on the belief that the Germans had gone into winter quarters before Moscow, having failed to capture the Soviet capital. Since the Russians had not been defeated, the Japanese ran the risk of a two-front war if they attacked that winter. By the same token, he would have considered there was a grave danger of a Japanese offensive had Moscow fallen.

This was the substance of an hour-long "bull session" between the two men, according to Harsch's reminiscence to the author. That Saturday morning Kimmel's rationalization sounded plausible enough to the correspondent. Singularly, Kimmel, so far as there is documentation, had not made a point to any of his staff of linking the likelihood of hostilities in the Pacific with the war in Russia.

That panic gripped the second deck of the Navy Department immediately after the attack on Pearl Harbour is beyond reasonable dispute. One officer, then in intelligence, now in a high post in the Navy, told this writer that he went to his office safe one morning to find that a number of the "magic" dispatches were mysteriously missing. He never retrieved them.

ONI, in fact, had done such a thorough housecleaning of its top-secret and secret as well as not-so-secret files that, according to another officer on duty at the time, not even a departmental organization chart of November and December, 1941, could ever be found.

Yet another informant from the same intelligence office, now a prominent Washington attorney, was baffled on arriving at his desk on December 8 to discover orders which would have shipped the able Far East expert, McCollum, off to command a small oiler in the Caribbean. The orders were, providentially, cancelled within the day.

These conceivably were not so much wilful attempts to destroy evidence, cover tracks and remove witnesses on the part of the Navy after the attack, as they were the result of headlong, blind, unreasoning fear. However, even this charitable supposition can be debated. Obviously, the Navy had been guilty of dire errors of both omission and commission. Its leaders, a number of whom could well wish they had never been born, passionately desired to pull the curtains, draw the blinds, and shutter the windows.

But it was too late. Much of the fleet had been sunk. The blot was on the record. And the ink was indelible. Commander Safford was to spend part of his ensuing naval career in planning to defend Kimmel at a court-martial which never occurred and, then, with no such vehicle, in attempting to show that a "winds execute" had been monitored the Wednesday before the attack. This message, if the evidence of Takao Yoshikawa, a Japanese naval spy in Honolulu, can be believed, arrived concurrently with the bombing of Pearl Harbour. According to Yoshikawa, Consul Kita himself was breakfasting with him as the pair "silently listened to the eight o'clock news on Radio Tokyo." Amid routine announcements, they heard "a single phrase twice repeated ... 'east wind rain' ... that meant that the Imperial Council in Tokyo had decided for war with the United States."

Safford, after having been awarded $100,000 by the government for his cryptographic inventions, retired in the quiet Georgetown section of Washington. In civilian life he remains employed in the same general field of analytical work that brought him mingled fame and despair.

Admiral Richardson, whose disagreement with Roosevelt over basing the Pacific Fleet led to his replacement by Kimmel, has taken vows of silence, informing the author, "On January 15, 1941 (upon being relieved of command of the Pacific Fleet), I resolved not to write or to assist anyone in writing for publication, anything in relation to the events leading up to the Japanese attack on Pearl Harbour." And in the confidential circle of his friends at the Chevy Chase Club, he has been heard to implore, as only this lusty old naval officer can implore, "God give me the strength to keep my mouth shut!"

Even as Churchill said in 1939 of Russia, our experience at Pearl Harbour—*why* it happened—remains largely "a riddle wrapped in a mystery inside an enigma." Seemingly, it was a sneak attack that never should have succeeded. Having broken the Japanese diplomatic code, how could the United States have been so oblivious of Tokyo's intentions?

There persist many enigmas. The most important and baffling appear insoluble since many men who could bear further witness to the tangled trail leading to December 7 have gone to their graves. Their number includes Roosevelt, Hull, Stimson and Knox, Hopkins, Sumner Welles, Donald Nelson and Budget Director Harold Smith, General Marshall, General Short, Admiral King, Admiral Turner, Admiral Wilkinson, Admiral Noyes, Admiral Newton, Admiral Halsey, Admiral Bellinger and Admiral Zacharias, as well as Rufus Bratton, Otis K. Sadtler and FBI agent

Robert L. Shivers.

The author had the privilege of talking with Ellis Zacharias some months before his untimely death. It is hard to believe that the surprise effected at Pearl Harbour would have been possible had Zacharias been Chief of Naval Intelligence. Zacharias himself was to damn Kimmel's staff for "short memories and incorrect conclusions." He was, in a way, voicing criticism of the "hang it on Washington" group of immoderates. To this day, those who contemplate Pearl Harbour tend to radically divergent viewpoints, on one extreme attributing wilful intrigue to Washington in "allowing" or even "arranging" for the island to be attacked and on the other over-simplifying the catastrophe through a bland espousal of the doctrine of "inevitability."

These two passages from the Congressional inquiry represent, in contrast, a relatively dispassionate appraisal.

The first:

"... secret diplomacy was at the root of the tragedy. The United States had warned Japan that an advance into Malaya and the Dutch East Indies would mean war with this nation. The President gave Great Britain assurance of our armed support in such event. What Japan and Britain knew, our commanders in the field and our people did not know. Washington feared that national unity could not be attained unless Japan committed the first overt act. Accordingly, the Army in Hawaii was put on an anti-sabotage alert, a defensive posture containing the least possible risk of incident in Hawaii which Japan might claim was an overt act by the United States. The mobilization of

American public opinion in support of an offensive by the Pacific Fleet against Japan was to be accomplished, if at all, by a message to Congress, 'at the last stage of our relations, relating to actual hostilities.' .... Mr. Stimson's diary describes the plan succinctly: 'The question was how we should manœuvre them into the position of firing the first shot without allowing too much danger to ourselves.'"

The second, as contained in the minority report:

"In the future the people and their Congress must know how close American diplomacy is moving to war so that they may check its advance if imprudent and support its position if sound. A diplomacy which relies upon the enemy's first overt act to insure effective popular support for the nation's final war decision is both outmoded and dangerous in this atomic age. To prevent any future Pearl Harbour more tragic and damaging than that of December 7, 1941, there must be constant close co-ordination between American public opinion and American diplomacy.

"Eternal vigilance is the price of liberty even in the atomic era ... no war comes in a moment. War is the sum of many minor decisions and some that are major."

With respect to unravelling the snarled diplomatic threads, the investigation has "sadly failed to live up to the lofty prospectus with which it was launched," the same report concludes. And it would seem, that governmental departments want it to remain just that way. Still stamped "secret" are many vital papers of the State Department (the Cordell Hull file, for example) bearing a date later than *January 1, 1942*.

The same holds true of a vast hoard of Army and Navy documents—especially reports of "Boards"—of World War II vintage gathering dust in the Alexandria annex of the National Archives.

There are a few specialists, *circa* 1941, who insist that their memories as well must bear the "secret" tag. A leading cryptanalyst, in retirement, hinting at a kind of passive brainwashing, with his pension as a lever, maintains he has been ordered not to discuss those long-ago codes and ciphers. However, the National Security Council, which he indirectly accused, has denied not only the allegations but any interests in the World War II period.

Most who have acute memories of Pearl Harbour, and with special, personal reasons, feel unfettered and eminently free to talk. Sherman Miles, for example, who remains both vocal and graphic in his recollections, has this basic philosophy on the riddles which, like bacteria, have multiplied from the evolvements of December 7: "Show me two men who say they agree on all points on Pearl Harbour and I will show you at least one liar," adding:

"I still do not understand how our years of indoctrination, planning and training found that great fortress and fleet dozing on that Sunday morning. I agree with Senator———that we have not gotten to the bottom of it."

The one-time G2 chief asks further, "Why were the carriers *Lexington* and *Enterprise* away? ... Why hadn't the overhaul of the other two, the *Saratoga* and the *Hornet;* been hastened?"

As it turned out, the old battleships, too slow to keep up with a modern task force, were almost a case of "good riddance." What really counted was the loss of personnel. If the Japanese aviators had concentrated on fuel tanks and port installations, especially repair yards—which they did not—the United States would not have been able to mount its counter-attack for many more months than was actually the case.

"Regardless of anyone's opinion of President Roosevelt," writes Colonel Dusenbury, who was Bratton's assistant, "(I'm a Republican myself), it is inconceivable that he could have wished war with Japan. He was certainly enough of a strategist not to want war on two fronts.

"Re Kimmel's views as to the President's intentions, it is wise to reflect that the principals were fighting for their official lives and some for their reputations. The situation was confounded by a lapse of four years of the stress of war, which demands concentration on the immediate problems and plays havoc with minute details of occurrences during that period."

From his home in the hills of Sharon, Connecticut, Admiral Hart re-emphasizes:

"The 'winds' dispatch—I have not thought it of much importance in any respect. I think my reaction at the time was that it was something to be watched but that we had already been told enough. . . .

"MacArthur, Brereton and all other commands on or around the Pacific had the same information and directives. Actually, the vital thing was the 'war warning' dispatch, as we of the Navy called it. In that dispatch were ten all-important words; the remainder was not very important and could well have been omitted. The ten words were: 'This is a war warning. Execute an appropriate defensive deployment.'

"Really it was quite simple. We were told that we were to await the blow, in dispositions such as to minimize the danger from it and it was left to the commanders on the spot to decide all the details of said defensive deployment. I don't think it was necessary to tell us anything more than we knew on the measures to be taken subsequently."

At Winter Park, Florida, General Brereton expresses the opinion that "General MacArthur was of course the recipient of all the confidential information coming our way. He, however, took precise pains to see that his commanders were kept abreast of the situation as he saw it.

"I have a definite impression that we in the Philippines seemed to be much more aware of the impending action than was true in the Hawaiian Department. A comparison of our state of readiness as recorded in the Brereton Diaries with what seems to have been the status in Hawaii I think shows that we were really convinced that attack was imminent. And I think that this was what General MacArthur had decided, and I don't see how more precise intelligence could have come at the time than what we had.

"Of course we were highly sensitive and nervous. It seemed inevitable that we would be attacked massively and quickly. We knew from our own sources of the Jap concentration in Takao and in Camranh Bay."

Admiral Stark, at his estate in Washington, emphasizes that he feels Naval Operations transmitted this sort of "precise intelligence" to his Pacific and other outposts. He remains loyal to all those he dealt with in the final, moribund months of peace: Roosevelt, Hopkins, Hull, Marshall, Turner, Wilkinson and others.

McCollum, who retired as a rear-admiral and now runs a real estate business in Arlington, Virginia, has an abiding curiosity about *why* things happened when they did, without anywhere nearly enough persons being prepared. In a letter to this author, he mentions:

"These word codes ('east wind rain,' for example), if such they could be called, were not used by the Japanese prior to the outbreak of war and were not effective as a war indicator. Again it seems to me that we are over-emphasizing code decryptions. To my mind then and now there were a number of much more definite and concrete indicators of war; for instance, the burning of codes and other papers by the Japanese embassies and consulates located in what we now call the Western Democracies and a number of others."

From Honolulu, two Army intelligence officers who chose the islands as home after retirement have conveyed their thoughts in retrospect. George Bicknell observes:

"I have always had the opinion, and I might be wrong, that the commanding general of a situation such as we were facing in those days had the responsibility of making up his mind what should be done and not having to rely on what somebody back in Washington might have said. After all, he was put out here to command the Hawaiian Department, and under the war plan, to protect the naval base at Pearl Harbour. Therefore, if he decided it was necessary to go into a full alert, I see no reason why he should not have done so, and then tell the General Staff in Washington what he had done and why. I may be wrong in this but I still feel that it was his responsibility and that he should have taken whatever steps were necessary and certainly going into an alert against sabotage did not help the situation in any way."

Of the actual attack, Bicknell recalls that he was awakened by a sound "of what I thought were firecrackers at first, and then looking from my window down onto Pearl Harbour, saw the attack actually in progress.... I made a very fast trip to Shafter and was somewhat disappointed with what I had observed there. I presume it may be just the fact that I had higher aspirations of what the Army would do in case of an emergency, but there certainly was no great sign of any organization or understanding of an emergency situation.

"What seemed to impress me, and I can still remember it vividly, was the fact that we had been going through manoeuvres year after year in order to meet a situation which might arise, and now the situation was upon us, and I could see little effect of the training which we had been going through in the confusion that existed at that time."

Kendall Fielder, Bicknell's one-time senior, lauds Short's "high state of training" which, the retired Brigadier-General believes "paid off when the first real combat took place—Guadalcanal where the 35th Infantry of the 25th Division saved the day." Fielder continues:

"The Marines got a lot of credit as they always do but the 35th actually saved the day as has now been recorded in history. General Short was relentless in his demand for superb physical fitness and thorough knowledge of weapons and their use. Both the 25th and 24th which he reorganized and trained were just about our best here in the Pacific."

Fielder still believes "there have been few officers of my acquaintance so dedicated or capable" as General Short, adding, "It was too bad he had to be made a scapegoat and never got to lead troops in combat. He would have been, in my opinion, one of the greatest of our World War II combat leaders."

On the surprise element, Fielder asserts:

"I have never known for sure what information Washington had, if any, that was not transmitted to Hawaii, but I'm sure no one there considered an attack on Pearl Harbour probable. Therefore, I can only conclude that even if all information available had been sent to the commanders here it would have had little effect on the outcome of the attack. We no doubt could have shot down a few more enemy planes and saved a few of our own bunched together on the ground to minimize sabotage danger. But in the absence of knowledge that a carrier-borne attack was a definite threat, a surprise strike was bound to succeed. As for the battleships, the destruction of which was the real object of the attack, they were vulnerable so long as bottled up in the harbour. And had they not been in the harbour the attack would have been delayed until they were. For there was no way during peacetime to prevent Japanese agents from observing the coming and going of the fleet and knowing when the battleships were moored at Ford Island."

Concerning secrecy between the Army and the Navy:

"As to the exchange of classified information between the services, there is little question but what Navy Intelligence officers withheld some. However, it had mostly to do with movement and activities within the Japanese fleet and was derived from intercepted and decoded messages. The argument was always that to divulge the information might give away the fact that the Japanese codes had been broken.

"So far as I was ever concerned, the only really important bit of information withheld concerned the Japanese task force which struck Hawaii. It had been under constant surveillance through radio intercepts and suddenly nothing was heard from it. When it took off from Hokkaido towards Hawaii under complete radio silence, and therefore its whereabouts unknown, the Army should have been informed. The reason given for not passing it along was that it was felt that any Japanese aggression would surely be towards Indo-China or the Philippines, and the task force had headed south.

"If the Army Intelligence had known there was a strong Japanese carrier task force on the loose with radio silence and its whereabouts unknown, we couldn't have done much except man the anti-aircraft positions, issue plenty of ammunition for each gun and disperse the planes on the ground. And of course have fighter pilots on standby. No doubt this might have resulted in more Japanese casualties, but I'm sure that so long as the fleet was in Pearl the attack would have done enough damage to permit Japanese aggression to the south while the battleships were being repaired.

"They constituted the only threat to Japanese plans to take the rubber, oil and tin available in Malaya, Borneo, Sumatra, etc., which they so desperately needed."

Relative to General Marshall's Sunday horseback ride:

"Why shouldn't he take a little early-morning exercise? Since everyone from the President down has said they did not expect a Japanese attack on American soil, why should he not take any type of exercise necessary for his fitness on a week-end? Had he been at his desk he could have done nothing to minimize the attack. Sure, relations were severely strained, a crisis expected soon, but when? Surely not on that particular Sunday morning. Was everyone to crawl in a hole and await the gong? That is not the way Americans do business.

"My belief is strong that no one person or group of persons was responsible. As a nation, we were very cocky and smug. We looked down on the Japanese and never dreamed they would dare strike American soil, and we thought our Navy was invincible. It is easy to say that this person or that group was guilty of negligence or dereliction of duty. But the question has not been settled and it never will be. During the period following the war, one political party tried to pin the blame on the President and the administration—the other on the military leaders. Neither succeeded."

Commander John J. Rochefort does not share Fielder's opinions. He has written from California:

"The area commands, including both Pearl and the Philippines, were not given 'sufficient warning' nor were they kept advised as to developments. If one is inclined to be charitable, one could say that Washington was guilty of a serious error in judgement. This is not to be construed as criticism of Washington because they had other problems in Europe. But if they withheld information from the military commands in the Pacific, and I believe they did, they must accept the responsibility for what later occurred. Their handling of the Japanese note of December 6 indicates a complete lack of knowledge of the Japanese mind, or a pre-meditated plan to withhold vital information from responsible military officers. . . .

"As one cognizant of most if not all of the developments during 1941, I agree with Admiral Kimmel to the extent that he was not being furnished information affecting his command, and available in Washington through Communications Intelligence. . . .

"I choose to believe that: (a) December 7 was the result of Washington policy and the resultant serious error in judgement; (b) that responsibility for this must be placed on the wartime Commander-in-Chief; (c) it was imperative at that time, for the good of our country, to place the blame outside Washington, and; (d) all the ingredients for a repeat performance have been present since 1945. . . .

"It is an age-old tradition that the C.O. of a ship is liable if the ship is lost. For this reason, Admiral

Kimmel must be held responsible for his losses at Pearl Harbour. However, if the losses were due in part, or in whole, to errors by his superiors, then those superiors must be held responsible. Admiral Stark knew what measures for protection Admiral Kimmel had taken, and was quite familiar with the dispositions. With this information at hand—upon the receipt of the so-called Fourteen-Part Message of December 6—Admiral Kimmel should have been informed instantly by the Navy rather than by an antiquated Army communications system. If Admiral Stark's actions were based on orders received from his superior [President Roosevelt] then that superior must accept the final responsibility."

And so the controversy has raged for more than twenty years. Even though Pearl Harbour's legacy of suspicion, confusion and outright recrimination persists like some enveloping miasma, certain "ifs" which could easily have changed history are now apparent:

> IF Roosevelt had not ordered a witch hunt in those last days to discover the source of the Chicago *Tribune* story....
>
> IF he had not been ill with a sinus infection that week-end or his Cabinet had been composed of healthier, younger, more able men....
>
> IF Stark had not replaced the telephone receiver on Sunday morning when, apparently, he had started to call Kimmel....
>
> IF Marshall had not taken his customary Sunday morning horseback ride....
>
> IF Marshall's last-minute warning had not been transmitted by ordinary commercial cable....
>
> IF the Army, Navy and State Department at all levels

had been allowed to interchange all important intelligence matters. . . .

IF G2 and ONI and possibly Operations as well had not assumed that no "major element" of the fleet was in Pearl Harbour that Sunday or, indeed, if it had been unequivocally clear which commands possessed "purple" machines and which did not. . . .

IF there had been less jealousy, less chaos on the second deck of the Navy Department and vastly improved liaison at the War Department especially within the Chief of Staff's immediate echelons. . . .

IF there had been overtime provisions for the Civil Service decoders. . . .

IF the Japanese expert, Zacharias, had not been "punished" with sea duty, as but another manifestation of the clique system festering within the Navy. . . .

There are other ifs. It appears a reasonable assumption, however, that had *any* one of these ten ifs not existed, the chances of a successful surprise attack would have been proportionately diminished.

There persists, long after the books of the last investigator of Pearl Harbour were closed, a question that has never been satisfactorily answered—why, during those twenty-four hours before the bombs fell, had there been such apathy in the War and Navy Departments and in the White House, especially in the White House? This paramount question must be considered wholly apart from the subject of local failures and omissions within the Hawaiian commands.

Did the President's health, not especially good that week-end, have a direct bearing on his attitude? Or was his sinus attack merely coincidence? That Roosevelt sat back and waited Saturday and Sunday, even after having read the first thirteen parts on Saturday evening and commenting "this means war," is a matter of record. Whether his apathy can be called deliberate becomes a matter of conjecture.

What *was* on Roosevelt's mind that week-end; what had been on his mind ever since his gloomy prophecy to his Warm Springs neighbours the preceding week-end? What had the President discussed that week with such personages as Lord Halifax, who called twice at the White House, or with Dr. Hu Shih minutes before the attack?

Winston Churchill was at his persuasive best when he expressed his "deepest fear" that Japan would attack some segment of the Empire, while "constitutional difficulties" kept the guns of the United States cold. Certainly Churchill had emphasized such concerns and others at the all-important Atlantic Charter Conference. Afterwards there was a definite change, a marked toughening in the United States' approach to the Tri-Partite powers. Following the Pearl Harbour attack the British Prime Minister observed that the end result was a "vast simplification" of the problems of Roosevelt, his Cabinet and his top military advisers.

With all the blunders that had been made both in military planning and in diplomacy, there was still time left—even as late as Sunday noon in Washington—for America to put its guard up, and not be hit while totally comatose. Yet, the known opponent continued to feint with open menace, unchallenged and, to all purposes, undetected.

Ultimately, as with the captain of a ship, the Commander-in-Chief must shoulder the responsibility for what befalls his nation. He cannot in conscience or in rectitude stand aside and point, much less allow others to be sacrificed by proxy. This he cannot do no matter what the derelictions of his subordinates.

And, what were the Commander-in-Chief's responsibilities for December 7? Frustratingly little is known of the White House's inner workings on that week-end. As a consequence, the pitfalls of surmise are all too numerous. Nonetheless, the blank spots and the contradictions of that brief, squandered period all centre around one source.

If further evidence is discovered on the Pearl Harbour disaster, and the author believes it someday will be, it will in all likelihood bear direct relationship to the decisions made—or not made—during the late Saturday and early Sunday hours in the Executive Mansion. For President Roosevelt, already returned twice to the nation's highest office as a man of action, failed to act in those final hours of grace when action of the highest magnitude was both indicated and demanded—urgently.

Pearl Harbour was our Pacific Waterloo. Almost four years were required to turn defeat into victory. Somehow, the stigma and the shame persist today, as well as the plaguing suspicion that there might have been some fine lines separating blunder from intent.

The December 7 attack was a Waterloo, yet one which—astonishingly—failed to beget a comparable St. Helena.

APPENDIX

THE TEN-POINT NOTE

The Government of the United States and the Government of Japan propose to take steps as follows:

1. The Government of the United States and the Government of Japan will endeavour to conclude a multilateral non-aggression pact among the British Empire, China, Japan, the Netherlands, the Soviet Union, Thailand and the United States.

2. Both Governments will endeavour to conclude among the American, British, Chinese, Japanese, the Netherlands and Thai Governments an agreement whereunder each of the Governments would pledge itself to respect the territorial integrity of French Indo-China and, in the event that there should develop a threat to the territorial integrity of Indo-China, to enter into immediate consultation with a view to taking such measures as may be deemed necessary and advisable to meet the threat in question. Such agreement would provide also that each of the Governments party to the agreement would not seek or accept preferential treatment in its trade or economic relations with Indo-China and would use its influence to obtain for each of the signatories equality of treatment in trade and commerce with French Indo-China.

3. The Government of Japan will withdraw all military, naval, air and police forces from China and from Indo-China.

4. The Government of the United States and the Government of Japan will not support—militarily, politically,

economically—any government or regime in China other than the National Government of the Republic of China with capital temporarily at Chungking.

5. Both Governments will give up all extraterritorial rights in China, including rights and interests in and with regard to international settlements and concessions, and rights under the Boxer Protocol of 1901.

6. Both Governments will endeavour to obtain the agreement of the British and other Governments to give up extraterritorial rights in China, including rights in international settlements and in concessions and under the Boxer Protocol of 1901.

7. The Government of the United States and the Government of Japan will enter into negotiations for the conclusion between the United States and Japan of a trade agreement, based upon reciprocal most-favoured-nation treatment and reduction of trade barriers by both countries, including an undertaking by the United States to bind raw silk on the free list.

8. The Government of the United States and the Government of Japan will, respectively, remove the freezing restrictions on Japanese funds in the United States and on American funds in Japan.

9. Both Governments will agree that no agreement which either has concluded with any third power or powers shall be interpreted by it in such a way as to conflict with the fundamental purpose of this agreement, the establishment and preservation of peace throughout the Pacific area.

10. Both Governments will use their influence to cause other Governments to adhere to and to give practical application to the basic political and economic principles set forth in this agreement.

THE FOURTEEN-PART MESSAGE

Part 1

The Government of Japan, prompted by a genuine desire to

come to an amicable understanding with the Government of the United States in order that the two countries by their joint efforts may secure the peace of the Pacific area and thereby contribute towards the realization of world peace, has continued negotiations with the utmost sincerity since April last with the Government of the United States regarding the adjustment and advancement of Japanese-American relations and the stabilization of the Pacific area.

The Japanese Government has the honour to state frankly its views, concerning the claims the American Government has persistently maintained as well as the measures the United States and Great Britain have taken towards Japan during these eight months.

It is the immutable policy of the Japanese Government to insure the stability of East Asia and to promote world peace, and thereby to enable all nations to find each its proper place in the world.

Ever since the China Affair broke out owing to the failure on the part of China to comprehend Japan's true intentions, the Japanese Government has striven for the restoration of peace and it has consistently exerted its best efforts to prevent the extension of warlike disturbances. It was also to that end that in September last year Japan concluded the Tri-Partite Pact with Germany and Italy.

Part 2

However, both the United States and Great Britain have resorted to every possible measure to assist the Chungking régime so as to obstruct the establishment of a general peace between Japan and China, interfering with Japan's constructive endeavours towards the stabilization of East Asia. Exerting pressure on the Netherlands East Indies, or menacing French Indo-China, they have attempted to frustrate Japan's aspiration to realize the ideal of common prosperity in cooperation with these regions. Furthermore, where Japan in accordance with its protocol with France took measures of joint defence of French Indo-China, both American and British Governments, wilfully misinterpreting it as a threat to their own possessions, and inducing the Netherlands Government to follow suit, they enforced the assets freezing order, thus severing economic relations with Japan. While manifesting thus an obviously hostile attitude, these countries have strengthened their military preparations perfecting an encirclement of Japan, and have brought about a situation which endangers the very existence of the Empire.

Part 3

Nevertheless, to facilitate a speedy settlement, the Premier of Japan proposed, in August last, to meet the President of the United States for a discussion of important problems between the two countries covering the entire Pacific area. However, the American Government, while accepting in principle the Japanese proposal, insisted that the meeting should take place after an agreement of view had been reached on fundamental and essential questions. Subsequently, on September 25, the Japanese Government submitted a proposal based on the formula proposed by the American Government, taking fully into consideration past American claims and also incorporating Japanese views. Repeated discussions proved of no avail in producing readily an agreement of view. The present cabinet, therefore, submitted a revised proposal, moderating still further the Japanese claims regarding the principal points of difficulty in the negotiation and endeavoured strenuously to reach a settlement. But the American Government, adhering steadfastly to its original assertion, failed to display in the slightest degree a spirit of conciliation. The negotiation made no progress.

Part 4

Thereupon, the Japanese Government, with a view to doing its utmost for averting a crisis in Japanese-American relations, submitted on November 20th still another proposal in order to arrive at an equitable solution of the more essential and urgent questions which, simplifying its previous proposal, stipulated the following points:

(1) The Governments of Japan and the United States undertake not to dispatch armed forces into any of the regions, excepting French Indo-China, in the South-eastern Asia and the Southern Pacific area.

(2) Both Governments shall co-operate with a view to securing the acquisition in the Netherlands East Indies of those goods and commodities of which the two countries are in need.

(3) Both Governments mutually undertaking to restore commercial relations to those prevailing prior to the freezing

of assets.

The Government of the United States shall supply Japan the required quantity of oil.

(4) The Government of the United States undertakes not to resort to measures and actions prejudicial to the endeavours for the restoration of general peace between Japan and China.

(5) The Japanese Government undertakes to withdraw troops now stationed in French Indo-China upon either the restoration of peace between Japan and China or the establishment of an equitable peace in the Pacific area; and it is prepared to remove the Japanese troops in the southern part of French Indo-China to the northern part upon the conclusion of the present agreement.

Part 5

As regards China, the Japanese Government, while expressing its readiness to accept the offer of the President of the United States to act as "Introducer" of peace between Japan and China as was previously suggested, asked for an undertaking on the part of the United States to do nothing prejudicial to the restoration of Sino-Japanese peace when the two parties have commenced direct negotiations.

The American Government not only rejected the above-mentioned new proposal, but made known its intention to continue its aid to Chiang Kai-shek; and in spite of its suggestion mentioned above, withdrew the offer of the President to act as the so-called "Introducer" of peace between Japan and China, pleading that time was not yet ripe for it. Finally, on November 26th, in an attitude to impose upon the Japanese Government those principles it has persistently maintained, the American Government made a proposal totally ignoring Japanese claims, which is a source of profound regret to the Japanese Government.

Part 6

From the beginning of the present negotiation the Japanese Government has always maintained an attitude of fairness and moderation, and did its best to reach a settlement, for which it made all possible concessions often in spite of great difficulties.

As for the China question which constituted an important subject of the negotiation, the Japanese Government showed a most conciliatory attitude.

As for the principle of non-discrimination in international commerce, advocated by the American Government, the Japanese Government expressed its desire to see the said principle applied throughout the world, and declared that along with the actual practice of this principle in the world, the Japanese Government would endeavour to apply the same in the Pacific area, including China, and made it clear that Japan had no intention of excluding from China economic activities of third powers pursued on an equitable basis.

Furthermore, as regards the question of withdrawing troops from French Indo-China, the Japanese Government even volunteered, as mentioned above, to carry out an immediate evacuation of troops from Southern French Indo-China as a measure of easing the situation.

Part 7

It is presumed that the spirit of conciliation exhibited to the utmost degree by the Japanese Government in all these matters is fully appreciated by the American Government.

On the other hand, the American Government, always holding fast to theories in disregard of realities, and refusing to yield an inch on its impractical principles, caused undue delays in the negotiation. It is difficult to understand this attitude of the American Government and the Japanese Government desires to call the attention of the American Government especially to the following points:

1. The American Government advocates in the name of world peace those principles favourable to it and urges upon the Japanese Government the acceptance thereof. The peace of the world may be brought about only by discovering a mutually acceptable formula through recognition of the reality of the situation and mutual appreciation of one another's position. An attitude such as ignores realities and imposes one's selfish views upon others will scarcely serve the purpose of facilitating the consummation of negotiations.

Part 8

Of the various principles put forward by the American Government as a basis of the Japanese-American agreement, there are some which the Japanese Government is ready to accept in principle, but in view of the world's actual conditions, it seems only a Utopian ideal, on the part of the American Government, to attempt to force their immediate adoption.

Again, the proposal to conclude a multilateral non-aggression pact between Japan, the United States, Great Britain, China, the Soviet Union, the Netherlands, and Thailand, which is patterned after the old concept of collective security, is far removed from the realities of East Asia.

The American proposal contains a stipulation which states: "Both governments will agree that no agreement, which either has concluded with any third powers, shall be interpreted by it in such a way as to conflict with the fundamental purpose of this agreement, the establishment and preservation of peace throughout the Pacific area." It is presumed that the above provision has been proposed with a view to restrain Japan from fulfilling its obligations under the Tri-Partite Pact when the United States participates in the war in Europe, and as such, it cannot be accepted by the Japanese Government.

Part 9

The American Government, obsessed with its own views and opinions, may be said to be scheming for the extension of the war. While it seeks on the one hand, to secure its rear by stabilizing the Pacific area, it is engaged, on the other hand, in aiding Great Britain and preparing to attack, in the name of self-defence, Germany and Italy, two powers that are striving to establish a new order in Europe. Such a policy is totally at variance with the many principles upon which the American Government proposes to found the stability of the Pacific area through peaceful means.

Whereas the American Government, under the principles it rigidly upholds, objects to settling international issues through military pressure, it is exercising in and upon other nations pressure by economic power. Recourse to such pressure as a means of dealing with international relations should be condemned as it is at times more inhuman than military pressure.

Part 10

It is impossible not to reach the conclusion that the American Government desires to maintain and strengthen, in collusion with Great Britain and other powers, its dominant position it has hitherto occupied not only in China but in other areas of East Asia. It is a fact of history that the countries of East Asia for the past 100 years or more have been compelled to observe the *status quo* under the Anglo-American policy of imperialistic exploitation and to sacrifice themselves to the prosperity of the two nations. The Japanese Government cannot tolerate the perpetuation of such a situation since it directly runs counter to Japan's fundamental policy to enable all nations to enjoy each its proper place in the world.

Part 11

The stipulation proposed by the American Government relative to French Indo-China is a good exemplification of the above-mentioned American policy. That the six countries—Japan, the United States, Great Britain, the Netherlands, China and Thailand—excepting France, should undertake among themselves to respect the territorial integrity and sovereignty of French Indo-China and equality of treatment in trade and commerce would be tantamount to placing that territory under the joint guarantee of the governments of those six countries. Apart from the fact that such a proposal totally ignores the position of France, it is unacceptable to the Japanese Government in that such an arrangement cannot but be considered as an extension to French Indo-China of a system similar to the Nine Power Treaty Structure which is the chief factor responsible for the present predicament of East Asia.

Part 12

All the items demanded of Japan by the American Government regarding China such as wholesale evacuation of troops or unconditional application of the principle of non-discrimination in international commerce ignore the actual conditions in China, and are calculated to destroy Japan's position as the stabilizing factor of East Asia. The attitude of the American Government in demanding Japan not to support militarily, politically or economically any régime other than the régime at Chungking, disregarding thereby the existence of the Nanking Government, shatters the very basis of the present negotiation. This demand of the American Government falling, as it does, in line with the above-mentioned refusal to cease from aiding the Chungking régime, demonstrates clearly the intention of the American Government to obstruct the restoration of normal relations between Japan and China and the return of peace to East Asia.

Part 13

In brief, the American proposal contains certain acceptable items such as those concerning commerce, including the conclusion of a trade agreement, mutual removal of the freezing restrictions, and stabilization of the Yen and Dollar exchange, or the abolition of extraterritorial rights in China. On the other hand, however, the proposal in question ignores Japan's sacrifices in the four years of the China affair, menaces the empire's existence itself and disparages its honour and prestige. Therefore, viewed in its entirety, the Japanese Government regrets that it cannot accept the proposal as a basis of negotiation.

The Japanese Government, in its desire for an early conclusion of the negotiation, proposed that simultaneously with the conclusion of the Japanese-American negotiation, agreements be signed, with Great Britain and other interested countries. The proposal was accepted by the American Government. However, since the American Government has made the proposal of November 26 as a result of frequent consultations with Great Britain, Australia, the Netherlands and Chungking and presumably by catering to the wishes of the Chungking régime on the questions of China, it must be concluded that all these countries are at one with the United States in ignoring Japan's position.

Part 14

Obviously it is the intention of the American Government to conspire with Great Britain and other countries to obstruct Japan's efforts towards the establishment of peace through the creation of a New Order in East Asia, and especially to preserve Anglo-American rights and interests by keeping Japan and China at war. This intention has been revealed clearly during the course of the present negotiation. Thus, the earnest hope of the Japanese Government to adjust Japanese-American relations and to preserve and promote the peace of the Pacific through co-operation with the American Government has finally been lost.

The Japanese Government regrets to have to notify hereby the American Government that in view of the attitude of the American Government that it cannot but consider that it is impossible to reach an agreement through further negotiations.

ACKNOWLEDGEMENTS

The author owes a debt of gratitude to many in addition to those whose help is clearly evident in the narrative of the book itself. There are a few, highly placed today, who have aided the author on the firm condition that their names would appear nowhere in this study.

I wish, however, to thank a number of persons even though their names may already have appeared prominently in the book—especially Admirals Stark and Bloch. I have relied heavily on interviews with these two distinguished officers, living not far from each other in Washington, and who can mention with pride that they were midshipmen when Dewey captured Manila Bay.

In addition, I wish to acknowledge the help of:

Vice-Admiral Walter S. Anderson, U.S.N. (ret.), of New York; Rear-Admiral John R. Beardall, U.S.N. (ret.), of Winter Park, Florida; Francis Biddle, of Washington; Barry Bingham, editor and publisher of the Louisville *Courier-Journal*; Blair Bolles, of Washington; Paul S. Burtness, Department of English, Northern Illinois University, author with Warren U. Ober of a recent study of the Pearl Harbour attack; Charles K. Claunch, former White House usher, of Orlando, Florida; Elizabeth B. Drewry, director, Franklin D. Roosevelt Library, Hyde Park; Allen W. Dulles; Colonel Trevor R. Dupuy, of Washington; Rear-Admiral E.M. Eller, U.S.N. (ret.), Chief of Naval History; Joseph C. Grew, of Washington; Mrs Charles S. Hamlin, of Albany; General Thomas T. Handy, U.S.A. (ret.); Richard H. Hansen, Lincoln, Nebraska; Joseph C. Harsch, of

London; John Henry, the *Evening Star,* of Washington; Admiral R. E. Ingersoll, U.S.N. (ret.), of Washington; Admiral Alan G. Kirk, U.S.N. (ret.), of New York; Rear-Admiral Edwin T. Layton, U.S.N. (ret.), of Tokyo; Dr. Rudolph Marx, of Los Angeles; Ferdinand L. Mayer, of Bennington, Vermont; Vice-Admiral John J. McCrea, U.S.N. (ret.), of Boston; Lieutenant Oden L. McMillan, U.S.N., musician then on the *Pennsylvania*; John E. Masten, of New York, assistant counsel for the Congressional inquiry committee; Mrs. Ross T. McIntire, of Coronado, California; Rear-Admiral Irving H. Mayfield, U.S.N. (ret.), of La Jolla, California (since deceased); Edwin R. Murrow; Mrs. Leigh Noyes; Hal O'Flaherty, of Kensington, California, former managing editor of the Chicago *Daily News* and one-time naval officer in the public relations department; Rear-Admiral Paulus P. Powell, U.S.N. (ret.), of Washington (since deceased); Rear-Admiral Joseph Redman, U.S.N. (ret.) of Washington; the late Mrs. Eleanor Roosevelt; Mrs. Otis K. Sadtler, of Washington; John Semanko, of Harrisburg, Pennsylvania; Rear-Admiral Roscoe E. Schuirmann, U.S.N. (ret.), of Washington; Rear-Admiral John F. Shafroth, U.S.N. (ret.), of Washington; Vice-Admiral Alexander Sharp, U.S.N. (ret.), of Washington; Vice-Admiral William R. Smedberg III, U.S.N., Chief of Naval Personnel; Lawrence B. Smith, of Phoenix, Arizona, son of the former Director of the Budget; Mrs. R. Inez Turner, of Phoenix, Arizona; Miss L. Lucile Turner, of Carmel, California; Egon Weiss, U.S. Military Academy Library; Vice-Admiral Charles Wellborn, attached to the United Nations, New York; and Leonard Withington, Chamber of Commerce, Honolulu.

I owe particular appreciation to George P. Brockway and Burton L. Beals, of W.W. Norton & Company; and John Hale, of Robert Hale, Ltd., London.

Principal libraries consulted include the District of Columbia Public Library, Library of Congress, the National Archives, the Franklin D. Roosevelt Library, of Hyde Park, the Army and Navy libraries in Washington, and the New York Public Library.

BIBLIOGRAPHY

The following are among the many source books consulted, in addition to the forty volumes of the Joint Committee on the Investigation of the Pearl Harbour Attack, Congress of the United States, Government Printing Office, Washington, 1946, which also reproduced the proceedings of the prior investigations: the Roberts Commission, the Hart Inquiry, the Army Pearl Harbour Board, the Navy Court of Inquiry, the Clarke Inquiry, the Clausen Investigation, and the Hewitt Inquiry.

Allen, Gwenfread. *Hawaii's War Years*. Honolulu: University of Hawaii Press, 1949.

Biddle, Francis B. *In Brief Authority*. New York: Doubleday, 1962.

Brereton, Lewis H. *The Brereton Diaries*. New York: William Morrow & Co., 1946.

Burns, Eugene. *Then There Was One*. New York: Harcourt, Brace & Co., 1944.

Burns, James M. *The Lion and the Fox*. New York: Harcourt, Brace & Co., 1956.

Burtness, Paul S., and Warren U. Ober. *The Puzzle of Pearl Harbor*. Evanston & Elmsford, Ill.: Row, Peterson & Co., 1962.

Butow, Robert J. C. *Tojo and the Coming of The War*. Princeton: Princeton University Press, 1961.

Churchill, Winston. *The Grand Alliance*. Boston: Houghton Mifflin Co., 1950.

Cooke, Alistair. *A Generation on Trial*. New York: Alfred A. Knopf, 1952.

Davis, Forrest. *How War Came*. New York: Simon and Schuster, 1942.

Fabricant, Noah. *Thirteen Famous Patients*. Philadelphia: Chilton Co., 1960.

Farago, Ladislas. *Burn After Reading*. New York: Walker and Co., 1961.

Feis, Herbert. *The Road to Pearl Harbor*. Princeton: Princeton University Press, 1950.

Grenfell, Russell. *Main Fleet to Singapore*. New York: The Macmillan Co., 1952.

Hull, Cordell. *The Memoirs of Cordell Hull*. New York: The Macmillan Co., 1948.

Ickes, Harold. *The Secret Diary of Harold Ickes*. New York: Simon and Schuster, 1955.

Karig, Walter. *Battle Report*. New York: Farrar and Rinehart, 1944.

Kimmel, Husband E. *Admiral Kimmel's Story*. Chicago: Henry Regnery Co., 1955.

Konoye, Fumimaro. *The Memoirs of Prince Fumimaro Konoye*. Tokyo: Okuyama Service, 1945.

Kurusu, Saburo. *Treacherous America*. Japan Times, Tokyo, 1942.

Leighton, Isabel (ed.). *The Asprin Age*. New York: Simon and Schuster, 1949.

Marshall, Katherine Tupper. *Together*. New York: Tupper and Love, Inc., 1946.

Marx, Rudolph. *The Health of the Presidents*. New York: G. P. Putnam's Sons, 1946.

McIntire, Ross T. *White House Physician*. New York: G. P. Putnam's Sons, 1951.

Millis, Walter. *This is Pearl*. New York: William Morrow & Co., 1947.

Morgenstern, George. *Pearl Harbor*. New York: The Devin-Adair Co., 1947.

Morison, Samuel E. *The Rising Sun in the Pacific*. Boston: Little, Brown & Co., 1948.

Nelson, Donald M. *Arsenal of Democracy*. New York: Harcourt, Brace & Co., 1946.

Payne, Robert. *The Marshall Story*. New York: Prentice-Hall Inc., 1951.

Roosevelt, Eleanor. *This I Remember*. New York: Harper & Brothers, 1949.

Shalett, Sidney and James Roosevelt. *Affectionately, FDR*. New York: Harcourt, Brace & Co., 1959.

Sherwood, Robert E. *Roosevelt and Hopkins.* New York: Harper & Brothers, 1948.

Smith, A. Merriam. *Thank You, Mr. President.* New York: Harper & Brothers, 1946.

Stimson, Henry L. *On Active Service in Peace and War.* New York: Harper & Brothers, 1947.

Theobald, Robert A. *The Final Secret of Pearl Harbor.* New York: The Devin-Adair Co., 1954.

Toland, John. *But Not in Shame.* New York: Random House, 1961.

Tugwell, Rexford G. *The Democratic Roosevelt.* Garden City, N.Y.: Doubleday & Co., 1957.

Tully, Grace. *F.D.R., My Boss.* New York: Charles Scribner's Sons, 1949.

United States Department of State. "Summary of Conversations," Memorandum prepared by Department of State, 1942.

Watson, Mark S. *Chief of Staff, Prewar Plans and Preparations.* Historical Division, U.S. Army, 1950.

Whitehead, Don. *The FBI Story.* New York: Random House, 1946.

Wohlstetter, Roberta. *Pearl Harbor, Warning and Decision.* Stanford, Calif.: Stanford University Press, 1962.

Zacharias, Ellis. *Secret Missions.* New York: G. P. Putnam's Sons, 1946.

Numerous periodicals were reviewed, including the *Atlantic Monthly, Collier's, Current History, Harper's, Illustrated London News, Life, Newsweek, New Yorker, Reader's Digest* and *Time.*

A great number of newspapers also provided invaluable background, including the Baltimore *Sun,* Chicago *Tribune, Christian Science Monitor,* Honolulu *Star-Bulletin,* Honolulu *Advertiser,* Louisville *Courier-Journal,* New York *Times,* New York *Herald Tribune,* San Francisco *Chronicle,* St. Louis *Post-Dispatch,* Seattle *Post-Intelligencer,* and the Washington *Post* and *Evening Star.*

INDEX

A
Astor, Vincent, 134, 155
Australia prepares for attack, 125

B
Baukhage, H. R., interviews Kurusu, 151
Beardall, John, R., 116, 192, 205-6, 210, 236
 visits Wilkinson, 155
 discusses 14-part message, 185-6
Belin, Ferdinand Lammott, 129, 132
 entertains Kurusu, 190
Bellinger, Patrick N. L. jr., 108, 246
Betts, Thomas J., 76, 200
Bicknell, George W., 96, 104, 108, 252-3
 comments on paper burning by Japanese consulate, 138
 comments on use of KGMB, 140-1
 confers with Short and Fielder re Mori message, 170-1
Biddle, Francis, 21, 132, 234
Black, Hugo, 235
Bloch, Claude C., 43, 46, 98, 108, 112-13, 225
Bratton, Rufus S. ("Rufe", "Togo"), 76, 92, 192, 197, 208-15, 246
 "winds execute" message, 120
 receives 14-part message, 135-6
 on locale of American fleet, 159
 confers with Miles, 187-8
 receives 13 parts of 14-part message, 180-3
 receives "one o'clock" message, 198-202
Brereton, Lewis H., 249-50
 and preparedness of air force, 174-8
Brown, Wilson, 110 *seq.*

C
Casey, Richard G., on results of Roosevelt-Halifax conference, 152
Chiang Kai-shek, 23
Churchill, Sir Winston, 16, 20, 26, 245

cables Roosevelt, 152
speaks to Roosevelt, Dec. 7, 237
Creighton, John M., 177

D

Deane, John R., 217
Donovan, William J. ("Wild Bill"), 129, 232
Dunn, James, 129, 133, 191
Dusenbury, Carlisle C., 182, 199, 249

E

Early, Stephen T., 229, 233
Edison, Charles, 155
Elliott, George, 223
Enterprise, 101, 248

F

Fabricant, Dr. Noah, 206
Fielder, Kendall J., 96, 107, 120, 138, 252-4
and Mori message, 146-7
confers with Short and Bicknell *re* Mori message, 170-1
Fourteen-part Message, 127-36, 148, 180-94, 210-16, 228, 259 Appendix
Friedman, William, 81

G

Gerow, Leonard T., 75, 79, 121, 188, 191, 203, 212
and Bratton discuss 14-part message, 135
Army Pearl Harbour Board, 239
Grew, Joseph, 22, 154, 159

H

Halifax, Lord, 15, 134, 251
confers with Roosevelt, 152
Halsey, William F. ("Bull"), 100, 110, 245
defends Kimmel and Short, 241
Harsch, Joseph C., interviews Kimmel, 243-4
Hart, Thomas, C., 42, 73, 133, 185, 203, 211, 249

and preparedness for attack, 174 *seq.*
Hirohito, 180, 218
Hitler, Adolf, 16, 83, 124
Hopkins, Harry, 17, 20, 36, 50, 134, 179 seq., 227, 246
Hull, Cordell, 15-17, 21-30, 36, 38, 61, 117, 129, 182-3, 191, 197, 217-18, 226-33, 245
receives Japanese note, 117-18
re note from FDR to Hirohito, 153-4
speaks with Nomura, Dec. 7, 216-17
speaks with Nomura and Kurusu, later Dec. 7, 226, *seq.*
Hu Shih Dr., 217, 259

I

Ickes, Harold, 36, 235
Ingersoll, Royal E., 189-92, 201
receives 14-part message, 190

J

Japan:
background of aggression, 21
presents a peace proposal, 23
Western assets of, frozen, 25
ten-point note sent to, 29
codes and ciphers, 80 *seq.*
rejects ten-point note, 124
sends "one-o'clock message", 199
attacks Pearl Harbour, 228

K

Kimmel, Husband E., 41-52, 70-1, 91-2, 100, 102-3, 108-12, 172, 241-2
King, Ernest J., 40, 241-2
Kita, Nagao, 83-4, 97, 243
Knox, Frank, 16, 29, 183 *seq.*, 226 *seq.*, 244
Konoye, Fumimaro, 24
régime of falls, 24
Cabinet resigns, 45
Kramer, Alwin D., 86, 180 *seq.*, 197-9

280

Kroner, Hayes A., 200
Kurusu, Saburo, 29, 71, 117, 129-33, 179-80, 190-1

L
Layton, Edwin T., 91, 102, 113, 172
Leahy, William D., 41, 155
Lend-Lease, 20
Lockard, Joseph L., 223

M
MacArthur, Douglas, 51, 79
 on preparedness of Philippines, 174
McCollum, Arthur H., 72-3, 82, 92, 119, 183, 192, 209 *seq.*, 251
McIntire, Dr. Ross T., 19, 134, 211, 218
 treats Roosevelt, 154
 and Roosevelt, Dec. 7, 206-7
Marshall, George Catlett, 20, 31, 50-6, 77, 90, 107, 123, 188, 191-2, 198, 201-3, 207-9, 212-14, 217, 230, 233, 245, 251, 255
 and "gaining time", 122-3
 on evening of Dec. 6, 156
 MacArthur tells of preparedness to, 173
 Katherine, 156, 198
Martin, Frederick L., 109, 140-1
Mayer, Ferdinand L., 129
 talks with Kurusu, 130-3, 179-80, 190
Mayfield, Irving H., 95-7, 103-5, 221
 concerned with Mori message, 172
Miles, Sherman, 75-8, 183, 192, 201-3, 212, 215, 228, 249
 on "winds execute" message, 120-1
 and Bratton discuss 14-part message, 135
 visits Wilkinson, Dec. 6, 155
 discusses 14-part message, 186-8
Mori, Dr. Motokazu, 141-2, 146
 Mrs. Motokazu, 141-6
Mori message, 137-46, 221
 Short, Fielder, and Bicknell confer on, 170-1

N
Nelson, Donald, 35, 116, 245
 hears of attack, 235
Newton, John Henry, 110, 245
Nimitz, Chester W., 40
Nomura, Kichisaburo, 22-5, 29, 47, 71, 117-18, 132, 207
 appointed as ambassador, 22
 and Turner, 60
 and Zacharias, 69-71
 visits Hull, Dec. 7, 226, 232-3
 converses with Stark, 229-30
Noyes, Leigh, 58, 62-4, 74, 75, 82, 88, 193, 202, 211, 245
 background of, 62-4
 and Turner, 62-7, 72
 on destruction of records, 118
 on "winds execute" message, 120
 hears of attack, 226-7

O
"One o'clock message", 195-204, 207, 209, 210, 211-12, 215-16
Outerbridge, William W., 222

P
Pearl Harbour *passim*
 Roosevelt uses as deterrent, 41
 Dec. 7, 221-6, 228, 229
Pershing, John J., 51-2, 55, 75
Phillipines, *passim*
 prepares for attack, 125-6
 Dec. 7, before attack, 172-8
Phillips, Walter C., 138, 240
Poindexter, Joseph B., 231, 234
Purnell, William R. ("Speck"), 175-6
"Purple machine", 81-2, 91-2, 124, 151, 176, 258

R

Rainbow plan, 106
Richardson, James O., 41, 110
  disagrees with Roosevelt, 245
Rochefort, John J., 95, 97, 120, 256
Roosevelt, Eleanor, 19, 155, 218
  on Roosevelt state of mind, 134
  on Roosevelt, Dec. 7, 234
    Franklin Delano, 124, 192, 198, 211, 238, 239, 245, 246, 249, 251, 255, 258-60
  on Dec. 1, 15-17
  physical condition of, 18-21
  on Lend-Lease, 20, 23
  Cabinet and "lieutenants" of, 21-38
  asks budget increase, 22
  and Stimson, 30-3
  on the Navy, 34
  and Hopkins, 36-8, 184, 218, 226-30
  and Stark, 39-42
  shifts Pacific fleet to Pearl Harbour, 41
  suspects clash with Japan, 115-17
  note to Japan concerning massed forces, 117
  confers with H. Smith, 134
  visits with Vincent Astor, 134, 155
  confers with Lord Halifax, 152-3
  sends note to Hirohito, 153-4
  is treated for sinus, 155, 206-7, 219
  on evening of Dec. 6, 179-80
  tries to contact Stark, 185
  receives 14-part message, 185, 192, 205
  meets with Dr. Hu Shih, 217
  and Hull, Dec. 7, 233
  on attack, 236
  disagrees with Richardson, 245
Rosenman, Samuel L., 20, 232
Russo-Japanese War, 63

S

Sadtler, Otis K., 245
  on "winds execute" message, 120-1
  entertains Dec. 6, 156
Safford, Laurence F., 82, 86-8, 119-20, 136, 148, 244
Sayre, Francis B., 176
Schuirmann, Roscoe E., 186-7, 196, 210-11
  Hull speaks to, 30
  visits Wilkinson, Dec. 6, 155
Schulz, Lester, 188, 205
  stands confidential mail watch, Dec 6, 155
  takes 14-part message to Roosevelt, 183-5, 192
Shivers, Robert L., 97, 103-4, 172, 221, 246
  and Bicknell re Mori message, 141-6
  phones J. Edgar Hoover re attack, 232
Short, Walter Campbell, 52-3, 55, 79, 92, 94, 96, 104, 107, 109, 111, 138, 221, 224, 245, 252-3
  and Marshall, 52-5
  and Mori message, 146-7
  and Fielder confer with Bicknell re Mori message, 170-1
  MacArthur's advantage over, 176
  Army Pearl Harbour Board on, 240-1
  relieved of command, 240-1
Singapore, *passim*
  prepares for attack, 126
  reports Japanese fleet movement, Dec. 6, 150
  before attack, 178
Smedberg, William R., 149
Smith, Harold, 134, 153, 205, 245
  Walter Bedell, 121, 188, 191-2, 218
Stark, Harold R. ("Betty"), 17, 20, 39-51, 64, 71, 90-2, 122-3,

149, 183, 185, 187, 188-93, 197, 201, 203-4, 207-9, 210-11, 215, 217, 228-30, 234, 239, 242, 250-1, 257
  background of, 39-42
  and Kimmel, 42-9
  McCollum advises, 73-4
  sends message to Kimmel, 135
  confers with Roosevelt on 14-part message, 188-9
  on alerting the Navy, 213-14
  hears of attack, 229
  on phone with Bloch, 230
  conversation with Nomura, 230-1
Statistics of men-of-war, 157
Stimson, Henry L., 16, 28-36, 38, 186, 192, 207, 233, 245, 247
  on U.S.-Japan negotiations, 28-9
  background of, 30-1
  and Roosevelt, 32-3
  re cable from Winant, 133
  asks statistics on men-of-war, 157
  on airforce as defence, 175
  on Dec. 7, 197, 216-17
  hears of attack, 228
  on chance of attack, 220
Sutherland, Richard K., 177

T
Ten-point Note, 29, 31-2, 124, 262-3
Theobald, Robert A., 243
Tojo, Hideki, 27
  Stark comments on rise of, 45
  replies to Roosevelt, 117-18
  Kurusu refers to, with Mayer, 131
  and War Cabinet rejects American proposals, 181-2
Tri-Partite Pact, 22, 27-8, 61
Tully, Grace, 134, 153-4, 238
Turner, Richmond Kelly, 58-62, 88, 91, 118, 183, 185, 193, 198, 201, 203-4, 211, 215, 217, 245, 251
  and Stark, 61
  and Noyes, 62, 67, 71-2
  and Wilkinson, 72, 149
  advised by McCollum, 73-4
  and possibility of attack, 122-3
  receives 14-part message, 190
  hears of attack, 229
Tyler, Kermit A., 224

W
Ward, 222-5
Wellborn, Charles, 123, 149
Welles, Sumner, 29, 233, 245
Wilkinson, Theodore Stark ("Ping"), 58, 67-8, 74-5, 118, 187, 190, 192-3, 196, 210, 245, 251
  and Turner, 72, 149
  entertains, evening of Dec. 6, 155
  and 14-part message, 187
  confers with Turner, 187
  on attack, 239
Willkie, Wendell, 115
Winant, John G., reports on Japanese fleet movement, 133
"Winds execute" message, 85-9, 120-1, 121-2, 123, 244, 249, 251
WPL-46, 106

Y
Yoshikawa, Takao, 244

Z
Zacharias, Ellis M., 68-71, 94, 246, 258
  and Nomura, 69-71

THE ONLY ALTERNATIVE IS ANNIHILATION ...
RICHARD P. HENRICK

SILENT WARRIORS (3026, $4.50)
The Red Star, Russia's newest, most technologically advanced submarine, outclasses anything in the U.S. fleet. But when the captain opens his sealed orders 24 hours early, he's staggered to read that he's to spearhead a massive nuclear first strike against the Americans!

THE PHOENIX ODYSSEY (2858, $4.50)
All communications to the USS *Phoenix* suddenly and mysteriously vanish. Even the urgent message from the president cancelling the War Alert is not received and in six short hours the *Phoenix* will unleash its nuclear arsenal against the Russian mainland. . . .

COUNTERFORCE (3025, $4.50)
In the silent deep, the chase is on to save a world from destruction. A single Russian submarine moves on a silent and sinister course for American shores. The men aboard the U.S.S. *Triton* must search for and destroy the Soviet killer submarine as an unsuspecting world races for the apocalypse.

CRY OF THE DEEP (3166, $4.50)
With the Supreme leader of the Soviet Union dead the Kremlin is pointing a collective accusing finger towards the United States. The motherland wants revenge and unless the USS *Swordfish* can stop the Russian *Caspian,* the salvoes of World War Three are a mere heartbeat away!

BENEATH THE SILENT SEA (3167, $4.50)
The Red Dragon, Communist China's advanced ballistic missile-carrying submarine embarks on the most sinister mission in human history: to attack the U.S. and Soviet Union simultaneously. Soon, the Russian *Barkal,* with its planned attack on a single U.S. submarine is about unwittingly to aid in the destruction of all mankind!

Available wherever paperbacks are sold, or order direct from the Publisher. Send cover price plus 50¢ per copy for mailing and handling to Zebra Books, Dept. 3591, 475 Park Avenue South, New York, N.Y. 10016. Residents of New York, New Jersey and Pennsylvania must include sales tax. DO NOT SEND CASH.

THE SURVIVALIST SERIES
by Jerry Ahern

#1: TOTAL WAR	(2445, $2.95)
#2: THE NIGHTMARE BEGINS	(2476, $2.95)
#3: THE QUEST	(2670, $2.95)
#4: THE DOOMSAYER	(0893, $2.50)
#5: THE WEB	(2672, $2.95)
#6: THE SAVAGE HORDE	(1232, $2.50)
#7: THE PROPHET	(1339, $2.50)
#8: THE END IS COMING	(2590, $2.95)
#9: EARTH FIRE	(1405, $2.50)
#10: THE AWAKENING	(1478, $2.50)
#11: THE REPRISAL	(2393, $2.95)
#12: THE REBELLION	(2777, $2.95)
#13: PURSUIT	(2477, $2.95)
#14: THE TERROR	(2775, $2.95)
#15: OVERLORD	(2070, $2.50)

Available wherever paperbacks are sold, or order direct from the Publisher. Send cover price plus 50¢ per copy for mailing and handling to Zebra Books, Dept. 3591, 475 Park Avenue South, New York, N.Y. 10016. Residents of New York, New Jersey and Pennsylvania must include sales tax. DO NOT SEND CASH.

BOLT

An Adult Western Series by Cort Martin

#10: BAWDY HOUSE SHOWDOWN	(1176, $2.25)
#11: THE LAST BORDELLO	(1224, $2.25)
#13: MONTANA MISTRESS	(1316, $2.25)
#15: BORDELLO BACKSHOOTER	(1411, $2.25)
#17: LONE-STAR STUD	(1632, $2.25)
#18: QUEEN OF HEARTS	(1726, $2.25)
#19: PALOMINO STUD	(1815, $2.25)
#20: SIX-GUNS AND SILK	(1866, $2.25)
#21: DEADLY WITHDRAWAL	(1956, $2.25)
#22: CLIMAX MOUNTAIN	(2024, $2.25)
#23: HOOK OR CROOK	(2123, $2.50)
#24: RAWHIDE JEZEBEL	(2196, $2.50)

Available wherever paperbacks are sold, or order direct from the Publisher. Send cover price plus 50¢ per copy for mailing and handling to Zebra Books, Dept. 3591, 475 Park Avenue South, New York, N.Y. 10016. DO NOT SEND CASH.

REACH FOR ZEBRA BOOKS
FOR THE HOTTEST IN ADULT WESTERN ACTION!

THE SCOUT
by Buck Gentry

#13: OGLALA OUTBREAK	(1287, $2.50)
#16: VIRGIN OUTPOST	(1445, $2.50)
#18: REDSKIN THRUST	(1592, $2.50)
#19: BIG TOP SQUAW	(1699, $2.50)
#20: BIG BAJA BOUNTY	(1813, $2.50)
#21: WILDCAT WIDOW	(1851, $2.50)
#22: RAILHEAD ROUND-UP	(1898, $2.50)
#24: SIOUX SWORDSMAN	(2103, $2.50)
#25: ROCKY MOUNTAIN BALL	(2149, $2.95)

Available wherever paperbacks are sold, or order direct from the Publisher. Send cover price plus 50¢ per copy for mailing and handling to Zebra Books, Dept. 3591, 475 Park Avenue South, New York, N.Y. 10016. Residents of New York, New Jersey and Pennsylvania must include sales tax. DO NOT SEND CASH.

HAUTALA'S HORROR—HOLD ON TO YOUR HEAD!

MOONDEATH (1844-4, $3.95/$4.95)
Cooper Falls is a small, quiet New Hampshire town, the kind you'd miss if you blinked an eye. But when darkness falls and the full moon rises, an uneasy feeling filters through the air; an unnerving foreboding that causes the skin to prickle and the body to tense.

NIGHT STONE (3030-4, $4.50/$5.50)
Their new house was a place of darkness and shadows, but with her secret doll, Beth was no longer afraid. For as she stared into the eyes of the wooden doll, she heard it call to her and felt the force of its evil power. And she knew it would tell her what she had to do.

MOON WALKER (2598-X, $4.50/$5.50)
No one in Dyer, Maine ever questioned the strange disappearances that plagued their town. And they never discussed the eerie figures seen harvesting the potato fields by day . . . the slow, lumbering hulks with expressionless features and a blood-chilling deadness behind their eyes.

LITTLE BROTHERS (2276-X, $3.95/$4.95)
It has been five years since Kip saw his mother horribly murdered by a blur of "little brown things." But the "little brothers" are about to emerge once again from their underground lair. Only this time there will be no escape for the young boy who witnessed their last feast!

Available wherever paperbacks are sold, or order direct from the Publisher. Send cover price plus 50¢ per copy for mailing and handling to Zebra Books, Dept. 3591, 475 Park Avenue South, New York, N.Y. 10016. Residents of New York, New Jersey and Pennsylvania must include sales tax. DO NOT SEND CASH.